Vintage Praise for Fruit of the Vine!

Cynthia is a great story-teller and has woven the true fabric of our wine-making region into a wonderful read. Entertaining, thirst-provoking, and a keen inside look at the lifeline of Finger Lakes wine.

—Holly Howell, Wine Columnist and Certified Sommelier

A fun and entertaining read. Cynthia really did her homework. Being part of the wine and grape industry makes it especially enjoyable for me.

—Scott Osborn, Owner, Fox Run Vineyards

Fruit of the Vine is fun, fresh and fascinating – just like the Finger Lakes.

—Valerie Knoblauch, Finger Lakes Visitors Connection

Joe –

Cheers!

– Cynthia Kolko

FRUIT
OF THE
VINE

CYNTHIA KOLKO

Fruit of the Vine / Cynthia Kolko
First Edition Paperback: April 2011
ISBN 10: 1-936185-27-X
ISBN 13: 978-1-936185-27-6
Interior Design: Roger Hunt
Cover Art: Miriam Grunhaus
Editor: Karen Adams

Readers may contact the author at:
www.cynthiakolko.com
www.twitter.com/CynthiaKolko
www.facebook.com/FruitoftheVine

Published by Charles River Press, LLC
www.CharlesRiverPress.com

10   9   8   7   6   5   4   3   2   1

Acknowledgements

Thanks to my husband and kids, and to David, Cecily & Jillian, Holly Howell, Sheila Livadas, David Pascal, and Lesley Perlet.

one

Bar-going knew no season in the town of Sawhorn. During the longer months, the warmer ones, tourists spilled into Loud's Tavern with certain predictability after a day of vineyard tours, eager for a refuge from the confines of whichever bed and breakfast held their luggage. Not that a good drink wasn't enough of an incentive.

But even in the marrow of winter, when white-outs bleached the roads of visibility and a fierce chill sifted into the pores of thick jackets like water through a sieve, the tavern was well-populated, standing much as it had through over two hundred years of wear and tear—to both the edifice and the patrons—enduring all that upstate New York could dish out, duly fulfilling its role as watering hole of choice for locals. Indeed, it was the only bar in town.

This Sunday evening, the last one of the year, was usual at first. The sun had gone down merely an hour previously. The day's football score was final, and the bottle-beaten bar was

Fruit of the Vine

rimmed with man butts standing, leaning, and perching on stools. Adam's apples bobbed with gulps of beer.

Jem Loud entered the joint, jacket on, cap sun-faded, arching his too-tall frame under the doorway, tripping over the heap of jackets shed by the overcrowded hooks near the door. His buddy Zack beckoned to him. Neither man had yet celebrated his twenty-second birthday.

Jem ordered, received, took a sip, sat down, and stood up as if pricked by a tack. He bent his torso over the splintered bar.

"Yo Bender! When are you going to fix this stool? My ass just got pinched in it again! Through my pants!"

Earl Bender chuckled. The bar's proprietor and Jem's second cousin, he was an unlikely hunk. Bender favored rumbling, flesh-jarring motorcycles and wore tight rock concert t-shirts, sleeveless ones that revealed biceps and triceps oddly bare of tattoos. A sour stench sometimes emanated from the tangled region between his arm and chest. A black moustache dominated his face and topped a rectangular smile of tall teeth. Somehow, he got women.

"Find yourself some heavier-duty pants," said Bender. "Yours are like paper towels. And get some boxers. Word around here is you like to freeball."

Bender cupped his crotch for effect and then with the same hand, fished a lime wedge out of a bowl, forcing the juicy slice into the neck of a beer bottle. He clonked it in front of a man whose facial color seemed derived from the red in his buffalo plaid shirt. Bender pointed to a lone stool at the end of the bar.

"Grab that one before one of these other fuckers gets it."
Jem dragged the good stool next to Zack like a wheeled
suitcase through an airport.

"Dude needs to take a marketing class," Zack said. "Bad for
business, insulting your customers."

Jem ignored Zack's complaint, as weak as it was. No one
had exactly stormed out.

"Bar has my name on it, think they'd have a decent place
for me to sit," Jem said.

The tavern was old as the town, with a white clapboard
façade that glowed at night in the soft wash of the streetlights
like a foggy billboard. It was named for Jem's forbearers,
English settlers who'd taken up where the French left off in
eradicating the Seneca from the area. The town itself could
have carried the name Loud—the clan was among the area's
first English pioneers —but instead was named for Elias
Sawhorn, a childless, wifeless farmer who died of diphtheria.
That was just like the Louds. Omnipresent but never remarkable.

Jem had well-proportioned features, a body lithe as a rubber band, and matte skin that bronzed in the sun like a ter-
racotta pot. Since the age of eleven or so, he'd worn his hair
in a grown-out crew cut. He only altered the style once,
briefly that past year, when he'd razored his favorite NASCAR
driver's car number into the side of it.

Zack, the color of toast, was six inches shorter than Jem
and bulkier, with muscles that responded to physical labor by
becoming pronounced. The two worked together at Hassler
Vineyard, out in the field or in the barn, working on the press

Fruit of the Vine

deck, the harvester, pumping barrels, even bottling wine. All the toting and lifting expanded Zack's biceps to what he called "guns." He weighed a lot on account of those muscles.

Before long, Jem felt the need to slink away to the back corner of the tavern. He opened the door stenciled with a silhouette of a man in a porkpie hat, adding his fingerprints to the smudged brass rectangle as he pushed.

It was hard to imagine a circumstance that could empty the tavern before closing time, and yet, while Jem stood whistling, drilling the urinal cake with his stream, all but two of the bar's lubricated patrons funneled out the door like hourglass sand. Jem swung open the men's room door to find Zack slumped at the bar like a lonely trucker.

"You sure picked a bad time to go to the can," said Zack. "The Brasserie is on fire."

Jem pulled a few dollars from a money clip engraved with his great-grandfather's initials and put the wrinkled bills on the bar, where they remained unclaimed. Bender had fled the joint along with the rest. Just outside the tavern, Jem peered like a prairie dog over the heads of the small crowd watching the blaze a block away on the same side of Main Street. A larger halo of people hovered around the Brasserie's periphery.

Sawhorn dwelled in the foothills of western New York, in a region of agriculture and lakes, country closer to Canada than the hubbub that swirled around New York City, though out-of-staters, particularly those from out West, seemed to think that this rural area and Manhattan were one and the same. Even folks from New York City itself sometimes my-

4

opically took "upstate" to mean those counties ringing the city.

Sawhorn's grape-growing operations, intertwined with forsaken farms, were sprinkled over thousands of painterly acres that radiated from downtown, a mere half-mile collection of buildings edging Main Street and its tributaries. Ornate Victorian homes, subdivided into efficiency apartments, hinted at latter-day prosperity that at some point turned forlorn and struggling. Old structures housed restaurants that were written up by the health department, shops that went out of business and a salon that almost guaranteed a bad dye job. A building originally erected as a jail now held a lawyer's office. With upstate New York claiming the highest tax rate in the nation, the only person in Sawhorn busier than a grape grower was a tax attorney.

The Brasserie, which occupied the bottom floor of a converted opera house—and whose name almost everyone mispronounced at one time or another, jokingly or not, as the brassiere—was the closest thing to chic Sawhorn had, with toile tablecloths, waiters in bowties, and menus containing foreign-sounding names for sauces. A foreign-sounding martial-arts school resided on the upper floor above the restaurant.

"Jesus. It's the Tae Kwon Do studio," said Zack.

"The hell is that?" said Jem.

Flames like orange Halloween streamers fluttered from the studio's windows. A pair of fire trucks from a neighboring town honked a series of jarring blasts as if announcing their arrival.

Fruit of the Vine

"Like karate," Zack said when they could hear themselves again. "They teach it up there." He pointed to the flaming second-story windows.

Jem had never noticed the sign—now reduced to ashes on the windowsill—that announced the studio to Main Street. He tended to walk slightly hunched the way tall young men do (especially the shy ones who subconsciously try to shorten themselves), eyeing the moist toes of his work boots.

It had taken some time before the fire upstairs registered with diners downstairs. While smoke leaked through the vents under the restaurant's crown molding, waiters ignored the thickening fog. They navigated around tables, holding trays high on flat hands as if nothing unusual were happening. Eventually one or two patrons stood up, looked around. They asked questions of the waiters or just of the air. Some motioned for the check.

Before long, all the Brasserie's patrons had left, some holding doggie bags they were careful to get packed before they fled. People assembled in the bank parking lot across the street. Chefs and wait staff formed a tight circle, like a group of hacky sack players. The lot was almost as crowded as Jem had ever seen it, rivaling even Sawhorn's annual fall grape festival, when this very pavement was rimmed with tents, vendors serving buffalo burgers, samples of pie, wine in Dixie cups, and grapes from small wooden crates. Sometimes, there was music too. Girls wore shorts. At this time of year, those same girls were cloaked in Michelin Man down coats or shapeless fleece sacks with sleeves.

Cynthia Kolko

Laura Fillmore waved to Jem and Zack, smiling as if it were a parade.

"It happened so fast," she said, gesturing to the flames, which seemed to intensify despite the blitz of water from the fire trucks' hoses.

The streetlamp washed over her freckled skin and bounced light off the enamel grapes pinned to her lavender hat. Her chestnut hair hung in a braid down her back like a branch. Back at Sawhorn Regional High School, Jem had shared a few classes with Laura, her cinnamon-glazed skin turning orange when the teacher called on her. Laura had the damndest laugh, ringing out in staccato notes, bouncing off the metal lockers like mallets hitting a glockenspiel. With his eyes seared shut, Jem would know who was laughing just by the sound. He had barely spoken to Laura in those days. He preferred instead to appear aloof, intriguing girls with his mysterious demeanor, an attraction tactic that worked just about as well as gravel in a birdfeeder.

"Were you in there?" asked Jem.

Laura's voice was low, almost masculine, like a young boy imitating his father's speech.

"Yeah. The owners gave me a certificate. Christmas gift. Said they appreciate me always bringing their pies on time. Guess it's good I got anything. Someone said the electrical system was probably overloaded. But who knows? Didn't look to me like there was a whole lot of electricity being used. All the dim lights."

The hoses' onslaught gained an advantage and the fire

Fruit of the Vine

slowed to an orange glow. A trio of firefighters entered the building. Plumes of smoke rose from the roof and disappeared into the tar-colored sky.

A dark-haired man stood, gaze tethered to the charred building, the sky salted with snowflakes that dissolved in the air by the frozen thousands before hitting the flames. Jem recognized the man's stance, designed, subconsciously or not, to let everyone know he was hot shit, at least in his own mind: balls pitched forward, shoulders back, pecs pushing his man-breasts taut against the inside of his shirt, arms hanging wide. It was Laura's brother-in-law, Joe Silla, the first name seldom mentioned without the last, the two forming an irresistible, easy-to-utter combination of vowels and consonants that sounded like the name of a B-movie monster. Jem pointed a hitchhiker thumb toward the man.

"Back in town?"

"House is done. They just moved into it," said Laura.

Her older sister Sandra's home sat in a freshly carved out subdivision whose brick-fronted houses featured two-story foyers hung with oversized glittering chandeliers like gilded octopi. Doorbells played classical music snippets.

"Where's Sandra?" asked Zack, whipping his head around.

Laura pointed to a frowning blonde in a knee-length fur. A fireman waving both hands like a crazy orchestra conductor bellowed at the assembled crowd.

"Everyone go home! Move out of here! Keep this place clear!" the fireman yelled.

"See you on the farm," Laura said.

Jem watched Laura retreat, her parka sitting high enough

on her waist to reveal the back pocket slits of her wool pants, the dressiest thing Jem had ever seen her wear, prom night included. With each step, alternately, one of Laura's butt cheeks pushed against the fabric of her pants so that the rounded outline could be glimpsed. Left, right, left, right.

"Give it up," said Zack.

"I could get her if I wanted to," said Jem.

"Too bad Joe Silla beat you to Sandra," Zack said.

"Not my type either," said Jem.

"Bullshit. You'd do a tree if it wasn't for the splinters."

Jem stood with gloveless hands in his pockets, looking at the blackened, smoldering opera house, still spitting sparks.

"Wonder what'll happen to the place now?"

"Who cares?" answered Zack. "It won't affect me. Won't affect any of us."

The cops re-opened Main Street. Sawhorn seemed to return to normal almost as quickly as the fire had erupted. The tavern refilled. People started vehicles, scraped ice from windshields.

Not a few Sawhorn residents hoped the oncoming year might offer something of a different existence, a break from the staid, an improvement that still allowed the comfort of the usual. It was a noble dream, yet change wasn't something one could order up just the way you wanted it, like a beer. Sometimes change came at you with the force of water from a fire hose. And damn if you weren't prepared for a soaking.

two

Orange daylilies spread like a rash from the side of the road and then fell dormant. Leaves browned. It was the time of year when the honking traffic of southbound geese all but silenced the rhythmic chug of the grape-picking machines, and the time of day when the grass fringing the driveway hung defeated under the weight of dew.

This place was Hassler Vineyard, a small grape farm and winery named for Laura's long-deceased grandparents, European Jewish immigrants who outran the impending Holocaust not by foresight, but by hope and doggone luck. Here in Sawhorn, they rammed locust posts into barely-yielding earth and planted grapes in rows north to south. They tied vines—hands scathed crimson from handling fence wire—and lost grapes to extreme weather or wandering critters. Made a go of it, but never a success of it. They ingested so many grapes themselves, you'd have thought they urinated pink.

It was still a small operation. Too insignificant to be reviewed much. Not prestigious enough to be included on the usual wine trails or major bus tours. It drew enough tourists in the summer to stay afloat, but hardly droves of them. The regional guidebook for that year, 1991, listed it as "Hessler Vineyard" and offered no more information than the address, a blurry photo of Manette Hassler looking cross-eyed sniffing a cork, and an admonishment to watch for potholes on the driveway.

In the morning's florid shine, Jem worked the crusher, dumping crates of grapes into the receiving hopper. The contraption was buttressed by a large red barn, its pointed overhang piercing the sky like loose barbed wire.

Nearby, Laura kicked open the rusty creaking front door of her domicile, an old tenant house on the property that she had cutesied up with grape motifs. As the door swung, bees scattered, stalwarts hanging onto summer's errant threads. Laura's hands shored up a high stack of pie boxes. She'd started this business as a teenager, rolled out the dough on a pine farm table, spooned the purple filling into shallow pans. It was something to do, something to make. She'd sold the oozing pastries from a stand at the base of the bumpy blacktop driveway that had been paved and repaved, her father's idea of a luxury. And she didn't risk getting sunburned or frostbitten sitting out there, thanks to an honor-system box that she knew no one would steal.

"Jem!" Laura called over the hum of the crushing machine, face obscured by the boxes.

Jem trotted, unhitched Laura's truck cap door, lifted it high as the hinges allowed.

Fruit of the Vine

"Going to be a record harvest for concords this year," said Jem. He eyed the pie boxes.

"Joe Silla," Laura said. "They're for Tap. His new bar. Restaurant, I mean. He calls it a bistro. You been in there? He slicked up the joint like mad."

"Naw," Jem said. Grape juice gave his soil-caked work boots the tinge of a cordovan stain.

"Beats that old depressing Brasserie," she said.

Jem heard his father Ed's complaint tumble out of his mouth. "Beat it a little better if he didn't use our money for all that slicking up. If he hadn't scammed a tax break for saving the opera house after it burned."

Laura placed the boxes into the flatbed and closed the cap.

"I can't complain too much about anyone who gives me business. Be back soon," she said. "Joe likes to get his pies first thing."

"Bet he does," said Jem.

Laura sat in the driver's seat, swung her left leg in as she slammed the door, which was painted raspberry and festooned with grape-laden vines that formed a green and purple crest around the words "Lulu's Delights." The truck flew down the long driveway until it rounded the bend out of sight. Jem retreated to the machine in his spattered shirt.

Manette Hassler Fillmore, Laura's mother, owner and boss of Hassler Vineyard, emerged from behind the barn. "Jem, come see me in my office when you're in a good place here," she said and left as quickly as she appeared.

Zack peered around the barn's weathered corner. Manette was out of earshot.

Cynthia Kolko

"Ever wonder why Manette likes you so much more than me?" he said. "Think I got the hint."

"Don't say it," said Jem.

Zack scraped grape stems into a compost bin.

"You started the same day I did," said Zack. "Day we walked here from town. Eighteen years old."

Jem remembered. They had spent the summer driving too fast and drinking too much. One night, the two sat on the hood of Zack's car, downing beer and pissing in the grass. Zack, lousy with drunkenness, turned the ignition, drove a half mile and smashed the car into the guard rail that girded the bridge over the Mohawk River. Jem blackened both eyes when he hit the windshield. Zack got stitches on his forehead, a brace on his right arm, and an earload of hell from his mother.

Replacing Zack's totaled car was an expensive prospect. And both fledgling men itched for the means to break out of the confines of their parents' homes. They heard that the Hassler operation needed help. Several hands had left and so much rain fell between August and September that the grapes were threatening to rot on the vine. It was 1991, and the law had no problem with teenagers working at wineries, so long as they didn't drink the stuff. Jem and Zack applied, rifled through a box of field gloves in Manette's office, and started working. They earned twice the minimum wage, which in Sawhorn went further than one might guess. Rents in town were not exorbitant, and the supply of used cars exceeded the demand.

"And now I got to answer to you," said Zack. "I'm not say-

ing you don't deserve it. Just gives you a complex sometimes. Makes you look for answers."

"You act like I get off on being your boss," Jem said.

"Hardly my fault. Just doing my job."

A long driveway entered the Hassler property and fanned
into a parking lot for vineyard workers and customers of the
drab but kempt wine shop, set up in a converted small barn,
from which wine and wine accessories were peddled. Laura's
house sat close to one side of the shop, and Manette's office
was housed in the back of the shop. The big red barn obscured much of the horizon behind both buildings.

Jem found Manette sitting at her desk wearing steel-
rimmed half glasses a shade or two darker than the hair
pasted to her head. She mopped a few dewy beads from her
forehead. As much as she hated desk work, it offered one of
the only occasions she got off her feet. Even lunch was a
stand-up affair at the kitchen counter, though during harvest
she often skipped the meal altogether. Daylight was something not to be wasted. Manette punched numbers into an
adding machine which spit a centimeter of paper spiral each
time she hit "enter." She looked like a short, female Woodrow
Wilson.

"Mind if I get a drink?" said Jem.

"Go ahead," said Manette.

Back from Tap, Laura loaded pies into the pastry case. Her
father, Sanford Fillmore, stood behind the counter, face like
a faded stop sign with cottony tufts above the ears, white
beard forked like a divining rod. Whenever he spoke, his jaw

hinged open and shut, giving the beard an up-and-down ride. Jem took a bottle of cola from the refrigerator case.

"Put it on your tab?" Sanford asked.

Jem dug into his pocket, found his money clip and some loose coins.

"I got it. How much do I owe?"

Sanford opened the cash drawer, retrieved a scrap with the letters "IOU" scrawled at the top.

"Seventy-five cents. Give me a dollar and we'll call it even."

Jem handed Sanford a dollar fifty. As Sanford turned to put it in the register, Jem moved his eyes down Laura's frame, taking a rest on her chest and her hips before ascending back to the face.

"Getting late," Jem said to Laura. "Don't you deliver to a bunch of restaurants on Tuesdays?"

"I'm in slo-mo," she said, jerking her limbs like a sluggish robot. "Got some time yet."

In the office, Manette held her glasses and shook them at Jem as she spoke.

"The blue harvester doesn't seem so healthy to me. Yesterday it was chugging like it was going to faint. See if you can figure out what's wrong. Chardonnay grapes are almost ready to go. All I need is for the old coot to crap out during harvest."

"See what I can do," Jem said.

"Just do it soon," said Manette.

Before joining Hassler Vineyards, Jem had spent after-school hours working at a mechanic shop, the name of which gave passers-by a howl: Loud Motors. Jem's uncle owned the place and had his two sons working there, both sporting

Fruit of the Vine

fingernails so permanently rimmed in black they may as well have been tattooed. The four Louds fixed anything that ran on gas. By the time Jem was a high school junior, Loud Motors had expanded to ten employees, six garage bays, and a gasoline pump.

After the uncle's serial smoking cost him his life, the cousins found a mountain of debt and sold the business to pay it off. Jem stayed on for only a month after Loud Motors sold, working his butt off for the new owner, a cheap, miserable man who docked Jem's pay for staying in the bathroom too long. Jem might have made vehicle repair a career if not for the weight of the depression—like a boulder attached to his heart—every time he saw that bastard in his uncle's coveralls.

Laura poked her face into Manette's office.

"Mom, I forgot to tell you that Yankee broke a bunch of bottles last night. But don't worry. I cleaned it up. All the purple paw prints."

"I told you to keep that mutt out of the shop," Manette said.

"You can only control a dog so much," said Laura.

A sinister gust flogged the building's exterior. The office walls groaned.

"Before you go home today, take a look at her in the barn," Manette said to Jem.

"Ma'am?"

"The harvester. Take a look at the harvester."

Outside, the arms of Jem's jacket rippled. The wind carved shallow rivulets in his hair. A few dozen leaves raced down one of the rows and spiraled into the air like passengers on

16

a wild amusement park ride. Cold whipped Jem's face. He drew his shoulders up, retreated into his shirt.

From over the hills came a low roar like a stadium of cheering football fans. The sound evolved into a racket of honks and squawks as a black-and-white screen of Canada geese flapped low in the sky. Maple trees flipped their leaves undersides up, like blackjack cards. Songbirds that lacked the wherewithal to fly south flitted under pines whose lower needles had long ago perished and fallen. Dense gray puff-balls eclipsed remnants of clear sky.

"We're going to get dumped on," Jem said aloud.

At the edge of the parking lot, a duo of pickers' rusted pick-ups bookended the shiny tricked-out truck of the pickers' contractor. Laura emerged from one of the rows, sidestepping between two of the parked trucks with a handful of green grapes. When she spotted Jem studying the clouds, she approached him.

"Chardonnay's not ready," she said. "Take one. See what you think."

"Manette measured the brix yesterday," said Jem.

"Bah. That fancy refractometer she uses. I do it the old-fashioned way."

That refractometer was a curious device. Manette wore it dangled from a cord around her neck like a coach's whistle. Sometimes she even twirled it.

Jem plucked a grape from Laura's open palm. His stomach rumbled with the thought of his bologna-on-white in the barn's fridge.

Fruit of the Vine

"They're not ready," said Laura. "But Mom won't listen to me."

From a loudspeaker mounted to the top of the red barn, a synthesized predator squawked an admonishment to any snack-seeking critter.

"Wait for the birds to start eating the grapes," Jem said. "They always know when they're sweetest."

Snow started. Flurries swirled like aimless fruit flies, so wispy they seemed to be alive, flying on even the slightest wind for a minute before floating down to the earth.

The abandoned Loud Farm stood at the pinnacle of a hill, perched adjacent to a stain of woods, the farmhouse a lonely shepherd of weeds.

"How did you find this place?" said a woman, hands cradling hips, floorboards whining under boots edged with mud.

"Jogging," said Joe Silla. "No one drives here early in the morning except guys going to work at the vineyards and all. Least they know that much. Wee hours are the best time to get in gear. Carpe diem." He thumped a fist to his chest.

The woman scrutinized an Orion's Belt of oozing splotches on the ceiling and then touched her finger to a brown drip line running down one wall.

"No one's lived here for a while," she said.

"Hardly blame them," said Joe. "Place stinks."

"How'd you get in?"

"Wasn't hard."

"This house isn't exactly private," the woman said. "The road is right there. No trees blocking the view. People can see."

"Stop worrying already. No one's breaking in on us in this dump," said Joe. "Aren't any bums in Sawhorn."

"Depends who you ask," said the woman. "And what if someone drives by when I'm coming through the yard?"

"Why in hell would you stroll on up through the yard? Come undercover through the woods and around back like today."

"It's a whole lot of trouble just for—"

"Just for what? Your idea, doing this. Finding someplace out of the way."

"I meant a nice hotel. Not a shanty."

Joe looked over the blonde land toward the woods, trees largely skeletal except for the evergreens. The dark sky heaved with moisture.

"Holy Mother of God," Joe said, stalled at the window. He wiped it with his hand.

"What is it?" said the woman, pressing the toe of her boot into a soft baseboard.

Joe said nothing. He gaped out the window, suspended in regard, his mind churning with the possibilities. He smiled.

three

A snowstorm just after Halloween was nothing new. Still, it caught Sawhorn off guard. Shovels and boots wouldn't make it into the stores for at least another week. And the Quik Mart hadn't yet erected its annual front-entrance display of rock salt; still there was a pile of cut-rate pumpkins and misshapen gourds. Snow tires lay in the dusty corners of people's garages.

Loud's Tavern was populated with working stiffs. The tavern was a comfortable jacket-over-the-chair, ketchup-in-packets kind of establishment. Broken-in like old work boots. At the tavern, no one asked what type of cheese you wanted on your burger. There was only one kind available.

The tavern's walls were fogged with yellow tobacco stain and hung with matted, faded photos of ancient farmers. Dotty negative dust eclipsed portions of some images: men standing in front of the tavern or other Sawhorn buildings (most of which still existed), men posing proudly next to horses, men sitting on stoops, men smoking pipes. Men who

Cynthia Kolko

always appeared older than their present-day counterparts. In one picture, a horse-drawn cart trudged along a row of grape plants. In another, a big-skirted, improbably cheery matron poured liquid from a pitcher.

Sitting at the bar with Zack, Jem watched Laura's profile chatting with Bender, who leaned both cheeks of his jeans against the back of the bar.

"I can't figure that shit out," said Jem. "Talk about robbing the cradle."

"Maybe he's hung like a horse. Twelve-incher. Like me."

Jem winced.

Laura took her jacket from the back of a stool and left. Bender resumed his usual position behind the bar, his arms folded.

"Least she ain't crashing upstairs with Bender," said Zack.

Jem winced again.

"I heard Joe Silla hired Roy to cook at Tap," Zack said.

Jem put his beer down and sucked the inside of his cheeks between his molars. "Can't imagine who'd want to work for Joe," he said. "And isn't Roy just about ready to retire?"

"Who can retire anymore?" said Zack. "And Roy's only like sixty. It's just because his face is so craggy he looks older. I say it's a good move for Joe Silla, hiring him. Quite a chef. Made the Brasserie what it was. All that arranging stuff on the plate. Different textures and shit. Taught himself too, what I hear. Didn't go to cooking school. Smart guy."

"When did you ever eat at the Brasserie? Little fancy for you, ain't it?"

"Mother's Day."

Fruit of the Vine

The phone rang. Bender picked it up.

"No. She just left," he said, the off-white handset dappled with greasy fingerprints. "Call back if she doesn't show in the next fifteen minutes."

Bender hung up and wiped a wayward dollop of mustard off the bar.

"Manette," Bender said to Jem's inquisitive face. "It'll take Laura a little while to get home in all this snow."

In the glow of the streetlamps, snowflakes spun in swirls like the broad strokes of Van Gogh's Starry Night. Jem turned the ignition on his aged truck and cranked a U-turn out from the tavern. He retraced what he guessed were the snow-dusted treads of Laura's truck. A fluttering guitar jam squealed from the radio in the cab. Windshield wipers beat out a metronome's rhythm. The truck rumbled up the sloping road, snow-dusted grape plants hemming the way. Jem scanned left and right, seeking the red lights of Chevy truck buttocks.

The sign for Hassler Vineyards wore a hat of snow, the driveway a white satin sash spread out before him. He clicked off his lights in an attempt to make his entrance clandestine. He inched up the driveway. The cracked blacktop was bumpy under the afternoon's snowfall, which was packed like hard supermarket frosting by a lousy plow.

Jem came within a thousand yards of Laura's house and stepped out of the truck. The weather slapped him across the face. He turned the collar of his field coat up vampire-style. The remorseless wind came in bursts, blowing flakes across the driveway, pelting Jem's face with tiny cold pinpricks. He

22

thought he would have seen the lights of Laura's house, but the landscape was slate black. The wind came up again, turning Jem's view to television static. A yellow orb glowed in the distance like a flashlight under the covers. Jem's work boots slid out from under him and he landed on his rear.

"Shit," he said. "Fucking…"

Closer, Jem could see the porch railing bathed in a yellow haze like campfire. Laura's parked truck was sprinkled with cold dandruff. Jem wiped the melted snow that beaded his face. A square of light, murky with frost, showed the outline of curtains. Jem crouched under it. He whisked his glove across the bumps of ice, clearing enough smoky condensation to allow a look.

He heard rustling behind him. Coyote? The flank of a rifle cracked into Jem's frozen cheek. When he opened his eyes, Laura stood over him holding a rifle with one hand on the trigger and the other on the barrel. Laura shivered. She was clad in the same shirt, cords and sneakers she wore at the tavern. No time to dress for shooting a prowler. Jem put his glove to his temple, removed it and saw blood on the heel of his hand.

"You scared me, Jem."

Laura put an arm under Jem's shoulder. She tried to drag him up and toward the house, but Jem said he was fine to walk. He wavered like a flagpole in the wind.

"Can't do that, Laura." Jem spoke in thick words, his lips numb. "You hear something outside, don't just come out like that. Trying to capture someone. Bad idea. Call the police. Find your dad. You'll get killed doing crazy stuff like that."

23

Fruit of the Vine

"What were you doing? Speaking of crazy stuff," said Laura.

"Just wanted to be sure you got in okay. The weather."

The snow picked up again, falling as if from a gigantic flour sifter. Laura stuck out her tongue, unable to resist letting dots of cold land there. It was almost a reflex.

Jem washed his face at Laura's scalloped bathroom sink and put a bandage over the cut. His feet thawed on the tile. In the kitchen, Laura drained water from ramen noodles and plopped them in a bowl without the seasoning.

"Want some?" she called.

"That's all right," Jem said, shaking his head. "But thanks for the…sink." His face reddened. He hunched.

Jem trod back to his truck, his footsteps erased by the wind. He turned the ignition. Nothing. He waited, tried again. Again. Nope. The mirrors were glazed with white.

"Shit."

Jem considered sleeping in the truck. He had a blanket in the storage hopper. He could do it. He'd been winter camping in a flimsy tent. Or how about walking home to his apartment in town? Only a few miles. A blast of wind rocked the truck.

"Fuck Bender," said Jem.

He plodded on foot back toward the nimbus on Laura's porch. Flecks swirled and cold re-established its grip on his extremities. His gashed cheek throbbed under the bandage. Laura answered the door wearing a sweat suit and a ski hat topped with an enormous yarn pompom.

"Now what?" she said.

"Truck's dead."

Laura disappeared into her bedroom, leaving Jem idling in the front room. Moisture from his boots soaked Laura's tan and purple rug woven with grape motifs. Laura returned with a thin blanket. A brown cord and plug dangled from it like a garter snake.

"You can sleep on the couch if you want," said Laura.

"You sure?" Jem said. "I can always ring your parents' bell."

"Dad gets ornery when his sleep is interrupted. I'd drive you home, but the roads are a disaster."

She pointed to an arrangement of decorative couch pillows. Jem selected a faux deerskin one, laid it flat.

"Mind if I watch a little TV?" he said.

"Whatever you want," said Laura, taking the remote from the coffee table and bouncing it onto the couch.

"I'll leave first thing in the morning." said Jem. "Get Zack or someone. I know half-a-dozen guys with access to a dozen tow trucks."

"Okay, then. Goodnight." said Laura.

"You sleep in that hat?" asked Jem. "Doesn't the pompom get in the way?"

"It's on top of my head, not under it."

From the couch, Jem flipped through channels. He watched a young woman talk with concern about the storm and suggest that people stay home, get ready to shovel in the morning, and expect lengthy commutes. The station cut to a shot of snow blowing over a road, a car's hazard lights flashing red in the distance, translucent flakes over the scene

Fruit of the Vine

giving the look of a pointillist painting. Jem clicked it off and lay supine under the blanket from waist to ankles, head on the deerskin pillow, trying to picture what Laura might wear to bed if the weather were balmier. He felt a stir in his jeans and forced his mind to his dead truck. Shit. He'd miss the Bills game tomorrow on account of that fucking heap.

In the early morning, Jem turned the knob of Laura's bedroom and peeked in. A body-shaped lump topped by light brown hair slept motionless under the quilt. The woolly hat lay discarded on the floor. He closed the door and released the knob.

Jem suited up into his boots, jacket, and gloves. Still dark. Crescents of snow gathered between the porch rails and posts. Driveways, grass, tree limbs: white. Jem pulled up his collar and lumbered hunchbacked down the driveway. A hearty gust blasted snow off some pines in the distance, dusting Jem's cheek with cold powder. His truck sat ahead like a pitiful abandoned artifact on a frigid frontier. Jem skidded on an ice patch that sent him floundering, but he didn't fall. He yanked on his truck door, only to find it frozen shut. With a jackknife from his pocket, Jem chipped ice from the door seam and then pulled again. The door's bolts creaked in short pops like an angry hammer, snow and icy shards raining onto the driver's seat.

Jem turned the ignition. No good. Tried again. Dang.

The thing started. Yes!

The motor hummed. Shit. Laura will think I faked it.

Jem brushed off the windshield and headlights. He let the

26

Cynthia Kolko

defrost kick in enough to clear a blob out of which to see. Ten minutes later, a sheet of ice the shape of Arkansas slid down the windshield. Jem pulled out onto the main road.

In the oncoming lane, a tall red pickup beaconed, the barred teeth of its radiator grille partly obscured by a lead-colored plow raised off the road like a massive shield. Russ, the driver, flicked his lights as he neared Jem. They'd graduated in the same class at Sawhorn Regional. Russ's dad was a mean drunk. During Russ's childhood, whenever the Bills were losing a game (which was often), Russ's mom put the kids to bed early. Out of harm's way.

They stopped in the road, window-to-window. As Jem laboriously cranked his window down—the truck was stiff with cold, like an old man—Russ squinted into the wind striking his quizzical eyes and swishing his hatless mop. His vermillion face was centered in his already-open window like a framed Norman Rockwell portrait, spoiled only by the stippled and brailled beard of scars and acne, a plague since puberty, that hammocked his dry shingled lips. Mere months prior, Russ was one of the last holdouts of his generation to cut off the fringe of his mullet.

"Coming from Hassler, eh," said Russ, grinning.

"Yeah," said Jem.

"Good thing you got out of there before I plowed it."

"Yup," said Jem. "You watching the game later?"

"I might. You watching with Zack?"

"Yeah. You get a chance, come by."

Shame flickered in Jem for not having set the record straight on why he was leaving Hassler at that early hour. Be-

27

Fruit of the Vine 🌿

fore Russ's tires hit the vineyard's driveway, he'd already have summoned on the CB any other plow guys he figured were awake. By the time the sun rose, the story of Jem spending the night at Laura's place had run through Sawhorn like a spark flying down a line of gasoline.

🌿

The storm had subsided for the time being. Sawhorn's small armada of street plows created lips of snow that edged the roads, narrowing the driving lanes and forcing cars to travel close to the middle line. Concealed patches of ice made it a treacherous commute. But the residents of Sawhorn had done all this before.

Jem came home to a ringing phone. He braced himself for an inquisition about Laura.

"Hello?"

"The old Loud place. Front porch fell off," said Sanford's gravel-throated voice.

"Aw shit," groaned Jem. "Sorry. Anyone out there now?"

He squinted at the thermostat, turned it up a few degrees.

"No. Manette told me about it. Said I should meet you out there. Clear it and such."

"I can take care of it myself," said Jem.

"Not alone you can't. Least I can do, help out."

Bright sun often fooled Jem into thinking the weather was balmier, but the second he left the house, a chill knifed him down to the skin. He sheltered his eyes with a hand salute. His truck lumbered down Main Street, past the usual audience of businesses hung with closed signs. He rattled over the railroad tracks and bumbled over shards of stray ballast. Jem turned onto pock-marked Franklin Road. Wipers pushed the snow off Jem's windshield. Ahead, the Loud farmhouse loomed like a ghost. It had been the home of Jem's great-grandmother, Elba Loud. Jem recalled being inside the place as a boy, looking at a wedding photo of Elba surrounded by a sampling of family. He'd practically memorized that photo, searching for a glimpse of himself in the staid faces, a familiar chin or set of eyes. At some later point, it became too much house for Elba. She moved to Sawhorn Meadows, a subdivision of patio homes for retirees, leaving the weary Loud homestead abandoned, the neglected fields behind it dry and weed-woven. The land wasn't worth a lick, Jem's father Ed said. Too arduous a drive from even a minor metropolis, no railroad station nearby, and too far from the closest thruway exit. Jem remembered the U-Haul loaded with Elba's furniture and Ed explaining how she "needed neighbors." What didn't fit from the old homestead was crammed into dusty heaps inside Ed's restorations shop. Or it was junked.

The house hadn't been vacant for all that long. Six or seven years? In that time, Jem hadn't stopped to check it out even once. That was Ed's responsibility. Ed hadn't taken very good care of the place, not by a long shot. The house sagged. The garden went to hell. The property faded like an old photo left in the sun.

Jem stopped in front of the weeping house. Sanford hadn't arrived yet. The porch lay slumped on the ground like a driver asleep at the wheel. A scourge of weeds, alive despite

Fruit of the Vine

the snow, had crept into every available crack in the house, driveway, front walk and steps, and seemed to have created new cracks. They grew rampant. Jem thought that if the human race ceased to exist, this is how the world's new reality would emerge. Man-made structures—roads and buildings—would be overtaken, repurposed, knocked asunder not by animals or even insects (as scientists on a cable TV show surmised), but by plants.

Jem stepped over split boards, a cache of displaced balustrades like toppled statues. For the first time since the porch was built, a portion of the stone foundation of the house was visible, though gangly plants obscured most of the cobbles. Jem crouched on a teetering plank and ran his hand across the foundation's exposed stones. He came across a piece of flint protruding from the petrified mortar. Jem pulled out a chiseled arrowhead. He put it into his pocket.

Faint notes sounded over a motor. A country-western balladeer crooned, then ceased. Sanford walked across the yard around the rubble to Jem.

"Called Don. Help get the place cleared. What an eyesore," said Sanford.

"I'll take a look inside," said Jem.

"Careful, now. Place isn't stable," said Sanford.

Jem stepped over the jagged-toothed cavern left by the collapsed porch. He stood in the parlor. Amazingly, the panes in the front window were intact, marred only by the starbursts of a dozen bullet holes. Cigarette butts and beer cans crowded one of the parlor's corners. Jem creaked up the steps to the second floor, narrowly missing a dead mouse.

Cynthia Kolko

The house was utilitarian, built by people who wasted nothing. Jem realized how little he knew about this property or his family history, not to mention the people who lived on this land before them. In longhouses? Jem wasn't sure. He only knew that the past was something he shouldered, something that weighted him down like a sack of grain.

When Jem came back outside, Sanford's friend Don looked up from his work and smiled. He had a nice set of teeth for an old guy, whiter and straighter than most. He was built like an aged linebacker, his nose red, his chin protruding and bulbous with a thin cleft that made it look like a miniature pair of buttocks. Don heaved planks onto a flatbed with the deliberate hands of a man who refused to let age slow him down.

"Talked to your Dad this morning," Don said. "Doesn't want to rebuild the porch. Didn't seem interested. You'd think a guy who restores antiques would want to see his family place fixed up some."

Jem dug into his pocket for his work gloves and began to help clear the debris. He wasn't surprised at Ed's reaction. Jem's mother fled to the South when Jem was four years old, leaving his father Ed to raise him alone. Ed, too young for the horrors he'd experienced in Vietnam, drank just little enough to keep from being a drunk. He bemoaned his lot, bitter about how time progressed without him and he got stuck wallowing in the dregs. Instead of trying to dig out of his depressive state, he settled into it, like wearing days-old clothes he just couldn't muster up the energy to wash.

After clearing and boarding up, Jem drove his truck back to

Fruit of the Vine

town. Aside from Ed's own pickup, its jolly red paint job out of character for its sad-sack owner, Jem's vehicle was the only one parked on this side of the street for fifty yards. He slammed the truck door shut, rusty shards sprinkling the pavement. A hand-lettered sign spelled a single word above the shop's door in an old-fashioned newspaper-style typeface: Restorations.

"Dad?" Jem called, entering the shop, his stomach percolating with dread.

"Come on back," said Ed's voice from within.

Jem snaked through drifts of seatless chairs and drawerless dressers. A thatch of table legs leaned in a corner. An imposing art nouveau armoire, streaked with green paint and sporting 1970s-era shiny mirrored pulls, stood against a wall behind a card table draped with a gossamer sheet of dust.

In the rear, Ed leaned over a dining table, buffing a water ring off the mahogany. His motions were gruff, laborious, his face a hard grimace. Ed's dog Percy, lounging near Ed's feet, lifted his eyes and nothing else as Jem entered.

Ed Loud seemed to age right before your eyes as you walked toward him, a year or two with each step as the wrinkles were revealed, until you stood next to a white-haired man who could just as easily have been over sixty as his actual age, forty-five. Ed's once-shiny platinum hair had dulled, his ruddy complexion embattled by sun exposure and pocked like a lemon peel. Ed could get sunburned walking from his house to the end of the driveway for the mail.

Restoration was a fitting vocation for Ed. It was calming, solitary, filled a need to have some control over times long ago, effecting a rebirth in the furniture, if not in him. Jem liked it too. But for him, it was more like recycling. It was making something beautiful from something scarred; sharing a piece of the earth and passing it on. Both the elder and younger Loud found satisfaction in polishing something from the past and making it shine in the present. It was one of the few traits they shared; the others were a love of sports, a taste for amber beer, and an irritation with inefficient service people.

"Just came from the old place," Jem said.

Ed was silent, his eyes on the dining table, his left hand moving in short wipes.

"Could be a nice place again," said Jem.

"Too many other fish to fry," said Ed, eyes to the table. "Bills to pay." Ed gestured to the masses of decrepit furniture. "Could use your help here once in a while. But I'll survive. Don't worry 'bout me. I'll just hang back and eat your dust. I've acquired quite a taste for dust, after a lifetime of dining on it."

Jem's throat tightened. It felt like it had atrophied to half its normal width. Jem never got used to it, that uncomfortable feeling that seeped through him in the presence of his father.

Jem held fast to a certain anger at his father that waned at times but never truly departed. As Jem saw it, Ed fell into a tub of depression with no will to climb out and too much pride to ask for a hand. As if help were something shameful. That was wrong. Nothing, no one, got anywhere without help. Folks living in a farm community knew it better than anyone. Most of them, anyway. Nothing got built, grown, or picked without a crew of people working together.

Fruit of the Vine

Jem returned to the Loud Farm. The sky, heavy and gray, cast a smoky shadow over the land. He let his truck idle on the road as he entered the small cemetery on the corner of the property. Sawhorn and its surroundings were replete with the name Loud chiseled into grave markers. But here, there were only Loud headstones. It was a family plot. Time was, such conventions were not unusual. Dying was so much a part of frontier life that a family cemetery made as much sense as a family kitchen, though several graves were of a more recent vintage. Fifteen or sixteen simple headstones were in this cheerless place, some unreadable, some with barely distinguishable words. Some tilted forward, leaned right or left, bases ringed in weeds. A few flags waved weakly from the ground, Ed's one concessionary maintenance. He had a soft spot for veterans.

Jem tried to make out the lettering on the headstones. 1805–1810. No name. Virginia Loud 1778–1815. Few unmarked stones. William Ward Loud 1800–1817. William Everett Loud 1772–1823. Jeremiah Loud 1760–1827. A small rectangle level to the ground had one word: Berl. Or was it Earl? Hard to tell. One stone's severed top leaned against its base. Katherine Girard 1798–1819.

Girard. Jem's mother's maiden name. The name that appeared on both sides of his family tree. Jem couldn't help recalling the taunt kids had hurled at him as a boy: inbred. A bad birthmark he couldn't remove. He hunched.

The land was rife with plants overgrown enough to pierce the snow and despoil the white carpet. The woods were a threadbare shirt, sharp branches replacing the green canopy, the ground a mess of discarded leaves and sporadic white patties. Down the street, wood boards sealed the old homestead's wounds. Jem felt the arrowhead in his pocket poke him. He placed it at a more comfortable lie.

A blue pickup disgorged Roy. Jem extended his hand, but Roy didn't take it.

"Just wanted to look around," said Roy. "Heard about the house. That it's fallen onto hard times."

Part Seneca, Roy stood just under six feet tall, eyes like black marbles, high cheeks seemingly carved in a face wooden as poplar bark, parentheses etching either side of his mouth. Roy was sixty, never married.

"All set for the time being," said Jem.

He thanked Roy for his offer of help, though there was none. Roy stared into the trees, masses of dark pines, brown trunks, dark slivers of distance. There was rustling. Roy's heart quickened. He fixed his eyes onto the spot in the woods he thought contained the sound: snapping kindling, pine boughs parting.

Joe Silla barged out of the woods, his tan suede coat dotted with drops of melted snow. Roy's excitement drooped.

"What is this, a pow-wow?" said Joe to the two men who stood in similar poses: hands in pockets, leaning on one hip with the opposite foot pointing forward.

"Got a death wish?" Roy asked. "Where's your orange vest?"

The chill gripped Joe's toes inside a pair of designer boots that looked rugged but were more suited to driving a heated SUV than for hiking. His face had numbed.

Fruit of the Vine

"No hunters here," said Joe. "A million 'posted' signs. Like a square fungus on every trunk."

"Think anyone pays attention to those?" said Roy.

"What's everyone doing here anyway?" Joe's heavy lips moved sluggishly, like someone had turned a knob that slowed his motor.

"About to ask you the same thing," said Roy.

"I'm wondering what either of you are doing," said Jem. "Sure, there's not much going on in this town. But poking around to check out a collapsed porch doesn't seem too entertaining to me. Like watching red wine age in the barrel."

A curl of wind wafted the scent of Joe's cologne to Jem, who was reminded of the smell of the inside of a new pine fishing basket. Not a bad scent.

"Why were you traipsing in the woods?" asked Roy.

Joe scrunched his face, angry at Roy's probes.

"Good exercise," said Joe. "Keeps the physique up."

"You two can look around all you like," said Jem. "Case the joint, for all I care. You find Sasquatch tracks, let me know later. I'm going home."

The exhaust from Jem's truck formed a cloud that lingered over the road before the surrounding air claimed it.

"What is it you have up your sleeve, Joe?" asked Roy. "You up to no good?"

"Told you. Checking out the house. What about you?"

Roy was silent.

"Oh, no questions for Roy," said Joe, waving both arms theatrically in an x motion. "You just ask. You don't answer."

"This is a historic piece of property," said Roy. "It's the site

36

Cynthia Kolko

of a Seneca Village. Big battle between the French and the Seneca. A massacre, actually. Came here to pay respects. Honor my heritage."

Joe dropped his arms. "Cut the shit, Roy. You're like a-hundreth Indian."

"More like a quarter."

A chill shook Joe, whose lips were taking on a blue tint.

"You should have worn a hat," said Roy. He pulled the edges of his own cap further over his ears.

"Tell me what it is you're looking for," Roy said. "Something you've seen?"

"If you're going to keep asking me questions all suspicious like, might I remind you who you work for? And what I know about you?"

Roy sighed. "How could I forget," he said, under his breath.

Joe shivered. His jacket undulated in the wind.

"Want a ride home?" asked Roy.

"I'll walk."

With Roy gone, Joe tried to walk the land, take a self-guided tour of the Loud property. The ground was uneven under the snow, and his fancy boots weren't made for the terrain. The result was laborious plodding rather than the refreshing stroll he pictured earlier from the warmth of his home office. Joe's toes seemed to have disappeared inside his boots, replaced with painful cold. His leather gloves weren't doing the trick either. His ears throbbed.

There were animal tracks, but Joe didn't know what creature had left them. He spotted a pile of dung pellets that sunk a divot into the snow. It looked like the droppings of his

Fruit of the Vine

kindergarten class bunny back in Maryland, the one the kids took turns bringing home each weekend, the one that pushed its rear end against the bars of its cage, spewing tiny spherical poops all over Joe's family room while leaving its own cage pristine. The one his parents moved to the garage until Monday morning.

Joe walked toward home on the road's shoulder. A car sped past, dangerously close. Joe dodged the car by bounding onto the road's snowy edge, twisting his foot on a rock. He let out a howl to whichever God was listening and hobbled on, his ankle swelling in the designer boots. By the time Joe reached his car, parked some fifty feet into a snowy fire road, he was hopping on his unhurt foot, numb to the bone. With the heater on full blast, Joe started a slow thaw.

"Where were you?" Sandra screeched when Joe stumbled into the house.

Her nails were freshly manicured, hair coiffed. Sandra was a formerly pretty young woman who, at some point between high school and her mid-twenties, transformed herself into a grotesque bombshell-type with bleached hair blown to twice its normal volume, plumped lips, and an absurd boob job. Lots of women had fakes, but not in Sawhorn. Not like those. Her body was made obsessively taut by exercise and possibly liposuction. Sandra looked like a caricature, an exaggerated cartoon. But to those who favored an over-processed look, whoever they may have been, she was an eye-popper.

"Thought I'd park and take a walk," said Joe.

"In this cold?" said Sandra. "You're not dressed for it."

Cynthia Kolko

"I realize that now," said Joe. He hung his coat, still stiff with cold, on a wooden hanger in the hall closet.

"You could have died out there," said Sandra. "And why are you limping?"

Joe pulled off his boots. The swelled ankle was bruised purple.

"Oh God. You got hurt," said Sandra. "I'll get some ice."

"Don't think it'll help," said Joe. "Got to keep it elevated."

Sandra pulled a leather ottoman, factory-distressed for a rugged look, over to the couch where Joe sat. Joe lifted his foot onto it. Sandra brought him a plate of sushi, a selection of rolls with green nuclei and molded rice blocks holding waves of pink flesh.

"Damn," said Joe. "Sushi around here tastes like shit."

four

Ed's fingers bound a nosegay of miniature American flags. He stepped over the road's embankment, be-whiskered with a mess of weeds that, depending on their strength, size, or dumb luck, were matted with gravel, recoiled under snow, or standing at attention like porcupine quills. In the Loud cemetery, Ed plucked the weathered flags that sprouted from the base of some headstones, replacing each with a new one until only fresh flags waved in unison over the veterans' graves.

Ed shuffled through the snow to the old Loud house. He hadn't been close to it in years. It was expertly boarded up, polka dot nail heads trimming the boards. Amazing how the Louds bucked landscaping trends. No foundation plantings, shrubs, or ornamentals; just gray-trunked oaks lining one side of the driveway and the sketchy remains of Elba's perennial garden under the snow.

Ed felt a painful crackle in his chest that led to a coughing fit. Woozy, he put his free hand to his forehead. He trudged back to his red truck and, once inside, headed to the Veterans' Association to properly dispose of the old flags. He could just toss them in the trash, but hell if Ed Loud didn't handle the flag with the symbolic care required of a patriot.

My duty. Fucking goddamn duty. Plant flags for my favorite uncle. Uncle Sam.

Zack was due at Jem's place for the Bills game that afternoon, but Zack was not known for being prompt. Too busy straightening things: folding his shirts, toweling out the last drops of water from the sink, cleaning his hairbrush. Teachers, doctors, and employers thought his tardiness was due to being disorganized. Truth was, Zack was too organized.

"Got the good stuff this time," Zack said when he showed up, grinning under a beret, his gloves gripping a case of jaundiced beer in bottles.

"What's up with the hat?" said Jem, half-amused and half-disgusted.

"Sandra gave it to me. Someone left it at Tap. She said I looked like a poet in it."

Jem scrutinized Zack's dark face, the camel-colored beret, a piece of felt sticking up from it like an apple stem.

"You look like an acorn," Jem said.

Zack tore off the acorn hat and tossed it into Jem's garbage can.

"Shit. I knew it looked stupid," Zack said.

The two guys sunk into Jem's couch, sat gape-legged like

Fruit of the Vine

frogs. Zack wrenched a church key and let a bottle cap clink to the floor.

"Pick that up. You think this is a dump?" said Jem.

"Was going to, quickdraw. I ain't a slob," said Zack.

The screen played a commercial of a monkey dropping from a palm tree into a delighted crowd of bikini-clad women. Jem raked his crotch with four fingers.

"Fixed the harvester," said Jem. "Easy as pie. The fuel filter was plugged."

"You want me to stand on my fucking head?" said Zack.

The reason Jem and Zack were friends could be attributed, in part, to the phrase "misery loves company." The two found some kinship in their hard-luck circumstances. Zack's mother, Gidget Muff, hailed from a band of wandering craftspeople that rang doorbells looking for repair work in town after town, renting on short-term leases, bartering shelter for work, and occasionally camping out in their own vehicles. Solid as a boulder and tending toward the outspoken, Gidget met Zack's father, Miguel Santiago, when still a teen. She got pregnant and, after a slur-hurling ruckus involving both the Muff and Santiago clans, married him. Townspeople predicted all sorts of hardships, but against the dismal odds, the couple had stayed hitched and relatively prosperous. Gidget ran the local laundromat, working hard and earning a respectable living, though not the stuff of affluence. A sharp lady, she wrote a book, a childhood memoir called Now That That's Settled. Miguel, not interested in laundry, became a cop. For the better part of a decade, the Santiagos' life hummed along, each day as much like the previous one as if it had rolled off an assembly line.

One night Miguel stopped a speeder on Route 20. He was standing at the driver's window when a wayward semi shooting up the road picked him off like a kid kicking a pebble. Zack was five. Gidget took her meager savings and the life insurance check and bought the laundromat. A few years later, she added a dry cleaner's. Zack worked the pants presser and bagging machine after school, but the stenchy chemicals gave him massive headaches. He quit. Now even the suggestion of entering the laundromat elicited Pavlovian revulsion in Zack.

Jem and Zack had, at times, bandied about the prospect of fixing up Gidget and Ed, but always abandoned the idea for the sheer absurdity of it. Gidget was large. She had the most misshapen butt Jem had even seen, like sacks of onions strapped to her backside, jiggling and shifting when she walked, like they might break loose and spill all over the ground. Ed liked his women skinny as sticks.

The commercials were over and the game was back on. Jem had twenty dollars riding on the Bills. Ten point spread. The team looked promising as ever. There was hope for them yet.

"So," Zack said, "Spend last night at Laura's?"

"Yeah," Jem said, eyes fixed to the screen.

"You and Laura..?" Zack prodded.

"No."

"Her and Bender?"

Fruit of the Vine

"Yeah."

They spoke about yardages, the quarterback's injury, and how disappointing the rookie running back's performance had been this season despite his absurdly huge salary. And which of the two of them, Jem or Zack, would make a better on-air sports commentator. Then, aside from the sound of the television, silence.

"Porch fell off the Loud place," said Jem.

"Huh?"

"Up and dropped off."

"That must've been a mess."

"You ain't kidding."

"You get it cleaned up?"

"Yup. Sanford and Don took over. All under control."

"Could have come got me. I'd have helped you."

"I know."

Jem tried to use his tongue to dislodge some mashed up food that had settled between his molars, but decided that using his forefinger was more efficient. Zack stared at Jem's open-hinged profile.

"How'd you get that black and blue mark on your cheek?" asked Zack.

"Door," replied Jem.

"Door?" Zack said, incredulous. "What, you tried out a dance move and shimmied into the jamb?"

"Never mind, okay?"

Zack popped the top off another beer, spun the cap on the pitted coffee table.

"Saw your Dad at the hardware store," he said. "He had bags under his eyes. Looked all tired and shit. Sick, even."

"Tired? You talk to him?"

"Said 'Hey.'"

"It's his busy season, between summer antique shows and Christmas. Shop's loaded with projects needing sanding, staining, screwing. He can't handle all that work."

"Screwing? I can help, depending," said Zack.

No one heard Russ come in. He didn't knock. Just walked inside, scowling.

"What do you say you all come with me to Tap tonight?" said Zack. "Find some chicks for once. The tavern's a sausage hang. Too much man funk in there. Sick of that Bender. That 'stash of his."

"I don't know," Jem said, bristling at the thought of being out of his element among the starched collars and Joe Silla in the charred building he'd spiffed up, the halogen lights hung in a swirl on the ceiling and the martini of the day scrawled on a lighted wipe-board. Joe, flexing his arms behind the bar, declaring himself the hippest dude in town. Brandishing Sandra as proof of his manhood, congratulating himself for pulling such a hottie. They'd been married for several years already, but you'd think he'd just picked her up, bedded her, and was bragging to his friends about the conquest. Fucking Joe Silla.

"Come on," said Zack. "Break out of your comfort zone once in a while."

"If it sucks, I'm leaving. First five minutes," said Jem.

Fruit of the Vine

Jem would have resisted more or made an argument for the tavern, but he wanted to avoid Bender and any second-degree about Laura.

"Have fun," said Russ. "I ain't going same side of the street as that Euro trash joint. Especially with that fucking Indian in it."

A handful of years previously, Russ's sister got raped in the tattered farmhouse where their family lived. Someone said they saw Roy outside. But there was no proof. No other witnesses. No one got charged. The case went cold. The sister was seventeen now, a senior at Sawhorn regional. She was lanky like Russ. Great field hockey player, people said. Might even get a scholarship for it. She seemed well-adjusted, all things considered. Seemed to have moved past it all. But not Russ. He needed someone to blame. Not just for the rape, but for everything.

Joe poured black coffee for Ed, who was sitting at the card table in Joe's home office, and offered cream which Ed refused. Joe had the place built to resemble a gentleman's country retreat. Wainscoting in a dark cherry stain covered the walls below the chair rail and above it hung hunter green wallpaper festooned with pheasants, well-bred pointers, and knickers-wearing dandies on horses. The fireplace had been lit before Ed arrived. Over it, the oil painting of a Jack Russell terrier—as stately as any presidential portrait—dominated the room. Ed was surprised there wasn't a painting of

Joe in the frame. A pair of towering arched bookcases flanked the fireplace. Glare coated their glass doors, making it impossible for Ed to read the titles, though he guessed none of the books' pages had ever been turned.

Joe's desk was a finely polished wood semi-circle, devoid of papers or even a computer but topped with a leather office set: blotter, clock, and a pen cup containing one pristine Mont Blanc.

"What do you think?" Joe asked.

Ed eyed the numbers on the paper in front of him titled "White Deer Hotel and Estates."

"Pretty darn good."

He did a calculation in his head and liked them even more. The drawing for the proposed housing development looked like a kidney and attached urethra. Fifty rectangles edged the streets like boxes on a winding conveyor belt. There was a larger rectangle at the kidney's cusp. That would be the hotel.

"I like it," Ed said. "Nice name for a development too. Easier to say than "White-tailed deer."

He gulped from his cup, replaced it onto the leather-edged coaster. A brown drop painted a line down the cup's edge.

"Let your lawyer look at it if you want," said Joe. "I don't want to be accused of doing anything underhanded. Just making what I think is a fair offer. But don't take too long. I want this done fast. Cut and dry."

Joe led Ed to the front door. They shook hands.

"Call you in a week. That enough time?" Joe said.

"If it isn't, I'll tell you that when you call," said Ed.

Fruit of the Vine

Ed walked the path of ice-glazed flagstone pavers. In the breeze, a King Boris fir waddled like its namesake and sprinkled snow onto the coated ground. Ed slid his tarnished belt buckle behind the steering wheel and backed his truck out between the pair of brick plinths that flanked the driveway, an iron horse's head balanced atop each.

Look like puppets. Ed drove off, the afternoon light glinting off the sparkling snow.

The road split two lonely fields like a zipper. Pines pierced the distant sky. Thickets, homes to countless critters, rolled over the hill toward the old Loud place. In front of the house stood Roy's blue pickup. A gust stirred grounded flakes on the road's edge in a blast of cold confetti. The Loud homestead's roof was an expanse of rectangles, shingles outlined in white.

From atop another hill, a yellow house lorded over the scene, the monstrous Chateau Cobblestone homestead, catching the sky like cotton on a nail. Chateau Cobblestone was a massive winery, built by some Wall Street bigwig as more of a hobby than an investment, an experiment in a lifestyle for people who didn't need to derive a living from it, who imported a winemaker from France and MBAs to run the place while they themselves sniffed corks, went to competitions, and entertained friends in cavernous cellars lined with sweet-smelling oak barrels. Chateau Cobblestone had its own landing strip.

Cynthia Kolko

One blue state historical marker, erected in the 1960s, stood on the road opposite the Loud farmhouse:

LOUD FARM
Settled 1660
One of the earliest standing houses in region
built 1788

Roy scanned the neglected land and walked to the cemetery. Isaiah Loud. Roy remembered Isaiah leaning into the panel-backed truck to hand Roy's mother and father their pay for the week's work. Money they used to purchase milk, peanut butter, and cigarettes. Paid their rent. Girard, Roy read. He made an almost undetectable smile which quickly faded.

The sky darkened and the falling snow grew in size and quantity. The shingle rectangles were becoming filled in as if by a white crayon. Whorls of flakes spun like miniature tornados, touching down on the road and dissipating.

The sound of crumpling paper came from the woods' edge. A single buck, wearing a crown of antlers, strode onto the field behind the cemetery. The deer stopped no more than thirty feet in front of Roy, who watched the animal's pure white coat, its hazel eyes returning Roy's stare. The animal took a few steps, muscular but dainty.

Ghost Deer. We meet again.

The deer chewed what Roy imagined was the last green leaf left this season. Then the animal galloped across the field like a runaway bride until it became a speck at the field's far edge and melted into the brush.

49

Fruit of the Vine

The neon Tap sign glowed, its metal shanks connecting the huge letters T, A, and P, iced with red light. Jem hunched as he crossed the room in his stained field coat. He met up with Zack, who had taken a beer from the bartender, an attractive redhead who walked away behind the bar, one strap of her azure tank top slipping down her shoulder. Both Jem and Zack noticed.

"How about a snack? Roy cooks up some good shit," said Zack.

"Not hungry, just thirsty," said Jem.

Zack read the menu.

"Fancy," said Zack. "It's in cursive."

Russ entered the bar, looked sheepish. He joined the men.

"Look who crossed the street," said Zack.

"Thought you hated this place," said Jem.

"He'll go anywhere there's willing women to be had," said Zack.

Russ shrugged, conceding that Zack was right.

Ed sat in a kitchen chair, the beige vinyl seat framed in open-ended chrome pipes that scratched crevasses into any bare leg unfortunate enough to brush them. A collection of papers, clamped in a paper clip, rested in front of him on the glass octagon tabletop. The chrome fulcrum underneath reflected the lone working bulb in an acrylic tiffany-style light fixture from which a tousled ringlet of flypaper dangled, spotted with its spoils.

Ed took a swallow of beer, flipped the papers to the one earmarked by a blue post-it. He got up, rifled through a drawer stuffed with keys, receipts and business cards, found a U-Haul pen. He tested it by scribbling on a receipt, which he returned to the drawer before sitting down at the table.

He drank the last drop of beer, tossed the can into the sink. It clanged against the half-dozen other spent cans like cymbals of aluminum garbage can lids. Percy the dog, lying closed-eyed on the mat in front of the sink, briefly flinched one ear in response.

What's the difference? Land's not doing anyone any good.

He signed and dated.

Government will condemn the house, make me pay to get it repaired.

Signed again, dated. He closed the papers, went to the fridge, cracked open another beer.

Hell, someone's got to make money off that land. Might as well be me.

Ed walked to the living room, took the remote off a brown couch matted with dog hair, reclined and clicked through some channels.

Worked like a goddamn mule my whole life. Nothing to show for it.

He coughed a thick bronchial hack and sipped from the beer can. Percy lumbered in, circled an invisible spot next to the couch three times, lay down and twitched one ear. An image of a parasail over an expanse of turquoise water came

Fruit of the Vine

onto the TV. A gleaming beach edged the water. The show cut to a swarthy man, pink-shirted arms draping the shoulders of a pair of bikini-clad nubiles.

Yeah. I'm going to take a trip like that. Little piece of heaven.

Ed started to cough uncontrollably. He sat up, gave one final hearty hack and stopped. He wiped his mouth, looked at his fingers. A bright red smear.

At Tap, a band called Flipper was playing. Russ and Zack, pumped with several rounds of alcohol, danced on the section of floor cleared of tables and chairs for the event. Zack moved with a fluidity that transcended his blocky build. Russ yawed like a jerky windshield wiper. When the song finished, the two retreated to Jem at the bar.

"Next good tune, you're coming out there with us," said Zack.

"You know I don't dance," said Jem.

"He ain't happy unless Laura's in the joint," Zack said.

"Not true," said Jem. "Chick's out of her mind."

"Bender's chick?" said Russ. "Never mind her. Bark up a different tree. Some nice ones in here tonight."

"Nice trunks," said Zack.

"Woof," said Russ.

"Ho, ho!" said Zack, spying Sandra in a short black strapless dress, sashaying from the dance floor back to the bar. "Wait a minute! Check out what Sandra's wearing tonight.

Cynthia Kolko

Hoo! You should have seen the miniskirt she had on the other night. Let's just say I know that head of hair ain't her natural color."

Zack caught Sandra's eye, motioned for her to come over. Sandra's hair was freshly permed into a loose blond weeping willow.

"Hair," said Zack.

"You like?" Sandra shook her head so the curls bounced.

"Sexy," Zack said.

Sandra smiled, turned her eyes to the floor.

"You are the hottest woman in Sawhorn. Without question," said Zack.

"I don't know," Sandra said, gazing at Zack.

They stared at each other for a good five seconds before Sandra looked away toward Joe, who stood behind the other end of the bar, straightening the glasses that hung overhead.

Ten minutes later, Zack gyrated on the dance floor, bottle in hand, in front of Sandra, who shimmied her shoulders and tilted her pelvis to and fro in time to the thumping beat.

"Don't he know she's married?" asked Russ.

"Looks to me like she doesn't know she's married," said Jem. "You think she's good looking?"

"Fuck no. Can't figure why Zack's all hot for her," said Russ.

"Thinks he's supposed to be. Believes what he sees on TV," said Jem. "Besides, what woman doesn't he like?"

Joe glowered, eyes like slits, from behind the bar.

"Fucking Joe Silla," said Russ. "Needs to go back down South where he belongs. Damn transplant."

Fruit of the Vine

It was a sentiment not unheard of in Sawhorn. To many longtime residents, the town had slipped into a less-friendly state in recent years. The people were gruffer, more jealous of each other, more selfish, more into material goods. Crime was higher than before. People were less likely to report suspicious goings-on, less interested in others. There were too many people they didn't know, families for whom they had no reference, neighbors who couldn't be categorized. Ed called this phenomenon "city creep," and he pointed out its cause as everything from television to Wall Street mega-bonuses to fancy four-wheel-drive cars. City folks moved into town, set up summer retreats, eager to conquer a piece of the country. Truth, the region had been a popular vacation spot for as long as there were people who took vacations. But a more visible target of blame could not be found.

The Paynes, owners of Chateau Cobblestone, were a convenient example of city creep, with that beacon of a yellow house looming over Sawhorn like a king on a high throne. Mr. Payne erected the yellow monument to his own success on a sprawling vineyard which he paid other people to run. He called himself a farmer. Ed laughed, guessed it would be six months before Mr. Payne vacated his humidor room and moved back to the city. It had been four years since the construction of Chateau Cobblestone was completed. Yet in a way, Ed was right. The Paynes spent most of the year downstate. Mrs. Payne had her favorite spa shampoo shipped in. She could sometimes be spotted at the antique fairs, though they were better described as high-priced lawn sales that offered items that weren't quality when they were new: battered

Cynthia Kolko

factory-assembled secretary desks, "Jenny Lind" settees crafted of discarded chair spindles, water-stained reproduction Audubon prints. And fire buckets. Every dealer's booth seemed to have at least one fire bucket. Mrs. Payne rarely spoke to the vendors, lest she seemed interested. Word got around that she was aloof and snooty. It wasn't an altogether inaccurate description.

People around here are nice and all, Ed would say whenever the subject of city creep came up, but they'll never really accept folks who move here from somewhere else. They see them as a different breed. I know they bring money into town, but dang if people ain't happy when the summer's over. Gets back to normal. Around here when you ask someone what's new and they say nothing, that means everything's okay.

Jem sipped his beer.

"Know how Joe Silla's dad made his money?" asked Russ.

"He's a real estate guy, right?" asked Jem.

"Got a government contract building houses for the elderly. The kind your great-grandma lives in. Made him rich. The state decides they need more affordable housing. Someone's got to build it. Happens to us up here too. Albany's got the stickiest fingers yet. Them taxes we pay, they don't go to who needs it. We're paying for these guys' lifestyles. We should all get government contracts."

"Joe isn't from down South, you know. He grew up around D.C." said Jem.

"That counts as the South," said Russ.

"They just think they're Southern. Snows there like it's the

Fruit of the Vine

goddamn North Pole. But they don't have plows, so the whole city shuts down anytime a flake hits the ground."

"Fucking idiots," said Russ. "Get a damn plow, for crissake."

Zack returned to the bar and chugged the fresh beer that had appeared in place of the old one. A new tune started, its heavy backbeat reverberating through the room.

"Time to get down on the dance floor, Jem," said Zack.

"No way."

"There's a hottie out there with your name on her."

"Man," said Jem, pushing away from the bar and moving toward the dance floor, "I've got to stop drinking so much. Affects my judgment."

Soon after the three hit the floor, a pair of smiling girls danced in front of them. Zack, never one to resist an overture, moved in on the shorter one. Petite women made him feel taller. Jem moved his feet in time to the music, beer in hand by his side. Zack moved closer to the short woman, circling his hips.

"What the hell is this?"

A young man in a pinstripe shirt grabbed the arm of the short woman.

"Come on, Will," she said.

Will turned to Zack.

"I thought you guys all went South for the winter. With the birds and the old people. Shouldn't you be back in Mexico?"

Zack gritted his teeth. Like a ventriloquist, he barely moved his lips. "I've never been to Mexico."

Jem grabbed Zack's arms from behind, yanking him back.

Cynthia Kolko

The other dancers withdrew like ripples from a drop. A single fist rammed Will between the eyes. He folded to the floor. Russ held his hand like a smoking gun.

From his bed, Jem heard the mourning of an ambulance. In the distance, the wailing stopped and the siren of a cop car took its place. A few minutes passed. The ambulance started up again, louder as it passed Jem's apartment building, the Doppler effect like the crashing of a wave.

The call came at 5:30 a.m.

"Jemison Loud?"

"Yeah."

"I'm Marie, a nurse at Seneca General Hospital. Edward Loud was admitted last night. You're listed on his health care proxy."

"What happened? Is he okay?"

"You need to come down, Mr. Loud."

At intensive care, the nurse directed Jem to an empty waiting room. Jem sat in one of the room's stiffly-upholstered chairs and leafed through an elderly, dog-eared Newsweek against the backdrop of piped-in music, a broad falsetto melody punctuated by synthesized trumpet farts. He tried to read, but the music seemed to inch closer, gaining prominence until he could no longer concentrate on anything.

Jem approached the desk. The nurse greeted him with hard eyes and a scowl. Her identification tag showed a photo of a trim, smiling woman with feathered hair, hardly the heavy-set, tightly-coiffed specimen seated here.

Fruit of the Vine

"I'm Jem Loud. Here for my father, Ed. Got a call this morning."

"We'll be with you as soon as we can."

The nurse tilted her face down to a loose stack of papers. Jem almost re-entered the room of endless waiting, but about-faced the desk.

"I didn't call you, you called me. I got here soon as I could, and I'm waiting around. Don't have a clue what happened to my dad. His name is Ed Loud. As in Loud Road, Loud Farm..."

The nurse interrupted, "We treat all patients' families equally here."

"Equally bad," said Jem, hunching.

A creased-faced woman in a starched lab coat approached.

"Jemison Loud? I'm Dr. Hernandez, your father's physician. Come with me please."

Ed was asleep. His face was nearly the same shade as his bleached pillowcase, his barely-pink lips drawn into a thin frown. He looked shrunken and dehydrated as an apple doll.

Dr. Hernandez shook Ed's shoulder gently. "Edward. Edward."

"No one calls him that," said Jem. "Always been Ed."

Ed's eyes opened.

"Jem?"

"Jesus, Dad. What's all this?"

Ed coughed. His face reddened. After two or three earnest hacks, his pallor returned to bisque.

"Your father called 911 last night," said Dr. Hernandez. "He had trouble breathing and was coughing up blood. He has

Cynthia Kolko

cancer in both lungs. We want to remove one of them. But he won't let us."

"Remove a lung?" said Jem. "How will he live?"

"He'll use the other lung," said Dr. Hernandez.

Ed groaned from the bed. "I told them to stuff it. I ain't a fan of removing parts. Let me be buried with everything I was born with. Except maybe some teeth."

"Stop talking about being buried," said Jem.

Jem rebuked himself; he should have noticed how much Ed needed him and taken the initiative. He would have helped Ed with the shop, the house, anything. But hell, why didn't Ed just ask, just say something? And earlier, way earlier than the offhand complaint after the Loud porch fell off. Now here was Ed, terminally ill. He had probably been sick for years, sick as a dog, knew it, and never saw a doctor. He'd do something like that.

When Dr. Hernandez left, Jem took a manila folder from the Lucite holster mounted outside Ed's door. Jem read the chart, felt the blood drain from his lips. He heard a siren ring in his head. He hunched.

"Everything you need to know about my financial affairs, the house, the shop," said Ed, "It's all in a box on the top of the shop's closet. Take care of Percy. Poor dog's probably pacing around in his own doo. Your great-grandmother. Poor old broad. I take her on Sunday drives. Do that for me, Jem. Do that for her. For corn's sake don't let her starve."

Ed's voice petered out. He emitted a single painful-sounding cough.

Fruit of the Vine

"You're my only son, Jem. You know I love you. If I thought it would end like this, I'd a told you sooner."

"Would you stop talking like that? Be positive. Good chance to come out of this."

Doctor Hernandez re-entered the room.

"Gentlemen, I'm sorry but Mr. Loud needs to rest."

Jem leaned over Ed's lined face and kissed his forehead. Ed took Jem's hand, shook it, kissed it, closed his eyes. Coughed.

Jem drove home, felt his innards twisting, thought he may have to stop on the side of the road to relieve himself. When he got home, he spent an hour on the john, his buttocks red and sore in an oval shape when he finally got up.

He called Zack. The phone rang four times before the answering machine clicked on. A familiar "Hello?" interrupted the recorded message.

"You're not going to believe this," said Jem.

"What?"

Jem felt the tremolo of his vocal chords before he even spoke. He blurted the words all at once like a hasty guitar strum.

"Ed's not my father."

five

Jem met Zack at the tavern for an afternoon beer. "It kind of makes sense, don't it?" asked Zack from his chair at the table near the men's room, an unpopular seating location and therefore somewhat private.

"You ain't too much like your dad. You're way mellower. Always seems like he's got some kind of chip on his shoulder. And he's all high-strung like. Let's just say I wouldn't want to take him hunting. He'd be shooting every leaf rustle, every squirrel and chipmunk. Like Yosemite Sam, all wild and yelling 'yee-ha!' and letting bullets fly into the air like a crazy son of a bitch."

Jem thought back to an actual day of hunting with Ed, the two perched atop a plywood lookout Ed built, dry weeds on the ground piercing the sky like arrows. Ed shot at a deer and missed. The animal fled into the woods. Ed grunted as he flung his rifle, windmilling to the ground.

"You don't look like him neither," said Zack. "I don't mean

Fruit of the Vine

anything queer by this, but you're a good-looking guy. Like those models in the clothing ads. Only you got a goofier expression. And your ears are too big. And it looks like your hair's getting kind of thin. You know, you might end up needing a toop."

Jem closed his eyes, exhausted by the situation, Zack's blathering.

"Your dad, man, maybe he was something to look at when he was younger, but now he's a craggy old dude. And he looks like this." Zack held his pinky aloft. "Bet he's ninety-nine pounds with rocks in his pockets. You're thin, but you ain't hardly a toothpick like that." Zack shook his head. "Man. You could snap him like a branch."

"Right there in his chart," said Jem wearily. "His blood type's O. Mine is AB. It's impossible for him to be my father."

Jem remembered high school biology class, the unit on genetics, the bitter paper that only he, in a class of twenty kids, could taste. His recessive attached earlobes and hairless digits, one of which he pricked to drop blood on a card, to watch the red coagulate.

"He doesn't even know," said Jem. "Poor guy. Lost his mind in Nam. Lost his wife. Losing his life. And now he lost his son. In a way."

Jem saw a sixty-something balding man stumble over air on his way to the coat rack.

"My real father could be any geezer in here."

"Hell. Could even be Bender," said Zack.

"What am I, fifteen?"

"So ask your mom who it is."

Cynthia Kolko

"How? I don't know where she is. What her name is, if she got married again. Nothing. I don't even know if I really want to talk to her. Whoring around on Ed. This is just the latest piece of evidence."

"Still can't believe your dad's dying," Zack said. "That shit's surreal. One day you're hanging out at home, beating off on the couch. Next day you've got half your lungs, can't blow out a candle. Can't play kazoo worth a shit. You think things don't change. That stuff here in Sawhorn is pretty much just like it was a bunch of years ago. That your life is going to be like this forever. Then some shit goes down and everything's different. One thing makes other stuff happen. Like dominos. Before you realize it."

Bender came out from behind the bar looking like a referee, with a towel tucked in his belt. He leaned both hands on the table in front of Zack and Jem. Bender wore the sad, serious face of a scolded dog.

"Jem. Heard your dad's in the hospital. That sucks."

"I know."

"Possible to beat it. People do. If anyone can, it's a Loud."

"Thanks."

"You need something, let me know. My ma wanted to cook you dinner but I told her we didn't need you in the hospital too."

The three guys laughed. Jem was relieved to have the mood lightened. Bender twisted to face a group of men sitting at the bar, nodded to one of the guys, then turned back to Jem and Zack.

"Hey, what's Russ's real name?" Bender asked.

Fruit of the Vine

"Emmett," said Jem.

"Emmett?" said Bender.

"Emmett," said Jem.

"Yo!" Bender yelled to the group at the bar. "It's Emmett!"

Guffaws erupted from the bar.

"Emmett! Ain't that the Muppet Show frog? Yeah, Emmett the frog! Wait a minute. It's Kermit the frog! Oh yeah, Kermit. What a fucking name! Emmett! Piss-ant name! Little Lord Emmett! Fucking Emmett!"

Russ entered the tavern at that unfortunate moment.

"Emmett!" boomed the bar.

"Yo Emmett! What up? Emmett! Hey, froggy boy! Ribbitt! Emmett! How's it going, Emmett?"

Russ aimed a ferocious glare at Jem and Zack, and left about as quickly as he came. The group at the bar continued to yuk it up. Jem pointed to the rectangular bulge in Zack's chest pocket.

"Give me one of those."

"Thought you didn't smoke," said Zack, handing Jem a cigarette and lighter.

"I don't," replied Jem, lighting up. As a rule, he had to be rip-roaring drunk to use tobacco.

"The hell you doing?" said Bender. "This is the no-smoking section."

"Don't get your panties in a twist," said Zack, standing, his stool crashing to the floor behind him. "We're leaving."

"Got your twenty-two at your place?" Zack asked Jem.

Jem and Zack picked up Jem's gun, went to find Russ at his house—a converted trailer stranded on a patch of land like

64

a submarine lost at sea. A NASCAR flag beat the wind from a lone flagpole. A snow-blanketed mound of wormy apples ringed the property's only tree. Russ lived there alone. Owned the place.

Jem and Zack dawdled in front of the motionless door. Zack checked his bare wrist. "What time is it?" asked Zack.

"Don't have a watch. Two or three?"

Zack took a golf pencil from his front pocket, one of a cache of them he'd liberated from the public golf course where he caddied one summer during high school. He scrawled a note on the back of a scrap, "Shooting in Hassler woods till dark." He jammed it behind the weather stripping.

Thirty minutes later, Russ showed up in the woods carrying a six-pack of empties, a gun, a hammer, and a picture of Bender.

"Where'd you get this?" Zack asked, using his thumbs to iron the creased photo.

In the picture, Bender had an arm around half a girl. His opposite hand dangled. He looked drunk.

"Was in the garbage," said Russ. "At the tavern. Few months ago."

"You went through the garbage?" asked Jem.

"It was right on top," said Russ. "Little crumpled stack of pictures. Wasn't none of them flattering with Bender all half-cocked. I was in the right place at the right time. Knew they might come in handy. For bribery. Or revenge. Good thing I kept them, eh? Just wish I had pictures of all those other douche bags at the bar, making fun of my name. Fuck them. All of them."

Fruit of the Vine

He took a nail from his pocket and hammered the photo to a tree.

"I get to go first since I brought the picture," Russ said.

Russ was a damn good shot. First try, he blew a hole in Bender's moustache.

***

The nurse knocked on Ed's door.

"Visitor, Mr. Loud."

She peered into the room, checking if Ed were awake. Joe Silla pushed the door all the way open from behind her. He almost knocked down the startled nurse as he let himself in.

Ed's voice was weak. "Wasn't expecting you, Joe."

A monitor displayed Ed's heart rate as a picture of a hill. There was a beep every second or so, and the image morphed into another similar hill.

"Thought I'd see how you were."

"Been better," said Ed.

The monitor beeped.

"Where are we with the contract?" said Joe.

The hills got larger.

"Signed it," said Ed.

If it were appropriate, Joe would have done a tap dance.

"How'd you get a lawyer so fast?" he asked.

"No lawyer. Can't stand those bloodsuckers. You haven't lived here long enough, Joe, or you'd know that Sawhorn is a handshake community."

"Where's the document? Do you have it here?"

"Wasn't exactly carrying it around with me when the ambulance came."

Joe started to blink rapidly, as he tended to do when agitated.

"Don't worry," said Ed. "When I get out of here, you'll get it. No rush. Land ain't going to blow away."

At the hospital the next morning, Jem was surprised to see Ed standing with his hands propped flat against the reception desk like he was trying to keep himself from collapsing.

"You want to visit me, Jem, you better do that at home," said Ed. "I'm outta this quack bung hole."

"You're checking out?" asked Jem.

"This ain't a hotel," said Ed.

"He's releasing himself AMA," said the wrinkled nurse behind the desk. "Against medical advice."

She shook her head, weary from what Jem surmised was an arduous argument with Ed.

"What about the operation?" Jem asked.

"Screw that," said Ed. "We been over that yesterday. Remember? I'm leaving this world with all the original parts."

"But you need the operation. The cancer."

Ed put a slack hand on Jem's shoulder.

"Don't worry so much, boy. I'm going to be fine. Always am."

Ed walked away down the hallway, hair matted in back from lying on the pillow, his rear end non-existent in pants that looked several sizes baggier than they should be.

Fruit of the Vine

"Need a ride?" Jem called after him.

"Don's meeting me downstairs," Ed yelled back, his voice echoing in the stark passage.

At home, Ed turned down the thermostat.

Place is a hot box.

He put on gloves and a scratched leather jacket, lifted the squeaky garage door with both hands, fired up the motorcycle. A helmet hung on the cycle's handlebars. Ed lowered the helmet onto his head, removed its yellowed and clouded shield. Someone had either plowed the driveway, or the snow on it had melted; Ed couldn't tell. He and the cycle took to the road. Good a day as any. Clear roads. Ed inhaled deeply, felt the air filling him up like a drink of his own youth. Lungs worked fine.

Ed took in the back-roads scenery, took note of landmarks from his past. The dirt path that led to the canal where he first kissed his wife, Mary. The roadside gutter where he found his childhood dog hit by a car and left dying. An orchard's mint green farmhouse and the remote grove of trees where a hungry boy could steal an apple undetected.

Ed picked up speed, enjoying the blast against his face. The drop hanging from his nose flattened and formed a crust on his upper lip. He could just make out the Loud homestead's roofline on the horizon.

Ed took a hairpin turn unprepared for the white buck standing in his path. He catapulted over the animal and thudded to the roadside, his helmet smashing through the ice that glazed a deep water-filled ditch. The deer galloped away. Ed lay face down in cold water, unconscious.

❦

Ice pellets pinged Jem's windshield and ricocheted into the sky. The street that penetrated the Sawhorn Meadows subdivision curved gently, the houses lined up like toys on an assembly line.

Jem knocked at number thirty-four. Elba Loud. Ed's paternal grandmother. Jem's great-grandmother. Bender's great aunt. Jem pushed the unlocked door open.

"Gram?" Jem said leaning into the opening, feet on the welcome mat.

A stringy voice answered. "Son?"

"It's Jem."

"Who?"

Jem walked in, stood on a small square of tiles surrounded by carpet. Vacuum marks radiated from a random nucleus. Gram sat in a chair. It took some effort for her to get up, but once upright she took spry steps. Flickers of Ed shone in her face—the pale, almost colorless blue eyes; the twin lines running from outer nostrils to lip corners like road gutters toward the horizon, forming a trapezoid between nose and mouth, an almost stationary slab that vibrated slightly when Elba talked; the lower lip moving up and down as if on a hinge. Elba's white hair seemed transparent, pink scalp visible between the scant strands. Her two front teeth gapped just

69

Fruit of the Vine

enough to cradle a small cigar there, had she wanted to. She was thin like Ed. But where he was frail-looking, Elba was wiry, walking upright as the letter I, back taut, face angled toward the sky like a floodlight.

"I always forget how tall you are," said Elba. "Looks like you're still growing. Hope you don't have gigantism."

"I've topped out. Six-five."

"Always knew you'd be big. You were five weeks premature, but you were well over twenty inches long, like a full-term baby. You grew like ivy up the walls, but so thin, a breeze could have carried you away."

Elba's Audubon clock sounded the coo of a mourning dove.

"So. Your dad's got lung cancer. And then he crashes his motorcycle. Can't seem to stay out of trouble, that one." Elba extracted a wool overcoat from the closet. "Can't say I'm itching to go to the hospital."

Elba's hands fumbled with her coat buttons, but she secured them all and stepped into her boots, purposely purchased a size too large to make the task easier.

"I want to see the house afterward. Mrs. Carpin told me the porch caved in. Not surprised. Main house was built like a rock, but that porch addition. Slapped right up willy-nilly. Mrs. Carpin says the place looks like a flophouse. Couple of boards holding it together."

Elba pointed to Jem's boots. He anticipated a scolding for the puddle around them.

"You know what you never see any more? Rubbers. Young

70

men don't wear rubbers these days." Elba opened the door. "Mrs. Carpin worries when I don't tell her where I'm going."

Elba took Jem's arm as the two crunched the snow to the adjacent house. Jem rang the bell, waited. A wreath of artificial lilies hung by a brass hook engraved in cursive: Welcome, Friends. Jem re-pushed the button, heard the ding dong from inside.

"She isn't deaf, just slow," said Elba.

They waited in the cold air until the door opened.

"Come in. Don't want to catch a chill," said Mrs. Carpin.

The house was crowded with stuff, framed Hallmark prints obscuring the wallpaper, bits of lace draped over the arms of chairs, coffee tables and stands filled with what looked to be every figurine ever made—a dizzying collection of porcelain. Corner shelves and bookcases were similarly filled. Nothing was dirty, but everything was cluttered.

Mrs. Carpin's hair was a wavy pewter bonnet. Her body was bell-shaped, narrowly constructed on top and fanning out into buttocks that hung from her back like a shelf. A uni-breast similarly protruded from her sternum like a ledge upon which Jem imagined more figurines could be displayed. Legs terminated into feet encased in slippers of matted fleece embedded with lint, like a child's overwashed stuffed animal.

Jem bent to scrutinize a photo of Elba and Mrs. Carpin smiling in the midst of a mariachi band. The pair had spent Christmas on a "Yuletide Cruise for Seniors," as the ad called it. The price was cheap. All meals included. They took a series of flights to Florida and shared a cabin on board. A sal-

Fruit of the Vine

monella outbreak truncated the ship's voyage, which docked at Cancun to let a score of weary passengers disembark. When over half the remaining passengers fell ill, the ship about-faced back to Florida. Elba was spared sickness as she barely ate anything, but nausea sent Mrs. Carpin to the hospital. The doctor declared it anxiety, not salmonella. Doped-up on tranquilizers, Mrs. Carpin traveled back to Sawhorn in a blur of sleep. Jem and Ed had shared a rare laugh over the story. Jem wondered if Mrs. Carpin even remembered the photo being taken.

"Margaret, this is my grandson, Jem. He's taking me to see Ed."

"Elba, are you going senile? I've met him plenty. Pleased to see you again Jem, despite the circumstances. Terrible luck. Why don't you stay for a minute? I've got pecan sandies."

"Thanks, but we have to get going," said Jem, hand on the doorknob, rubber bands choking its neck.

"Oh, shoo!" Mrs. Carpin slapped the air in mock disappointment. A television show beckoned from around the corner.

Elba sat in the passenger seat of Jem's truck, her boots leaving tread marks on a manila folder in the foot well. The two Louds drove amid stitched-quilt squares of landscape bleached with snow. Leafless branches clawed the sky. A two-foot long snowy owl perched atop a telephone pole reigned over the road. It was months before buds would form, like tiny green peas on stems, the leaves breaking out like chicks pecking through their eggshells.

72

Cynthia Kolko

Elba directed Jem to an unmarked side road. "Turn here," she said. "I want to show you something."

Jem had been on this road numerous times; there were few stretches around Sawhorn with which he wasn't familiar. Joyriding was a popular pastime, especially for young men with wanderlust who lacked the gumption, not to mention the funds, to plan and carry out a real trip. Jem and Elba passed five minutes' worth of land, scraggly trees, downed fences, and homes: some neat, some worthy of a magazine cover, some ill-kept, some little more than shacks, often within yards of each other. Jem thumped his fingers on the wheel.

"This was a bad idea," he said. "I'm worried about the time."

"Ed won't even know we're there, let alone what time it is. Tell you the truth, I'm not sure I want to see him like that now. Not ever. Ignoring it is easier. God works in funny ways. An old lady like me is still living while everything around me goes to the dogs."

"Don't say that, Gram. We don't know how bad it is for Dad."

"It sure as Sam isn't good. Let's not sugar-coat it. We need to face it like men."

A crow holding a McDonald's wrapper in its beak flew into a leafless tree. The landscape became populated with houses, barns, a church. Small businesses were sandwiched between residences: a gift shop, a garage, a fabric store. Jem had passed these places countless times, but never noticed them as more than guides to his passage. Now, he wondered who

73

Fruit of the Vine

lived in these houses. Who built them? Who worked here? Had Gram been inside any of these buildings? Had his father hiked this road? Or his mother?

"Gram, you remember anything about my mom?"

"Why do you ask?"

"I don't know much about her except people say she was real good-looking."

"Average," said Elba.

"I've seen pictures. Looked pretty good to me."

"Everyone looks good when they're young," said Elba.

"Not true," said Jem. "I knew some homely girls in high school."

"Nobody has to be homely today, not with all the products in the stores."

"Well, you can't make a silk purse out of a sow's ear though."

"You can make a mighty nice sow's ear," Elba said.

To Jem, Elba's choice of words, her inflections, was like listening to his father.

"So was my mom a nice lady? All in all?"

"Now, what kind of nice lady runs away from her family? No. Not a nice lady. Selfish. Not dumb, but immature. She wasn't our type. You'd have had to be blind not to tell it wouldn't last. At first, Mary sat close to Ed when he drove, like a dog. So close she could rest her head on his shoulder. Before too long, she sat far away, practically hugging the passenger door, face to the window like she was about to be sick. Her dad and I were third cousins."

"I know," said Jem.

"Or second cousins once-removed. I can't remember how all that's calculated," said Elba. "We were cousins of some sort. Let's leave it at that."

Good idea.

The road narrowed as the vista grew wider. A Quaker cemetery broke the land, headstones huddled in the vastness. From a stop sign flapped a torn advertisement for weight loss supplements. A farmhouse occupied each corner of an intersection, signaling home for someone. More dead vehicles were disintegrating in their yards than there were graves in the cemetery. Elba leaned forward and squinted as though she were trying to read the blackboard from the last row of school desks.

"There!" she exclaimed. She pointed to a stand of pines. Just after the trees, like an exhibit behind a curtain, a structure was revealed. Jem wasn't sure what it was. A barn? Quaker Meeting House?

"It's an octagon house," said Elba. "Only one I ever saw. Victorian. They were supposed to be good for your health. It was a fad. Didn't catch on. Like Diane Keaton in Annie Hall wearing a tie and fedora. Ha ha!"

Jem had never seen Annie Hall.

A sedan, a snow-coated compact car, and a wheel-less pickup were scattered carelessly to one side of the building. A pile of stuffed garbage bags clogged part of the porch.

"Some slob lives there," said Jem.

"Look at the woodwork."

A piece of curlicue trim caught Jem's eye. "Standard decoration," said Jem.

Fruit of the Vine

"Architecturally significant, but it's cut into apartments. Maybe someone will fix it. Or have it moved. They do that, you know. Move houses."

"Cool," said Jem, admiring the cupola. He imagined Russ up there smoking a joint, watching for Roy so he could shoot him sniper-style.

At the entrance to the hospital parking garage, the ticket machine stuck its tongue out. Jem yanked the paper, slipped it between the sun visor and the car's roof.

Behind the hospital desk sat the on-duty nurse. When she saw Jem, her expression dropped.

"I'm Jem Loud, here to see—"

"Edward," said the nurse, completing Jem's sentence.

The nurse slid out from behind the desk. She was shaped like a bisected barrel, white pants below and a blue shirt above, her face round with a halo of yellow curls. She was like an abstract painting of a sunny, snowy day.

"I'm so sorry. He's downstairs already," said the nurse.

"Where's that?" said Elba.

"The morgue," said the nurse.

"What?" said Jem.

The nurse flitted her eyes between Jem's and Elba's. She was not the person who customarily broke this type of news.

"Ed had a motorcycle accident."

"We know about the accident," said Elba. You dumb cluck. "Cop said he was brought to this ward."

"He was dead on arrival," said the nurse. "Drowned in a puddle."

Cynthia Kolko

Elba sputtered, "And nobody told us? Of all the shoddy… Who's in charge here?"

Jem fell silent. He never prepared for the possibility that this day could come so soon. The nurse muttered something about a department head and scurried off, leaving the Louds alone in the vacuous reception area.

"I never heard of it," Elba said. "You know a good lawyer?"

"I don't want to get into a mess like that," said Jem.

"You're right. We should turn to God first," said Elba.

Jem wasn't so sure about the God part, but he didn't like the idea of getting involved in a lawsuit. Plus, he didn't know just who he'd be suing for what.

A second nurse appeared, dressed like the first nurse but about half the width. Her sensible shoes squeaked at each step. The large nurse trailed behind.

"Mrs. Loud. Mr. Loud. I apologize profusely. How this happened, I don't know. We have a strict procedure for notifying kin upon the passing of any patient, even one who dies en route. Somehow, this one slipped by."

The large nurse nodded gravely at Elba and Jem.

"Slipped by?" said Elba. "Is that all you have? Slipped by?"

"We're truly sorry. If we could do it again…," said the large nurse.

"Do it again?" said Elba. "You don't get many second chances in this world. Least of all when someone dies."

Jem and Elba returned to Jem's truck in the parking garage. Neither wept.

"My mistake, not seeing Ed first," said Elba.

77

Fruit of the Vine

"Wouldn't have made a difference. He died hours ago."

"Now, every time I see something octagon, I'm going to upchuck. Stop signs'll make me melancholy. I'll end up holed away in my house. Like a phobic. Have to get a few dozen cats, keep the newspapers stacked up so high you won't be able to see me."

Jem showed his ticket at the garage exit. The total flashed in LED numbers.

"Your father dies. They don't tell you. Then they charge you five dollars," said Elba.

Jem handed a crisp bill to the man in the booth and drove off so fast he gave the man a paper cut.

Elba talked for a half-hour about cousins, aunts and uncles, nephews and nieces. Which ones didn't like each other, which ones Ed didn't like and which ones didn't like Ed. Jem paid only sporadic attention, Elba's voice fading in and out of his consciousness like a weak radio signal. His thoughts wavered from the dread of a funeral to the arduous task of cleaning up his father's affairs to pangs of sadness. Yet he couldn't help the flitting euphoria of freedom at his father's death. This was the mark of adulthood he had heretofore yet to fully achieve. He silently chided himself for feeling it, but it was there nonetheless.

Jem clicked his right turn signal on. He wished he could throw a towel over the stop sign so Elba didn't have to look at it.

"Why are you turning here?" asked Elba.

"Way home," said Jem.

78

Cynthia Kolko

"What about the house?" said Elba.

"Haven't you had enough today?"

"If you don't take me to the house, I'll have to hire a taxi later. Is that what you want? Wasting an old lady's money? Some stranger driving me around in the snow?"

Jem sighed, U-turned. A sedan crawled in front of them, blowing snow off its roof like a traveling localized squall hindering Jem's view. Jem slowed and let some distance emerge behind the blizzard car. Then he passed.

"You know about the Loud property, right Jem?"

"Some," Jem said.

"Indians had a village. Big one. A community. Before the Louds. Before we were a country. It was a meeting place for the Iroquois. Mohawk, Seneca, can't remember the others. Right on that land. Amazing to think of it. There was an enormous battle. A bloodbath. French wanted the Indians out of their way, not for the land so much as for fur, I think. Who knows what they wanted? Maybe there were more furry animals running around back then. Can't say I've ever seen anything but squirrels around here. And deer. Lots of deer. People used to say the woods were filled with ghosts. Ghosts of the Seneca. Some said the people massacred on that land haunt the Loud property. If there are ghosts anywhere, I wouldn't doubt that they're there. The property's spotted with such horror. Cayuga. That's another."

Elba's words drifted across the screen of Jem's imagination like closed captioning. He always saw words like this, turned conversations into reading. It was how he got through school

Fruit of the Vine

without doing much studying. After a lecture, he'd just re-member what he had read, play it back. He attributed his spelling prowess to the same tendency.

"The Girards were around back then. And before too long, the Louds. In my day, this area was filled with Louds."

Elba circled a finger in the air. It was the same motion she used when she found something banal. It was usually ac-companied by the words whoop-dee-doo.

"Teeming with them," she said, the whirling finger now still. "Some folks look back at those days—the time when I was growing up—and call them the good old days. Thing is, they weren't all that good. People got sick. And we didn't have all the gadgets that make life easier. Things are better now. Doesn't seem like it sometimes, but it is. Sure as I'm sitting here. And yet, you've got people complaining up and down the flagpole like things are bad. They don't know what bad is. Most of them, you young people especially, none of you have ever been through war. Never truly been scared to death."

Jem thought Elba might let him have some silence for his thoughts, some peace in which to digest Ed's death, to pon-der the significance of knowing that Ed wasn't his biological father. That Elba, sitting here next to him, was no longer his grandma. But no such luck.

"Then again, nothing in New York is recession-proof," said Elba. "That's what Ed always said."

"Wine's a bright spot," said Jem. "Lifting this area up. Peo-ple come here more and more for the wine. Hassler is trucking along real well." Jem offered this as fact, though he didn't know squat about Hassler's finances.

"Wouldn't use that swill to clean my floor," said Elba.

Jem made a mental note not to give Hassler wine to Elba for Christmas.

"Chateau Cobblestone, though," said Elba. "That's another story. You ever tried the Riesling? Smoother than a spring lake."

Jem had. The stuff was damn tasty.

"Every day Sawhorn gets more well-to-do families," she said. "Vacationers and growers both. For the life of me, I can't understand why they'd build a huge house out here."

"Like I said. Hills, lakes, ponds. I'm not talking about the cities on the water with all the screaming jet-skis. The best land is the land no one wants. That hasn't been exploited. You just got to know where it lives."

He hadn't articulated that to anyone else, but it was how he felt. The Loud property. It was better now than it had ever been. Even the weeds were beautiful. Amber and gold. Some of them flowered three seasons, releasing billows of white. They were homes for rodents, a place for butterflies to breed. And they were strong. They could be woven into baskets, fashioned into weapons. They survived just about anything. And there was Franklin pond at the edge of the property: a sticky soup that was a haven for pesky bugs. But after spending an hour on its banks—with the birds, tadpoles, fish, vegetation—even the bugs, the nadir of the food chain, earned his respect.

"Sometimes people don't just want something to look at,"

Fruit of the Vine

said Jem. "They want a place that makes them feel good. Whether they're getting away from somewhere that's been bad, or just want something they can't put their finger on. Something that feels right, not that looks right. And there's no one who can tell them that. No one can sell it to them but their own soul. They find it in here."

Jem thumped his chest with his fist.

"You mind keeping both hands on the wheel?" said Elba.

As they approached the Loud property, Jem could feel Elba's anxiety as sure as if she blew it over him with a fan. When they passed Franklin pond, Elba breathed deeply, her thin bottom lip bent into a frown.

"You okay?" asked Jem.

"Was Ed who found him," Elba said, turning a stiff gaze out the window laced with grit.

Jem wanted to hear the story of his grandfather's death, though he dreaded the details. He knew the event had cast a sorry shadow over the Louds' already unsavory aura. He didn't know how it involved Ed. He'd long wanted to ask someone, but never dared.

"Weren't malls then. Just Epstein's store on Main Street. Isaiah, he had a shirt from there. Plaid. Different shades of blue. Beautiful shirt. His favorite. Ed. He and a bunch of boys, scrappy kids, they used to throw rocks at cans in the woods next to Franklin pond. Set up a whole shooting range there. It was hot that summer. Corn practically turned to popcorn on the stalk. Sunday, Ed comes home trip-trapping like a puppy up the path from the pond. He sees Isaiah's shirt in the scum near the cattails. Figures maybe his dad went fishing, got hot, took it off, shirt blew into the water."

Elba continued, "Ed wades into the pond, grabs the shirt, and Isaiah comes up with it. Baling twine tied to his waist. Seems he got an idea from a gangster movie. Tie yourself to a cinder block and jump in the water. Only the twine must've snapped after a while, and Isaiah's body floated to the top. He died the same week as that Jackson Pollock. Big news when that crazy Pollock, staggering drunk, crashed his car. You know who he was, right? Spat paint this way and that on a canvas, just a mess of drips. I've seen prettier drop cloths. Kindergarteners could do better. Sold those hideous pictures for a mint. To this day, I can't look at something paint-splattered without thinking of your grandfather. Same with water. Every time I look at a lake or even a really large swimming pool, I see Isaiah, sauntering out of the pond like he's fine, wearing his blue shirt, saying 'dang twine too weak. Block broke off.' And none of it ever happened."

Jem and Elba milled about the Loud homestead. Dried weeds like hands, pinwheels of matchstick digits, poked out of the snow, waved at the sky. The land breathed contempt, the house a colossal mockery to mediocrity.

"Should have taken Dad's keys," said Jem.

Elba skirted the house, uttering an occasional tsk tsk.

"Such a shame. Boy, it's just gone to pot."

She faced Jem, spoke quickly, her breath smoky in the chilly air. "This is all yours now, Jem."

"Pretty sure I can't afford to keep it."

Fruit of the Vine

"Rent it to grape growers. Great soil. Terroir, you call it? We used to have grapes growing here out back, on the way to the tree line. Near where the trash heap is. Native ones. Big sweet grapes. Size of eyeballs. Goodness, you had to pick them the minute they ripened, or the birds—cedar waxwings especially—they'd just peck 'em to death. Leave you with pits. And purple BM all over the porch."

Jem knew those grapes. He'd discovered them as a boy investigating the periphery of the Loud land, dreaming he was the lone survivor of a wrecked civilization, living on this sweet fruit that snaked like the head of Medusa over the discards of a rural existence: rusty tractor parts, fence posts, baling twine, and cleared-away rocks, a mess of garbage long reclaimed by vermin, weeds, sinewy trees, and those grapes spiraling atop the mess like a crown, twirling around the tires and all those metal parts. A sculptural combination of nature and man-made trash.

"Wouldn't never be enough to pay the taxes," said Jem.

Jem thought he saw Elba shiver slightly. He didn't know if it was the temperature or the memories that caused it.

six

Jem and Zack sat at the bar at Loud's Tavern. Jem's drinks had been free all evening, thanks to Bender and anyone else aware of Ed's death. The allure of free beer was too difficult to resist. Jem had consumed more alcohol this evening than he had in months.

"Nice guy, your dad," said Zack.

"You talking about Ed?" said Jem.

"I mean it. Yeah, he was kind of rough and depressed-like. But he did right by you, more or less. Best he could. You and me couldn't do much better. All that, and he wasn't your real father. That gives him a few extra points right there."

"If he knew I wasn't his, he'd have treated me different."

"Might as well put it out of your mind. Stuff like that is better left unanswered. Let sleeping dogs lie and all that crap."

Russ sidled up and put a hand on Jem's shoulder.

"Shit," Russ said. "Damn shit."

Russ shook his head. Kept doing it. Didn't know what else to do. Eventually, he stopped.

Fruit of the Vine

"You okay?" Russ said.

"Beer's helping."

"I always liked your dad," said Russ.

Ed had never liked Russ, thought he had the appearance of a nice kid, someone out of a '50s sitcom, but that there was something rotten inside him. Ed had never been a poor judge of character, thought Jem. But he tended to be absolute in his views. People were either good or bad. Jem forgave most offenses, chalked them up to being human. No one, Jem thought, was composed of all faulty parts or all angelic ones; everyone contained a helping of each. Yet, when it came to Ed himself, Jem let the bad outshadow the good. It wasn't so easy to forgive his own dad, to be sympathetic to his faulty parts.

"Shit," Russ said, withdrawing his hand. "Just wanted to stop in, make sure you weren't drowning in tears or nothing. I'd stay, but I've got to blow."

"Where you going?" asked Jem.

Zack answered, "Nowhere fast."

Russ grinned. "I got a date. Chick who works at the Quik Mart."

"The little blonde with the glasses?" asked Zack.

"No, the one with the big cans," said Russ. "See you tomorrow."

"I got to clean out all my dad's stuff," said Jem. "Going to be hell at least until spring."

"See you this spring," said Russ.

Jem became drunker before finally leaving the tavern on foot. He had plodded this sidewalk countless times, yet today it felt like a new route. Even the air smelled different. He had to concentrate on each step so he didn't waver like a wino. The shadow of a quick-moving male figure approached. Jem recognized the man's gait.

"Heard about your dad," Joe said. "Real sorry."

"Still can't believe it," said Jem.

"Tough stuff. Hey, he mention any contracts to you?"

"Huh?"

"Nothing about selling something?" Joe blinked rapidly.

"Furniture? I don't know what he had in the pipe. I still have to look over his papers in the shop. Had one of those filing systems where only he knew where everything was."

"You go through the stuff at his house?"

"Why? Something in there for you?"

"Just curious," said Joe.

As Joe walked away, Zack came out of the tavern, caught up with Jem.

"Hey, last time I was in Tap, I swiped a fancy napkin," Zack said. "Check it out, makes a great do-rag."

The instant Zack fashioned the paisley cloth on top of his head, the locks in a nearby car clicked loudly closed.

"Fuck this racist town," said Zack.

A rise in temperature melted the snow. Ed's funeral was a brief affair, the way Ed would have wanted. Word of mouth. A two-line obituary. Ed was buried in the Loud plot. Jem had forgotten to get a flag for the grave and made a mental note to do it later. He returned to work the next day.

Fruit of the Vine

Manette walked from the big barn wearing creases in her forehead. Her gray hair and light complexion contrasted with the building's paint like a single polka dot on a red dress, Japan's flag in reverse. Her plaid field coat hung long and boxy on her petite frame. She strode out to the field, her gait as wide as if she'd just stepped off a horse.

Before Jem worked for Manette, she'd been a cartoon to him. He pictured her flitting about the farm, saying things like "fiddlesticks" and "dagnabbit" as she bounced like a pinball to-and-fro along the rows. Now he found her to be a confident, no bullshit type. She made her own judgments from her own experiences coupled with a good dose of common sense. She had a demeanor some described as bitchiness, but Jem thought it a fitting counterpoint to the whirlwind of variables tossed upon the grape grower. Wimps got trounced in this line of work. Manette was a tough broad, to be sure.

Manette found Jem cleaning equipment to be stored until the next harvest, ten months down the road. She laid a gloved palm on his shoulder.

"Let's talk," she said.

Manette sat on an iron bench that flanked the towering barn like a too-short bookend. Jem didn't want to sit, but did anyway. He couldn't recall a time when he sat so close to Manette, his jeans almost grazing hers.

"You didn't have to come here this morning," said Manette. "We'd all understand if you wanted to take a little time."

"Keeping busy helps," said Jem.

Manette nodded, looking solemn. Lines in her face hinted at past frowns as well as smiles.

"How'd you like to be keeping a little more busy?" she asked.

"That'd be okay, I guess," said Jem.

"Time's come for me to slow down a little," said Manette. "Going to need help. You've been an outstanding field foreman. I'd like you to be vineyard manager. You'll do a lot of the stuff that I do now. I'll still be here, of course. But you'll need to do the legwork. Hours are long. No picnic, this job." Manette's voice trailed off.

Jem was just the way Manette liked them. As hardworking as an ant. When Jem got pulled down, or fell, he was the type to just get himself back up again. Mary and Ed Loud were another story. But every family had its rogue sheep—its unexplained aberrations, its storm-damaged elements. For all Mary and Ed's foibles, they'd turned out a fine son.

"Yeah," Jem said, halfway between a statement and a question.

"You seem surprised," said Manette.

"Not surprised. Well, maybe a touch. Wouldn't you rather get someone with a college degree?"

"College is overrated," said Manette, sitting with her legs apart. "Just an expensive reading list. You've worked here long enough, and you always learn fast. Course, it wouldn't be the worst thing to get some more education. In horticulture, for instance. You'd make a fine student. Smart as a whip, you are. Hope you know that."

Jem did feel himself more cerebral than his cohorts, though he never let on that he thought it. His kindergarten teacher had told Ed, in Jem's presence, that Jem was a boy who could do anything he wanted, if he put his mind to it. And now Manette was saying something similar. Jem enjoyed hearing it, even if he didn't quite believe it, or didn't think he should. He got so little validation of that kind, it was hard to take it seriously.

"Now to do this right, you'd have to live here on the property," said Manette. "There's an apartment above the wine shop. Rent will be part of the pay. No one's living there now, but it needs to be cleaned out first. Full of crap. And like I said, the job isn't roses. Hard work."

Manette unfolded her legs to stand, like opening a rusty bridge chair.

"You think about it," she said.

"All right," said Jem.

"All right you'll think about it? Or all right you'll do it?"

"I'll do it."

Manette smiled. It was quick. Just a flash of ivory before her lips returned to their usual neutral position.

"Glad to hear it," she said. "Come by my office before you go home. We'll work out the details. And, I'm sorry again about your dad. You can always come to me and Sanford if you need something."

Manette walked away. Jem hadn't noticed before how stooped over she was, like a late-season sunflower curving toward the ground. It made him straighten his own posture.

Jem caught up with Zack back out in the rows.

"Joe invited us to Tap," said Zack. "His personal guests. Says there's no hard feelings. Wants us back as customers.

Cynthia Kolko

Long as we don't bring Russ. He was pretty clear about that. No Russ."

"I'm not going back to that joint," said Jem.

"Come on."

"Never bothered you going alone before."

"I promised Joe I'd bring you."

"What, now you and Joe are all buddy-buddy?"

"He's giving us free booze all night."

❧

Tap's glass-topped bar, lit from within, displayed a collection of antique and vintage beer taps, highlighted and labeled like rare artifacts. Jem was fascinated with them.

"Didn't get a good look at these, last time," Jem said.

"One here from Prohibition, a bootleg job. Think it's down that way," said Zack.

Jem's gaze followed Zack's pointed finger in the direction of a 1930s tap which gleamed deep under a martini glass of pink liquid poised to refresh. A doll-faced woman sitting straight-backed, long hair like black silk, smiled a crescent of Chicklets in the guys' direction. Jem and Zack's necks snapped away. Jem regarded his hands on the bar, studied his knuckles. Zack stared down into the glass at the taps.

"Jesus," whispered Zack. "You see that?"

"Yeah."

Zack snuck another look at the woman. She gave him a closed-lipped grin and raised her eyebrows.

Fruit of the Vine

"She wants to meet us," said Zack.

"I'm staying here," said Jem.

"Pussy," Zack teased. "She's a city chick. That's the best yet. City chicks got farm fever. To them, it's like going to Europe and picking up a guy with an accent. We're exotic. A little piece of the country. They come out here trolling for rednecks."

"So we're rednecks?"

"Not me so much as you. Just look at you. Name might as well be Zeke."

"Isn't Zack a lot closer to Zeke than Jem?"

The woman rose from her stool and walked with her chest pointed toward Zack and Jem.

"Aggressive. I like that," Zack half-whispered, shuffling the menu away.

"Hi," the woman said, pink martini in hand. "You two from around here?"

"Yup," said Zack. "How about yourself?"

"Up from school. I live here sometimes. At my parents' place. Chateau Cobblestone."

Zack and Jem nodded in recognition.

"You on break?" Jem asked.

"You could say that. I've got one semester left, but I'm not going back anytime soon. Sitting it out. Had it with the books and those little preppy boys. They all wear the same ball cap and chew the same dip. Hang a Grateful Dead skull from the rearview, think it makes them bohemian. Then they graduate, cut their hair, and become like every other Wall Street stiff."

The woman inched closer to Jem. She stared, eyes brown with bull's eye stripe of hazel, luminous as a polished walnut settee. Her half-smiling lips were the color of an empire apple.

"I'm Meredith." The woman extended her hand. Jem took it.

"Jem."

"Jem?" she asked. "Is that Norwegian?"

Jem smiled. He'd heard that guess before, along with Finnish, Danish, Swedish, German, and Welsh.

"Short for Jemison. Family name," explained Jem.

Family lore had it that they were related to Mary Jemison, the "White Woman of the Genesee," though it was dubious, undocumented, impossible to prove.

Zack thrust his hand forward. He sensed the scales of favor tipping toward Jem but was not ready to concede so soon.

"I'm Zack."

"What do you do?" She asked both men.

"Work at Hassler Vineyards," Zack said.

"Me too," Jem said. "Field foreman."

Zack flashed Jem a scowl. He resented Jem flexing the muscle of his elevated employment, like a naval officer tapping the uniform stripes of his shoulder.

"I check the grapes, see if they're ready to be harvested," said Zack. "And coordinate some of the hand-picking. We did the pinots and the gewirtz a few weeks ago. Despite the cold. We're used to that. Doesn't stop the process. No siree."

"I know about Hassler. Seems like a cool place," Meredith said.

Fruit of the Vine

"It is," Zack said to Meredith's chest. "So where you usually live, when you're not here?"

"The city," said Meredith.

"Rochester?" asked Zack.

"New York," said Meredith.

"Oh, yeah? I went twice," said Zack. "While back. Jem's never been."

"You've never been to New York?" asked Meredith, eyes wide.

"Never had to," said Jem.

"You do have to!" said Meredith. She punched Jem's shoulder with perhaps more force than intended. He almost dropped his beer.

"Everything's there," she said. "There's so much to do. Culture. Best art galleries. The music scene is incredible. You can order Vietnamese food at three in the morning. Not Chinese. I'm talking authentic Vietnamese. Or Samoan, or Irish, or North African. You can get just about any newspaper you want. Yiddish, even. Greatest city on earth."

Jem shrugged.

"I've got to concede, it's beautiful here," said Meredith. "I've been all over the world, six continents, and this is as scenic, as peaceful, as anywhere. I hope you recognize that. Sometimes people don't appreciate what's right in front of them. But still, you've got to get out of this one-horse town sometime."

"I'm not into horses," said Jem. He tilted his bottle, emptying a drop of backwash between his lips. "Every time I drive somewhere out of state, people think I'm from New York

City. They say things like 'how's the big apple?' or 'how 'bout them Knicks?' I go along with it, tell them the city's great, never sleeps, all that crap."

"When you ever drive outta state?" asked Zack.

"You were with me, remember? Drove down to Florida? Slept at the rest stop? Then the time we went to Indianapolis speedway. And I've been to Pennsylvania before. Saw the cracked Liberty Bell with my dad. Ohio, too. And Canada. Course, Canada's not a state. But I've been there a bunch a times."

"To see the Canadian ballet?" asked Zack.

Jem gave Zack an admonishing look.

"Canada's colder than here, even. And man, it gets so damn cold here your nose'll freeze and fall off your face. Anyway, seems like too many mean people in New York City, if you believe the papers," said Jem.

"As if," said Meredith. "Every place has its share of jerks. Even Sawhorn."

Good point. Jem had adopted Ed's derogatory definitions. There were bloodsuckers, cocksuckers, jackasses, and bums. Jem had added "blowhards" to the list. Jerks? Maybe Joe was a jerk. But then, Jem thought of Joe not so much a jerk as he was a blowhard. Or a bloodsucker. Or a blowhard-bloodsucker hybrid. A blowsucker? Bloodhard? What about Zack? He might be a jerk. Self-interested, begrudging Zack. A bum, according to Ed. Russ? A jerk, for sure. And a bloodsucker. A bloodsucking jerk. Who was a cocksucker, then? Sanford? A bit hapless perhaps, but not a cocksucker.

"I don't know any jerks," said Jem.

Fruit of the Vine

"Reminds me of the time I was on vacation in Thailand," said Meredith. "At a resort. There was this French guy, and we were talking."

"You speak French?" asked Zack.

"Not very well. But he spoke English okay. This guy, he's from France, but he'd never been to Paris. Like, you'd think if he were that well-traveled to be in Thailand, he'd go to Paris. This is just like that, you never going to New York. Not that you're well-traveled. But you live here in the same state. And it's hardly a foreign country. You speak the language."

"I guess," said Jem.

"If you come visit me, I'll show you New York. My New York. It would be a blast."

Meredith's red blouse draped like the diaphanous wing of a butterfly. A black belt studded with silver medallions encircled her tiny waist. Blue jeans hugged her thighs.

"That an invitation?" Jem asked, heart thumping with the possibility of a crushing rejection.

Meredith turned her face to his ear, leaned in, her low voice little more than a vibration. "You bet."

Jem felt his face warm up. City girls are fast, that's for damn sure.

"When you're here, you live with your parents, then?" Jem asked.

"Yeah, but I have my own area in the house. My own apartment, with a separate entrance and a little kitchen. Sometimes I don't see them for days. I like it that way and so do they." Meredith laughed. "Maybe you'd like to see it sometime."

Cynthia Kolko

"Maybe you'd like to see my place," said Jem. "It's so close I could throw Zack from here and hit the side."

Meredith's hand flew to her mouth and a short string of giggles sifted through her fingers. Zack swiveled on his stool, swept the bar for other willing women, stumbling drunk women, rebounding women. Trolled the gutter. But closing time was approaching and most of the place had gone home.

Jem felt guilty for the impending hook-up, felt he should be mourning the loss of his father. In the days since Ed's death, Jem hadn't so much as stepped into his father's house to empty out the refrigerator, let alone begin attending to his new role as guardian of the Louds' ancestral farm. One of the first people who had called Jem the morning after that visit to the hospital was a lawyer with a copy of Ed's will. Jem was surprised that Ed had crafted an official one, since Ed trusted a lawyer as far as he could throw him, but there it was: all notarized and full of stiff language, leaving the whole of Ed's estate to Jem. Heaped on top of it all were his new responsibilities at Hassler Vineyard. And the constant prod of wondering who his biological father was. But alcohol had a way of helping Jem pull the covers over his head, to return everything back to the way it used to be.

"Be right back," Meredith said. "Don't go anywhere."

She strutted in the direction of the ladies room, the twin balloons of her buttocks tightly encased by denim. Pangs sparked Jem's jeans. A pretty face could hold Jem's attention, but a shapely rear all but sealed the deal. Zack's eyes—hard, jealous orbs, glazed with alcohol—met Jem's, dull green like sea glass.

97

Fruit of the Vine

"You fucking dog," Zack said. "You're going to fuck her, aren't you? Damn son of a bitch."

Jem grinned.

"Fucking stop smiling," said Zack. "Jesus. You get a fucking hot chick, and I get to go home and fuck my pillow."

"You get plenty of chicks," said Jem.

"When's the last time I got something like that? I'm going to settle up," said Zack.

Meredith returned from the ladies room with fresh lipstick and combed tresses, hips and arms tracing a figure eight as she walked. She nestled into the space between the bar and Jem's forearm. Jem's hand leaned on the bar. Meredith thrust her hip closer, sandwiched her hand on top of his.

At the register, Joe leafed through a stack of twenties. He faced Zack, who ticked his head in the direction of Jem and Meredith.

"Hubba," said Joe. "Sandra knows her."

Meredith spoke closely to Jem's face and smiled. Jem said a few words into Meredith's ear, put his hand on the small of her back as he steered her toward the coats. Meredith turned, her hair a lustrous swinging fringe.

"I've got a tab. Meredith Payne," she called to Joe, who nodded.

She said to Zack, "Nice meeting you, Jack."

Jem gave a cursory salute to Zack, who turned toward the bar. Meredith snapped a spotless white parka at the waist, put up the fur-trimmed hood, and the two stepped into the blustery air.

"That's a great buttocks," said Joe.

Cynthia Kolko

Zack looked at Joe quizzically. "Ain't 'buttocks' plural?"

"To me, it's one unit. But if you prefer, I can call it a great ass. How's that, okay?"

Zack nodded in annoyed agreement.

"Don't worry," said Joe. "Won't last. None of you hayseeds can handle her."

seven

Jem habitually arrived first to the vineyard. Zack tended toward the tardy. But this morning, Zack got to work even before the morning radio talk shows aired. As Jem exited his truck, Zack made a beeline for him.

"Dude. Know what happened to the porch at your family's old farmhouse? Same kind of thing happened at my mom's house. The little roof that hangs over the front stoop. It's the oil-based paint. Traps the moisture. Whole thing's rotted out. I got to go fix it after work today."

"Need some help?" asked Jem.

"Russ is coming already. He has that huge ladder. We just got to shore it up 'til spring. Make sure it ain't crashing down on the mailman or something. We don't want a lawsuit."

"Especially 'cause, you never know, the mailman might be your father," said Jem.

A palpable silence settled between them. Jem fumbled with one of his jacket's buttons, turned to walk away and start his work.

"So what happened with the chick?" said Zack. "You fuck her?"

Jem froze. "Maybe."

"Maybe?" said Zack.

"Damn, you're a nosy son of a bitch."

"She don't have a sister, does she?"

"I got her number. Why don't you call and ask?"

"Maybe I'll call and ask her what she's doing tonight. See if she'd like a little of this." Zack angled his palms around his crotch.

"Thought you got a roof to fix," said Jem.

"Like I ain't going to take a chick over a roof? Hell, I'd let it crash down on the mailman all day long. Let it crash on my own ma. What's her name again?"

"Meredith."

Zack nodded, grimacing like he was nauseated. "That's bad. That's a grandma name. Who the hell names their kid Meredith?"

"Jem?"

Laura's face beamed. Her cheeks were flushed. Her nose was so shiny it reflected the sun.

"Got a proposition for you," she said. "Don't feel obligated if you're not up to it."

"Proposition?" Jem's pulse quickened.

"Mom and dad gave me a little piece of furniture."

"Oh."

"I like the thing but it needs serious help. All wobbly, drawers stick, bubbly finish. Scratched. It's real old, and I don't want to ruin it."

Fruit of the Vine

"Want me to take a look?"

"Would you? I don't know what kind of time you've got. Your dad. New job."

"I'll see what's involved when I look at it."

"Mom and I have been cleaning out your new place," she said. "We had a boarder living there bunch of years back. Darndest thing. He smelled like kitty litter, but no cat. Place's been storage ever since. Should be real nice."

"Great."

Laura went back to her house. Zack looked confused.

"What new place?" he asked. "What new job?"

"Moving above the wine shop," said Jem.

"What?"

"Manette needs more help. Wants me living on-site. Got promoted. Pay raise."

Zack threw a glove to the ground, stomped away.

Joe picked up the Gideon's Bible from the motel room's coffee table and slammed it down with a resounding thud.

"You screwed him? You were supposed to be getting that contract for me. Not getting it on."

"He was cute," said Meredith.

"Not better looking than me though, right?"

"Of course not. And you know I'm a sucker for ambitious men. Not guys like him. Guys who don't try to better themselves. Who just let stuff happen and react to it."

Meredith sat down on the bedspread but thought better of

Cynthia Kolko

it and stood. She had seen a television news story about motel rooms. The reporter shined a black light onto the bedspread, revealing a host of bodily fluids and other unsavory remnants.

"I got enough ambition for this whole part of the state," said Joe. "That turn you on?"

"Yes," said Meredith. "Just not at the moment, if that's what you're getting at."

Meredith scuffed imagined bedbugs off her rear end, then looked at her hands as if she'd find the creatures crawling there. She thought of using the bathroom sink, but pictured a germ-laden room and drying, overly-scented soap that old ladies probably liked. She wiped her hands on her thighs.

"Did you see the shop?" asked Joe.

"Huh?"

"Jem's dad's shop! Didn't he take you there?"

"Oh, I guess I didn't realize."

Joe threw up his hands, sat in a barrel chair, his legs wide. He folded his arms. "Now I know why you dropped out of school."

"I didn't drop out. I took a leave of absence."

Joe spoke slowly, as if he were addressing a toddler, "He doesn't think this was a one-night stand, does he? He's interested in seeing you again, right?"

Meredith pulled aside a curtain with a cigarette hole in it. Outside, a vacant factory stood discarded in an ocean of cracked pavement. The workers had been replaced by foreign labor, places where taxes weren't high and compensation packages didn't cost as much.

Fruit of the Vine

"That's some view, Joe," said Meredith. "Once again, I said I wanted a nice hotel. Not a flea trap with a view of a home for rats."

"Close that! Someone could see you!" said Joe.

Meredith ungripped her hand, letting the burned curtain fall back over the window.

"I'm starting to feel weird about all this, Joe. Ever since that day at the Loud Farm, in that stinky old house, you've been a different guy. You're crazed."

Joe bolted to standing, spoke close to Meredith's face.

"We had a deal. Now, have him take you to that shop. You get that contract!"

"You can't push me around," said Meredith. "I'll tell Sandra."

"You do and I'll tell your daddy what you've been doing. Mommy too. They'll cut you off in a second. No more bank account for Merry."

"Stop patronizing me!"

Meredith shielded her eyes with her hand. Would they do that? Cut her off? They'd used the power of the purse for worse. They'd done it her whole life. They'd bought her a car when she'd gone out for the tennis team, then took it away when she'd been caught smoking. They used money as a reward, its absence as a punishment. She was sorry that these enticements and deterrents worked, but not sorry enough to rebel against them.

Joe's voice softened. "And remember what I told you about us? You don't want to ruin that, do you?"

Meredith sighed and sat down on the gross bedspread.

"Okay, I'll call him."

"It's in a green envelope. Like grass. You can't miss it."

Cynthia Kolko

From inside the abandoned warehouse, Roy Archer replaced his binoculars into the case. He stepped onto a crate and climbed—with surprising agility for a man who could qualify for membership in the AARP, let alone one who smoked as much as he did—out the window he had jimmied open to get into the building. Inside his blue pickup truck, Roy lit a cigarette, let the sweet nicotine do its work.

On the kitchen counter, Jem's answering machine blinked red, lighting the nearby window like a pulsing "no vacancy" sign. Jem pushed the play button.

"Hi Jem, it's me, Meredith. Just seeing what's going on. So. Give me a ring."

Jem headed out the door to the tavern.

"Yo! Here comes the big boss," Zack said when Jem entered the establishment. "Taking over Hassler while I'm still kicking the dirt around. Let's hear it for Jem Loud, folks. Good ol' white guy! Raise your glasses."

"What do you want me to do? Not take the job?"

A vein pulsed in Zack's forehead. "Just busting your chops, man. I'm happy for you. Really, I am."

Sitting hunchbacked on his bar stool, Zack read aloud from the newspaper personals.

"Whoa whoa. Look at this," he said. "'Up for anything.'"

"Must be a guy," said Jem.

Both men laughed. Zack closed the paper and pushed it across the bar toward Bender.

Fruit of the Vine

"Thanks for the birdcage liner," said Zack.

"Hey, Mom got a cat," Zack said to Jem. "Thing's got seven toes on the front paws. It's freaky-looking. Ma says it's from inbreeding."

Jem's face flushed.

"What's the matter? The 'inbred' thing? Get over it, man."

"I just get this feeling that that's what people think of me," said Jem.

Though his parents were distant cousins, their tangled bloodlines inclined Jem, their sole progeny, to feel himself a genetically-knotted chump worthy of whatever derision came his way. Inbreeding, Jem thought, meant dumb people. It spoke of a narrow existence, a lack of a desire to venture outside one's lair. Not that he was exactly a thrill-seeker.

"What people?" said Zack.

"People here in town. They look at me and think, 'there's that down-and-out Loud kid, the inbred.'"

Zack rolled his eyes. "No one's thinking that. Know why?"

Jem twirled his arrowhead between thumb and pointer finger.

"Why?"

"Cause they ain't thinking about you at all," said Zack.

"Even worse," said Jem.

"No it ain't. They're too wrapped up in themselves. Their own lives. They're worried about why their car is making that funny noise. Or what they're going to do about that toothache. They're sure as hell not thinking 'Jem Loud the inbred.' Dude, if anyone's thinking about you, they're wondering what you're thinking of them. You got to change your

Cynthia Kolko

glass-half-empty attitude. Look on the bright side. And ain't you overlooking something? Ed Loud's not your dad. Course no one else knows that. But that's gotta be a weight off your shoulders right there."

Sure. As if.

He'd been trying to put that fact out of his mind. Tried his damndest. Yet, it kept floating to the surface like a baking soda submarine. It seemed that at some point in most everyone's life came a desire to know about his or her ancestors: who lived before, what they had endured, what their vocations or their personalities revealed about their contemporary progeny. He had heard of this happening when people had children. Parenthood made folks more cognizant of the passing of time, more aware of their particular place in the epic of humanity. They created family trees, researched little-known branches, joined the Sons of the American Revolution.

Jem surprised himself with how much his wonderings—the ones he didn't successfully squelch—had focused lately not on his father, but his mother. He knew little about Mary Girard, remembered only brief, murky scenes that might be actual events or things concocted by his own imagination. Before Ed's death, Jem had felt disloyal conjuring up those memories or indulging in even the most fleeting curiosity about Mary. Word was that she'd died years previously. Ed said it was true. She wasn't "clean," as Elba had put it, was involved in risky behavior that certainly led to her demise. But Jem wondered if that was all speculation, with "dead" being a figure of speech. Was she just dead to them? And if she had physically passed on, what parts of Mary still lived in Jem?

Fruit of the Vine

What pieces of his personality had he inherited from her? He was well aware of much of the legacy she left: a broken, single father, a self-deprecating son. But what had she left under the surface, in the blood?

"Just cut the sad clown shit already," said Zack.

"Huh?" said Jem.

"You got this depressed look on your face," said Zack.

Jem shrugged.

"I stand corrected. Your glass is full. It's full of shit."

"It is shit," said Jem. "Sucks feeling like you don't belong in a town your family practically started. Like I snuck into a wedding and pretty soon someone's going to call me out."

"You feel like you don't belong? Try dyeing your face brown." Zack sunk a pointer into his own cheek. "Then see how you feel."

Bender sauntered over.

"Jem buddy, that Meredith chick was in here looking for you. She was all pissed off. But with women, you never know. Could have been on the rag and hating the males of the species for the week."

"She didn't like the bouquet Jem got her for her birthday," said Zack. "A big bunch of chlamydia."

Bender straightened upright as a radio tower. He grinned with half his mouth, a deep crevasse like a comma dripping from the corner. More wrinkles spread from his eyes. His skin looked craggy, with some blemishes staining the cheeks. Bender was not aging well.

"Fucking riot, this guy," said Jem.

eight

Jem ran the press, taking stock of the bin of grape skins, seeds, stems, and the occasional mangled leaf. He squatted to peer under the machine and check if any more juice was draining, the back of his jeans pulling perilously low. But he managed to keep from revealing himself.

"Jem?"

Laura's voice took him by surprise. He clambered too fast to his feet and tumbled ear-first against the open bin, coating his right temple and cheek with slippery grape skins.

"You okay?" Laura asked.

"Yeah," Jem said, mopping goo from his face. "Stupid, but okay."

"I can run home for a towel."

"I got one here."

Jem disappeared behind the press and returned with a cloth so blotched with oil and dirt that it looked like an artist's brush rag.

Fruit of the Vine

"That's not going to get your face clean," said Laura. She was wearing a knit cap with grapes knotted onto it.

Where does she find this stuff?

"I'll wash it in the bathroom," he said.

Laura waited outside the little washroom in the barn, listening to the running water and watching a spider spinning a web between the bathroom door jamb and one of the wooden ceiling beams. Laura wondered how many times this barn had been cleaned, really scrubbed from ceiling to floor? There must have been decades of filth caking all those crevices. This barn wasn't the oldest one on the property. It was built in 1910 or so. The oldest barn was the one attached to the main farmhouse, built around 1800. It wasn't so much a barn anymore as a garage, housing the Fillmores' pickup truck and sedan. It contained two large Dutch ovens from the barn's inception, big white domes like igloos that had fascinated Laura from as early as she could recall. What was baked in those? What were the ingredients? How did it taste? Baking, it seemed, had long piqued Laura's interest.

Jem emerged from the bathroom, the hair on his right side glistening.

"Remember when I asked you about that old piece of furniture, that dresser?" said Laura.

"Yeah," said Jem.

"I don't want to push or anything. I was just wondering when you were coming by. If you still want to do it, that is. No pressure if you want to bow out."

"Tonight's good," said Jem.

Laura looked relieved. "You could do it right in my house,

in the spare room, so you wouldn't have to worry about dust getting into every corner. Just close the door and open the window."

A trio of Indian corn cobs tied with a grape-motif ribbon hung from a nail on the door. Laura let Jem in. He dropped his jacket onto a nearby spindle-backed chair. The cushion was fashioned in quilt fabric printed with a crush of corks.

"You want something to drink?" said Laura. "Got soda, snacks. Think I got pretzels."

"Whatever, thanks."

Jem kicked off his boots onto the semicircle rug. En route to Laura's spare room, he snuck a snoop into the open door of her bedroom. A white chenille bedspread enshrouded a solid-looking log four-poster that must have required several burly men to carry inside. Filmy gauze curtains hung open, as taut as could be by grape-shaped holdbacks at the window. Jem imagined Bender supine on that bed, his dark hair contrasting against the pillow. Then he pictured Bender prone, lying over Laura, that disarranged moustache brushing her clean face. Jem wished the damn bedroom door had been closed.

In Laura's spare room, the old dresser emanated a musty odor that filled the cramped space. It was the smell of Ed's shop, and frequently when he was alive, of Ed. Jem hadn't stepped a toe into the shop since Ed's death. But despite Jem's attempts to avoid the place, the odor catapulted him there.

Fruit of the Vine

Jem ran his fingers behind one of the dresser's legs. Rotted. The handles on the two bow-front drawers were cheap replacements for whatever the originals were.

Laura brought Jem a can of ginger ale and a bag of pretzels. "Didn't have any Coke," she said. "This okay?"

"Fine," he said. Jem despised ginger ale.

Laura put the can and the pretzel bag on the floor next to a futon. Aside from the dresser, there was no table surface in the room.

"Can you get rid of those stains?" asked Laura, pointing at black circles on the dresser's top.

"Those are in the wood. I'd have to bleach the top to get rid of them. That's what I would do. Personally."

Laura moved closer to Jem. She scratched her fingernail over the stains. Jem caught a faint whiff of lavender from Laura's hair. It smelled like one of those toiletry shops, where they sell baskets of crèmes in opaque bottles and soaps shaped like flowers. It made Jem imagine Laura with her hair loose, wearing a lacy nightgown and slippers with bows on the toes.

"Just do what you have to. I'd rather have something I can use than this thing," Laura said. "I know people get all up in arms about antiques. But if you can't use it, what's the point?"

"My sentiments exactly," said Jem.

Laura left the room, Jem watching. When she was gone, Jem scrutinized the bag of pretzels. Honey mustard. Gross. He opened the can of ginger ale, sniffed the contents, set it back down.

The smell of baking pie traveled to the spare room. Jem's

Cynthia Kolko

stomach grumbled. Under the etched crystal of his watch, the time was 6:00. The pie scent drew Jem into the kitchen like someone pulling a leash. Laura was spritzing cleaner onto a paper towel.

"Bet you thought I was making grape pie," she said. "It's pot pie. This one's chicken."

"Chicken," Jem repeated.

"Want some? Be done in a minute."

Bender's mustached face flashed into Jem's mind. "Yeah, I'll have some, if that's okay."

"Okay with me," said Laura. "How's the dresser?"

"It'll take a while."

"No rush."

Above her head, between the ceiling and the wall, a piece of crown molding gaped open. The paint on it looked like it would flake right off.

"When did you move in here?" asked Jem.

"About a year and a half ago. Couldn't take living in the house with my parents. Needed space." Laura held up a palm as if she were stopping traffic. "I know I'm not that far away, next door. And yeah, I could live on another farm. Another vineyard. But I'm comfortable here. Plus, it's free."

"I can see why you like it," he said. "And your parents are good people."

"Weird, though, don't you think?" said Laura. "Not so much my mom. My dad's the odd one. You don't have a beard like that without having a screw loose."

Laura set the table with two grape-themed plates, plain napkins, two forks. She laid down a wrought iron trivet and

113

Fruit of the Vine

gestured to one of the spindle-backed chairs, the same kind as the one in the front hall only without the cork-y cushion.

"Go ahead and sit down," she said.

Jem watched Laura's hands, enveloped in pot gloves, remove the pie, gravy bubbling between the crust and tin. She cut the pie at the table with something resembling a miniature shield with a handle. Laura troweled a heap of gravy, vegetables, and collapsing crust onto Jem's plate. She scooped some pie for herself, got two wine glasses, and poured from an already-open bottle of table white. Jem sipped it. He took a bite of the potpie. It tasted sour. Laura picked at hers, ate scant forkfuls.

"Doesn't taste so good," she declared.

"Seems okay to me," said Jem, forcing another bite.

Jem noticed a spherical plastic head attached to a tie-dye cloth nestled between some cookbooks on a shelf.

"The hell's that thing?" he asked, pointing.

"That's Sunglo," she said.

She took the head from its wine bottle perch. The tie-dye cloth billowed below the plastic. Laura put her hand up inside the cloth and the head came to life.

"A puppet," said Jem.

"My sister has one too. We'd take them on all our trips. We used to not tell each other we had it, but as soon as we got down the driveway, we'd spring them out of hiding. I don't even know if Sandra still has hers."

Laura handed Sunglo to Jem. The face was almost worn away and encircled with a thick plastic border embossed with rays. The tie-dye cloth, which Jem could see was once a handkerchief, was secured to the neck with a rubber band.

"You carry this creepy plastic head with you on trips?" Jem asked.

Laura snatched back Sunglo. She stuck her hand inside the draping handkerchief and darted Sunglo around, bobbing its head up, down, side to side, the handkerchief catching the breeze.

"It dances," she said.

Jem watched Sunglo flit to and fro.

The night has come to this. Jem did not utter another thing about Sunglo, afraid that he might say something regrettable, call Laura crazy or such. Wine did that to him. Made him say things he later wished he could stuff back inside.

Laura placed Sunglo back onto the shelf. She sat facing Jem. He poured another glass.

"You ever think of going to school?" she asked.

"You mean like for viticulture? Manette doesn't think I need it."

"Not if you're working for her. But what if things change? What if you want to work for someone else? Or for yourself?"

"School costs too much," said Jem.

"You could get a scholarship," said Laura.

"Didn't think they gave scholarships to white guys."

"White guys get plenty of scholarships."

"I got enough work at the moment."

"Look beyond the moment. Think of the future."

Fruit of the Vine

Jem hated when a discussion turned to school or careers. He already regretted not enrolling in college or a vocational program, thought he'd pay for it for the rest of his days in earning potential. But somehow, when Laura brought up the subject, it wasn't all that agonizing. Quite the contrary. Whatever she talked about was fine with Jem. Anything. So long as she was talking to him.

"You could graduate in less time," said Laura. "Seeing as you got all this experience. I was thinking of going back to school myself. Not for the growing, but more on the wine-making side of the business. Enology. I need to have a real career. Can't bake pies forever."

"Not true. You can expand the pie business. Open a bakery. Become a caterer."

"The whole pie thing is starting to get stale. Pardon the pun."

"You kidding?" said Jem. "You're the pie lady. Swear I see you skip when you're holding those pie boxes. Like a leprechaun."

"I look like a leprechaun?"

"You look happy. Like those Keebler elves. No wait. That's not right. Oh hell. Sorry. Never mind."

Jem's face felt hot. His throat tightened.

Fuck. You fucking idiot.

"I'm just keeping busy so I don't get depressed," said Laura.

"What do you have to be depressed about? Health. House. Family isn't insane. And look at you. You're not exactly the Elephant Man." Glass half-full, he thought.

"Hard to explain," Laura said.

Jem saw the dark sky through the kitchen window, black-

Cynthia Kolko

blue rectangles edged in chippy white. Laura sighed and leaned across the table toward Jem as if she were afraid someone might hear her secret.

"So I'm living here rent-free. Utilities paid for. You think it's a great deal and all, but it's a trap."

"One person's confines are another person's framework," said Jem. "Heard my grandma say that once."

"I feel like I'm draining my parents," said Laura. "This state isn't the easiest for small business owners. No matter what you're selling. Let alone growing."

"So get another job," said Jem, wondering for a second if his new raise was difficult for the Fillmores to swing.

"Doing what? I'd make a lousy receptionist. And please don't suggest I work for Joe Silla."

"Course not," said Jem. "I still say open a bakery. Be your own boss like you want."

"Where'll I get the money to start? All that inventory. Food's got a shelf life. You know how many of those little coffee shops and stuff go out of business? It'd never fly out here. You and your gang, you're not going to go into a bakery and shell out three dollars for a cookie. You'll grab a six-pack at the Quik Mart and a fifty cent mini-pack of Oreos."

"Not wrong," said Jem, "But there are niches to be filled. Make it a tourist trap for all those bunches of ladies, the ones that come to the winery for tastings and bachelorette parties. They wouldn't stop into a bakery? They'd eat it right up. Chicks dig that stuff."

"They dig getting drunk," said Laura. "If you don't serve alcohol, you're up the creek."

117

Fruit of the Vine

"We can figure something out," said Jem.

"Another time," said Laura, rising from her seat. "If I don't get to sleep at a decent hour, I'll be a zombie tomorrow."

Jem put his plate in the sink. "You're too hard on yourself," he said over the sound of the faucet running.

"I'm twenty-two years old and still on the dole. I feel like the lamest thing in town."

Leaving the vineyard, Jem's truck rattled over potholes. Jem drummed his index fingers to the screaming radio music. A single "whoo" of a patrol car broke his reverie. He saw the spinning red lights in the rearview.

Shit.

Jem clicked off the music and pulled over. In the side mirror, he watched the officer amble closer and ultimately poke his face into the driver side.

"Well, this here truck was speeding so fast, I thought I was stopping Mr. Earnhardt, not Mr. Loud," the officer said. He waved his hand toward the Loud homestead like he was presenting a showcase on "The Price is Right."

"Kind of ironic I stop you right here, eh? Your forbearers in that cemetery there. Built this place. All them hardships they went through. And you speeding by like a bat out of hell, almost getting killed. Turning in their graves. Bet they are."

Jem's face flickered with anger. "I'm glad they're turning in their graves. It's good for the land."

"You know, Mr. Loud," said the officer, "when I used to see you in town with your dad, you were a little dusty-faced kid

Cynthia Kolko

without a peep to say to no one. Or were you a smart-ass back then too?"

The red lights danced across Jem's dashboard. Just stop it. Stop it here. Don't say anything. But the words, greased with liquor, spilled out.

"I've always been smart," said Jem. "Guess that includes my ass."

The officer's steely expression held steady.

"Know how fast you were going?"

"Forty-five," said Jem.

The officer shook his head.

"This is a forty mile per hour zone. Clocked you at seventy-one. More than thirty miles per hour over the speed limit. Real smart, Mr. Loud."

"Should be a fifty-five zone. No one's ever here except cops."

"License and registration."

The officer spoke close enough to Jem's face that Jem could inspect his teeth as he spoke. They looked like weathered barn slats, bleached on the fronts but stained darker between. Jem withdrew his license from the clip in his back pocket, shuffled through the glove box, pulled out a creased registration card and handed both to the waiting officer, who gave them a cursory glance.

"Step out of the car, Mr. Loud."

"Shit," Jem said.

"Keep your comments to yourself, Mr. Loud. Your punk jokes too. DWI is a serious offense."

119

Fruit of the Vine

Jem got out, slammed the driver's side door. He towered a good eight or nine inches over the officer. The cap teetering loosely on Jem's head added at least two more.

"Follow the white line there," said the officer. "One foot in front of the other."

Jem took a step on the weathered white paint line separating the wind-trampled shoulder from the road. He took another, another, felt as if he just stumbled off the teacup ride at the traveling fair that came to town each summer. Nausea welled up inside him. He gripped his knees with his hands and vomited at the base of the state historic marker. His cap fell into the mess.

Jem heard voices ping-ponging down the cinder block hall. He pushed his face against the bars, but couldn't see anyone. He retreated to the center of his cell. Soon, two men faced him from the free side.

"Slow night for the jail," said Bender, accompanying the same officer who'd booked Jem.

Bender curled his hands around two of the bars, admiring their heft. His eyes pierced Jem and then darted to the seatless toilet in the corner.

"You're the only one in here," said Bender. "No hoboes. No whores. No weed sellers. Nothing but one drunk cousin. Least no one else was riding with you. Or had the tough luck to be on the road. Lucky you ain't spending enough time here to get accustomed to it. Just got a big old ticket to pay. And a record."

The officer clanged open the cell door. Jem stepped out as if the head clearance was too low, but there was ample room.

"Hear your stomach got vacated," said Bender. "Rent's too high in there too. Just like the rest of the state."

Jem stooped further. He'd already talked too much. It only brought trouble. Trouble and Bender.

"You're a lot quieter now than you were an hour ago, Mr. Loud," the officer said. Jem's feet echoed shame and anger with each step down the hall.

"All I want for Christmas is a cousin who ain't in the pokey," said Bender.

He and the officer laughed together, the officer slapping Bender's black leather back like they were fraternity brothers.

The next morning at the vineyard, as Jem wheeled the compost spreader out of the barn, he heard Zack's throbbing truck before he saw it, felt the sub-woofer beat a rhythm in his chest. The truck was a tan low-rider loaded heavily in back with sandbags, Zack's yearly trick to keep the thing from fishtailing. The bed dragged so low on the ground that the truck looked like, in what had been Ed's description, "a shitting dog." But it did the trick, kept the truck driving straight.

"What happened to you?" Zack said to Jem. "Never

showed up. Didn't answer the phone. You hitting that Meredith again?"

"I was in the holding pen. Drunk driving."

"No shit! You can get major time for that."

"Blood alcohol wasn't high enough for a DWI. Barely even registered. I wasn't drunk. Wouldn't have even needed a breathalyzer except I had food poisoning and couldn't walk the line without puking. Bender came and paid the fine."

Zack looked at Jem's spotted boots and felt a touch queasy. "Easy to get off if your last name's Loud," he said.

Jem peeled off a purple-stained work glove, shook a collection of tiny dirt pebbles out of it, put it back on.

"Who you kidding?" said Jem. "Cop hates me. Been better off with a name like Santiago."

"Yeah right," Zack scoffed. "You ought to quit complaining is what you should do. You're white, male, and over twenty-one. If I was you, I wouldn't complain about nothing."

The YMCA was the only fitness club within a twenty-minute drive of Sawhorn. It wasn't the poshest place to work out, though management had tried to upgrade the facility to cater to more demanding, upscale—or upscale wannabe—types. Metal lockers had been replaced with wooden ones, manicure services were offered, and the women's locker room was renamed the Ladies Spa. It wasn't much of a change, but the establishment's limited budget had been

Cynthia Kolko

shaved each year until there were barely the funds to clean the carpet, let alone install a new one.

"The Y is gross," Sandra had said to Joe a few months prior. "All those fat ladies sitting under the hair dryers naked."

"Least they're not blow-drying their pubes like in the men's locker room."

Sandra pouted. "I knew we should have sprung for the walk-out lower level. We could have had a home gym built down there."

"Still can, but you have an unnatural fear of basements."

"I just like a window when I'm working out. Otherwise, it's like I'm in a cave."

"Could put in a bunch of mirrors. What else could be better to look at when you're working out than us working out?" Joe flexed a bicep. "Hell. Maybe I will install a gym in the house," he said. "Throw some top-of-the-line equipment down there. Make it like a men's club. The kind they have in big cities for all the execs." He flexed the other bicep.

But Joe had had front-burner stuff to deal with, and Sandra had been re-relegated to the Sawhorn Y. She trotted the treadmill holding hand weights, listening rapt through earphones to a TV talk show about wrinkle treatments. She kept a close watch on the machine's "calories burned" readout. She was trying to lose five pounds, thought her thighs were getting flabby and dimpled with cellulite.

After the treadmill, Sandra tackled the weight machines. She crunched, pushed, and pulled for an hour. She stood frowning before the locker room's full-length mirror in her

123

Fruit of the Vine

turquoise thong leotard. At least the black bike shorts underneath hide the thighs, somewhat. She poked the soft spot under one butt cheek, then the other.

She made a mental list of the foods she'd be able to eat on Thanksgiving. Sweet potato: No. Maybe half a sweet potato. Salad. Oh, go for a whole sweet potato. No! Stick to the diet! Have to be careful. A little red wine. What else? Cranberry sauce? Too much sugar, the way Mom makes it. Vegetables? No good. Mom cooks those carrots in butter. Why can't she learn to make anything fat-free? Drink a whole glass of water before leaving our house, before we get there. Fills you up. I'll eat less.

The day before Thanksgiving was a brisk business day for walk-ins, even at a small vineyard like Hassler. People were already in holiday shopping mode, and diehards who were fans of Hassler wine made a special trip to the vineyard for a Thanksgiving bottle or two, or for a tour with visiting relatives. The afternoon traffic, however, trickled to a drop, so Manette sent her employees home early, to no one's surprise. It was her holiday tradition.

Jem watched a tar-black SUV zip up the driveway towing its own shadow like a trailer. As the car stopped, it spewed gravel from beneath its tires onto the walkway of the empty wine shop.

"Hey Jem!" Joe called. "Roy and I are heading up to Chateau Cobblestone. Meredith's dad shot a deer. Twelve-

Cynthia Kolko

point buck! Isn't that the shit? Want to come? Plenty of room."

Roy Archer sat tall and stiff like a mannequin in the passenger seat. Jem opened the door behind Roy's and sunk his butt into the seat's leather dip. An instruction manual rested on what Ed used to call the "hump," but in this car was a humpless, dipless flat middle seat.

"New car?" Jem asked.

"Yeah, pretty slick, eh?" said Joe. "Bought it for winters. Right out of the show room."

"Looks like it's all loaded up," said Jem, noticing the crowd of knobs on the dash.

"You better believe it. All the options," said Joe.

Joe fiddled with the car's temperature control knob. He craned his neck toward the back seat but kept his eyes front. "You ever been to Chateau Cobblestone?" he asked.

"No," answered Jem. "But I've seen it from down below, obviously."

"Well, wait till you see the place up close and personal," said Joe. "It is plush. Beats Hassler with a stick. Beats it into the ground. To a pulp. Jem, you ought to get in good with Meredith. Case you need a job."

"I got a job."

"Don't be short-sighted, Jem! Did Sanford ever mention anything to you about the future of the place? Damn. What am I saying? Manette. Did Manette ever say anything about it?"

"What are you talking about?" said Jem.

"What am I talking about? I'm wondering why you aren't

125

Fruit of the Vine

talking about it. How long do you think Hassler's going to hang on? Look at their competition. In all the publicity about this region, all the fans, the tourists, the reviews, hardly a peep about Hassler. World-class wines being produced around here. Lots of them. More every day. It's essential to keep up just to get respect, let alone to stay afloat."

"We've got good product. And we're getting recognition at the shows. Lots of fans."

"Need more than that," said Joe. "It's about image. Even if you've got a great wine, you need an operation that plays the part. You need an image that supports the quality of the wine. One that's more high-brow. One that visitors can tell their friends about. Like the vineyards around here that get written up in international travel magazines. The ones featured in the wine snob rags. Even the ones with a cult following just in the Northeast."

"I don't like where this is going," said Jem.

"Some of the other places, not necessarily big ones, but small ones, same size as Hassler, they got these great winemakers on staff. They've got journalists covering them. A nicer store. Like Chipmunk Hill. The whole place just has a presence. One that can impress the world. Manette and Sanford are my in-laws, and I love them. I do. I'm secure enough in my manhood to say the word 'love' and not look like a simp. But I don't know if they have it in them. They need help if they want to take it to the next level."

"They're just as good as anyone in the business. And why does everyone has to have a certain kind of image? Every winery's different. Good thing too. Makes it interesting. Hassler is down home. More family. People like it. Who says we have to change anything?"

"Just stating what I've observed. I don't mean anything insulting by it," said Joe.

"What do you think, Roy?" asked Jem.

Roy's words stuck in his throat, parched from the pack of cigarettes he'd already smoked. When he finally spoke, it was as if someone were dragging the dry words out of him.

"The industry can support a wide range of players," he said.

The car passed the gilded Chateau Cobblestone sign and climbed the steep tree-lined drive. At the apex, the driveway forked one way to the tasting area and winemaking operation. The other way, which led to the private residence, was cordoned off by two shiny gates emblazoned with a pair of intertwining stylized letter Cs. Joe leaned out the window at an intercom mounted on a column mortared with smooth river stones. He bellowed, as if addressing someone hard-of-hearing.

"Joe Silla, Jem Loud, Roy Archer. We're here for Meredith."

The gates staggered open.

"Looks like they need to change the battery," said Roy.

The men parked and walked a winding flagstone path toward the front door. Yellow and periwinkle mums poked along the edge.

"Jem. Why don't you pick one of those and give it to Meredith?" Joe joked.

"Why don't you take one to your mom?" said Jem. "She can wear it in her hair."

"You ever seen Joe's mom?" said Roy. "She's got a military

Fruit of the Vine

buzz cut and thick-rimmed glasses. Looks like she's inventing the atom bomb. She makes Manette look like a toe dancer."

Jem and Roy guffawed, their breath billowing in the cool air like puffs of smoke.

"Lay off my mama, will you?" said Joe. "You'd be lucky to have a mother like her."

Jem contemplated the identical-twin marble fountains flanking the path. He stood face-to-face with one of the carved figures, a fig-leaf shrouded boy cradling a sprouting salad bowl over his head.

The doorbell sounded a lengthy series of chimes. A heavyset blonde woman let the men inside to wait. She said Meredith would be there in a minute, but with women, Joe quipped, a minute could mean a lot longer. Jem coughed. The echo of his voice boomed louder than expected in the barrel-shaped foyer, the lofty diamond-painted ceilings topped with thick scalloped molding like wedding cake fondant. In the hall's center, flora waved from a large gilded roman urn atop a shiny round table. The men shuffled their feet, put hands in pockets, scrutinized aesthetic details they (aside from Joe) would usually have passed without a glance.

"Well this is quite a scene," said Meredith, appearing in an arched opening in the foyer's curved wall. "Deers in the barn."

She led the group out an enormous side door equipped with thick iron hinges and a hammered handle that dwarfed her hand. Meredith opened the door of the stained wood barn like the lid of a coffin standing on its end. Inside, a deposed king of a buck hung by a rope from one of the barn's thick beams. Dangling by its back legs, the animal's body stretched downward as if it were galloping at top speed from the roof into the ground. The dirty floor under the deer showed a darkened flower shape, part blood, part shadow.

"Holy shit," Joe said. "Damn!"

Roy walked around the animal, touched the smooth hair of one of the haunches. He returned his hand to his pocket, frowned.

"Can I talk to you a second?" Meredith said to Jem.

The two retreated to a corner.

"What, did you forget about me?" asked Meredith.

"How could I do that?" said Jem.

"You never called me back."

"I've been busy is all. Way behind straightening out my dad's affairs. Working on refinishing a piece of furniture for Laura."

"Laura?" said Meredith. "Who's that?"

"The Fillmores' daughter. Lives on Hassler. Joe Silla's sister-in-law."

"Uh-huh. Well, you better be careful. I'm not waiting forever. I might just find someone else instead. It's not like I need to drag the lake."

Meredith went back to the carcass, leaving Jem standing in the corner like a scolded child.

"You calling the news?" asked Roy. "Get some publicity?"

"Dad doesn't want any," said Meredith. "He doesn't like attention. Doesn't like to be flashy or anything overblown."

Roy stifled a laugh, his snorts bouncing off the hand-carved beams of the cavernous barn.

Fruit of the Vine

"You guys can stay in here, but don't make it too long. Security'll kick you out," said Meredith.

Joe winked at Meredith and said, "No problem."

Jem and Roy stood in front of the deceased animal. Joe joined them, staring.

"You think you got animals like this wandering on your property, Jem?" said Joe. "Any idea what might be in those woods? You ever hear of any, like, discoveries?"

The comment hung in the barn's rafters, floating unanswered for several seconds before Jem spoke. "Never heard of anyone spotting this big guy before, so who knows what else is there. Probably a whole bunch of bird species. I don't know much about birds. There's been stories of white deer going back years. Centuries, maybe. Old stories of sightings. But those are probably myths. Unless you believe in ghosts. Never seen a photo of a white deer."

"Ghost deer," said Roy.

"What?" said Joe.

"My grandfather taught me a legend," Roy said. "Don't know where it's from, what tribe. But he liked it. Called it ghost deer. It's about a white deer who ambled around, the way deer do. Walked among a field of wilted corn, looking for a tasty morsel. But the deer pooh-poohed the corn. Didn't partake in it. He walked on and came across a field of bay leaves. He passed on those as well. He walked further and found more corn stalks. Decided those were too short. Snow fell and coated the deer, which by now was ravenous. Real hungry. He searched for any food, even wilted corn or the bay

Cynthia Kolko

leaves he had rejected just before. But nothing edible could be found. The deer turned white with cold. If only he'd been happy with what he had instead of constantly searching out the next best thing."

Jem was curious to see Joe's reaction. Joe was frozen. His face was a little frightened and perplexed, as if he were trying to make sense of a crazy dream. He had to force himself back to lucidity, back to his usual demeanor. He grinned, a signal that he had snapped back.

"Nice story, Roy," said Joe. "You ought to write it into a children's book. Make some dough."

Roy sighed.

"What tribe was your grandpa from?" Jem asked.

"Well, he was Seneca. But what's been passed down is that he was a descendent of the Wenro. Tribe near Lake Erie. Decimated during the beaver wars in the 1600s. The few survivors went to live with the Huron, or in our case, the Seneca."

"Beaver wars, eh?" said Joe. He chuckled.

Jem spoke in a hushed voice, "Unless I was in a contest, I couldn't shoot an animal like this. Too magnificent."

"Maybe Meredith's dad didn't know what he hit until after he shot," said Joe. "Doesn't that happen sometimes?"

"You serious?" Jem said at a normal volume. "You never shoot blind. That's how people get killed. Some idiot hears rustling, thinks it's an animal and just shoots before they see anything. Then you got a dead guy and the gun control folks come out of the woodwork looking to string you up by the balls as an example."

Fruit of the Vine

"Like when you came out of the woods at the Loud Farm," said Roy. "You could have been shot through the nose. What were you doing there again? Exercising?"

Joe rolled his eyes.

"Course in this case, we're talking about a bow," said Jem.

A rumble of wind struck the barn. The deer, a weak pendulum, swayed slightly in its wake. A field mouse, scurrying along a gap between the barn's wall and the floor, scampered into a corner.

"First day of bow hunting season too," Joe said.

"How you know when hunting season is?" asked Roy.

"My peeps down at Tap keep me informed," said Joe.

"What peeps? Who?" said Roy.

"Okay. I saw it in the paper this morning. Sports section," said Joe.

"Been fun and all, but I've got to get out of here," said Jem.

"Me too," said Joe. "Lots of work. Got a business to run. I'm a busy man. Busier than ten normal men put together."

Joe and Jem aimed themselves out the enormous door. At the threshold, Joe turned back to Roy.

"You coming?" he said.

"I'll just be a minute," said Roy.

Alone in the barn with the carcass, Roy stared at the animal's unseeing eyes. He wondered what the animal had known. What it may have seen in the Loud woods. Roy left the barn open to the chilly air, got into Joe's car.

"House is way bigger up close," said Jem.

"Ten thousand square feet. Not including Meredith's annex," said Joe, driving home.

Cynthia Kolko

"Ten thousand square feet for two people?" said Jem. "Isn't that excessive?"

"Waste of resources," said Roy.

"I say it sounds like a great way to stay married," said Joe. "Space between you and the missus. How come you never got married, Roy?"

"Yeah, that's too bad, isn't it?" answered Roy. "You know someone? It's not too late."

"I'll keep it in mind," said Joe. "Here's another question. How come you're not hooked on booze? I thought Indians were alkies."

Roy searched Joe's eyes for a twinkle, something that would indicate he was joking. He didn't find anything.

"You're a real fucking idiot, you know that?" said Roy.

Joe continued undaunted. "And your name isn't 'Horse Look Back' or 'Shot with Two Arrows' or something?"

Jem held a hand, fingers etched by fence wire, over his eyes, shaking his head. Some of the scratches were red or pink, others were black, and then there were the barely-detectable white scars. Jem's palms were similarly lined. They would give a soothsayer one hell of a challenge.

"Less than twenty-five Seneca speakers left on the planet," said Roy. "The language is almost gone. After a slow, painful death."

Jem uncovered his face. He listened to Roy's voice as the roadside blurred by.

"Parents named me Roy because it means 'king' in old Norse or such. But I'm not an etymologist."

"You mean the study of bugs?" asked Joe.

133

Fruit of the Vine

"That's entomology," said Roy. "Etymology is the study of language. My parents thought with the last name Archer, maybe I could be a king bow hunter. Like a living tribute to my grandfather and his heritage. But I never shot a bow my whole life. Plenty of guns, though. I was a good marksman as a boy."

"Yeah?" said Jem, turning his face from the window. "Want to go shooting sometime?"

"Where you go?"

"Me and Zack, we either go to the range or set up our own course in the woods behind Hassler," said Jem.

"Zack Santiago?" said Roy. "Kid's a loose cannon. Don't want to be around him and a gun at the same time."

"Don't blame you there, Roy," said Joe. "I don't trust that kid one bit." Joe's eyes narrowed. "Not one bit."

"Thought you had a change of heart about Zack," said Jem.

"Jem, you may be a hair savvier than the average guy, but you're no businessman. Zack buys a lot of booze. And like it or not, he's a draw for a certain kind of woman."

"What kind is that?" said Jem.

"The kind who go ape shit for that Latin Lover thing. Zack isn't exactly Adonis. Not like he's me. But he has an appeal among the ladies. And he buys them those fancy drinks. Specialty martinis—the fruity ones, the cosmos. They're big moneymakers. Every time you add a drop of flavored liqueur, you can jack up the price a dollar."

"That Russ is one scary kid," said Roy. "One day he'll turn out to be one of those crazy postmen who goes wacko and shoots up the Quik Mart. He's got it out for me. Always thought I was connected to what happened to his sister. Isn't anyone else thinks that but him. I was cleared in a second. But Russ. He found a verdict all on his own. Can't let it go. Doesn't want to, for some reason."

"He almost turned Tap into a fighting ring," said Joe. "I won't let him back. Not on your life. Can't trust him as far as I can kick his ass."

Jem shifted in his seat.

"Kid's frightening," said Roy, "but then I don't trust anyone too young to remember Nixon. Not even you, Jem."

"I remember Nixon."

"Get out," said Roy.

"We watched him on TV. I was only three. But I remember it. Something happened with the reception. Dad jiggled the rabbit ears, yelled at mom, and kicked a hole in the screen. I ran to pick up the pieces, try to put it back together. Got stitches on my hand. See the scar?"

Which line on Jem's hand was from the TV glass and which were from fence wire, Roy couldn't tell.

Back at Hassler, Jem ran into Laura.

"You busy all weekend or can you finish that dresser?" Laura asked.

"I can come Sunday if that's okay," said Jem.

"Hey, what're you doing for Thanksgiving?" asked Laura.

"Gram and I are going to the Apple Tree Inn in Geneva. We

Fruit of the Vine

do that every year. Gram wants to set a place for Dad. An empty chair and silverware. Sounds morbid to me, but I'll go along with it for her. I draw the line if she orders him food."

"Sorry I asked," said Laura.

"Don't be. Can't say it gets any easier, but I don't want everyone tiptoeing around me. You're having Thanksgiving here with your family I take it?"

"Plus one."

The main Fillmore homestead, which those in the know referred to as the "big house," stood off a ways from the wine shop and Laura's house. Its core was square-ish, with a barn attached like a tumor to the kitchen. Subsequent generations had added a pair of asymmetrical arms, one stubby, the other holding a porch with a side entrance and a string of tall windows that reflected the afternoon sun. The front door was red like a cold nose, with two windows jotted above it like eyes. The house resembled a colossal lounging beast.

At the threshold, Bender handed Sanford a bottle of wine wrapped in a shiny red bag. He shuffled his feet on the snow-soaked entry rug, which smelled like a wet dog. Sanford retreated to the kitchen.

"Good Lord," said Sanford, removing the wine from the bag and eyeing the label. "Would you look at this? Either he doesn't know anything about wine, or thinks we don't know anything. Not sure which is worse."

"Take this in there." Manette nodded toward the door, a

Cynthia Kolko

turkey teetering on a platter balanced on her knee, her blown-dry hair a millimeter pouffier than usual, which wasn't much.

Sanford sat at the head of the table. He dabbed a napkin to his tie, kelly green and embroidered with turkeys, one of them cooked with a curlicue of gray stitches resembling steam swirling up from it. He uncorked a bottle of Hassler's own wine. He passed it around the table, raised his glass and offered a prayer translated from the Hebrew—a Jewish prayer he liked to trot out at gatherings such as this. A nod to Manette. He thought it offered a connection between the past and the present, and expressed thanks for natural gifts.

"Blessed are You, Lord our God, King of the universe, who creates the fruit of the vine."

Joe downed the entire contents of his glass.

"Nice sentiment," said Joe. "Got to hand it to Jews to write something like that."

Laura rolled her eyes, but Manette ignored Joe's comment.

"I like to reinterpret it. Apply it to our industry. An Old World view," said Manette.

"How so?" said Joe.

"Here, the grape is king. But a great wine is about how it's made. What you do with what nature gave you is how you arrive at a great wine. The grape is an expression of where it came from and the wine is the ultimate result of that expression. Nature comes through the grape and through the wine. The earth makes itself known through nature."

"It's nature versus nurture," said Laura. "Like life. There's your genetics, your environment, and ultimately, what you make of it all."

137

Fruit of the Vine

"That's the fruit of the vine," said Manette.

"And the apple doesn't fall far from the tree," said Joe. "Hey, what does your dad do, Bender?"

"Time," replied Bender.

Laura side-jammed her elbow into Bender's arm, nearly spilling the drink he held.

"Really?" said Manette.

"No. Not really," said Bender. "After my old man and his wife split a few years ago—that was his third wife—he moved to North Carolina and turned some bad real estate deals. Never actually went to jail. Less you count one night's worth when they picked him up. He just got community service."

"Like those guys in the orange shirts who clean up the highway?" Sanford asked.

"Something like that."

"Don't feel weird about it, man," said Joe. "Lots of good people spend time on the other side of the law. Like Sanford's dad. Isn't that right? What did he do again, Sanford?"

Sanford replied curtly, "He was in business."

"Thought he was a con man," said Joe.

Sanford narrowed his eyes at Joe and then softened them. What was the use of denying it?

"He played cards," said Sanford. "Rode the trains."

Sanford peeled the foil off a tiny chocolate Jack Daniels bottle and bit into it, dripping a sticky thread of liquor onto his beard.

After dinner, Joe and Bender faced the football game, drinks in hand. Vestiges of Sanford's navy service dotted the mantle: a lopsided clipper ship in a bottle, a dusty uniform hat. The room smelled of burning wood, dried yarrow, and turkey.

"So," Joe said to Bender. "Getting serious?"

"Huh?" replied Bender.

"You. Laura. That'd be something wouldn't it? Us being brothers-in-law?"

Sandra peeked into the room. Her breasts were like two halves of a rubber ball encased in a mustard-colored turtleneck.

"Ready to go home soon?" she asked Joe.

"Whenever you want," said Joe.

"Fifteen minutes," said Sandra. She was gone.

"God only knows how I got so lucky," said Joe. "Isn't she something?"

Bender nodded silently and then added, as if he were reading from a cue card, "Sure is."

"You know," said Joe, "how when something interesting or funny happens, there's that one person you want to tell first? The first person you call or run to? You know who that person is?"

"Your mother?" asked Bender.

Joe flicked his chin toward the spot where Sandra had appeared a moment prior, gesturing with his glass as if he were toasting it.

"Your best friend," said Joe. "Sandra is my best friend."

Bender grimaced at the muddy fumble on the screen. "Why do I keep throwing money away betting on these clowns?"

Joe sloshed his glass, ice clinking.

Fruit of the Vine

"What's the spread?"

"Twelve. They'll never recover."

Bender swallowed the last drop of scotch mixed with melted ice. "I ought to just give up, know when I'm out-classed," he said.

He flipped a crumpled cocktail napkin into the fireplace, igniting a two-second fireball.

In the kitchen, Manette peered over the remains of the turkey. "Ridiculous, isn't it? All that work. Making such a big turkey. And it's over in an hour."

"It is kind of a non-holiday," agreed Laura, dry lips wine-stained where they met.

She spooned stuffing into a plastic container to take home.

"Christmas is no better," said Manette. "All that fuss, the forced buying."

"You say that because you didn't grow up with it," said Laura. "Who doesn't like opening presents?"

"You'd be better off buying what you want than waiting for someone to give it to you," said Manette. "Usually, they get it wrong anyhow."

She shifted her eyes sideways at Sanford.

"I like to be surprised," said Laura.

Sanford rinsed dishes at the sink. Tiny greasy droplets spattered up into his beard, reflecting the light like sequins each time he turned to load a dish in the washer.

"Joe sure doesn't hold anything back," said Sanford. "Think he likes taking jabs at people. Little pings. Getting to be a bad habit."

Cynthia Kolko

"That was the wine speaking," Manette said with sarcasm. Sanford didn't catch her joke.

"He's like that cold sober," Sanford said. "Of course if we drank that stuff Bender brought, we might all be speaking Pig Latin."

Laura put her hands on her hips, mouth agape.

Sandra stood on the front porch smoking, her long shearling coat open and billowing with the air currents like curtain panels in a breezy window. Her gloved hand, hanging by her side, moved the cigarette to her mouth and back again with such regularity, at a glance one might actually mistake Sandra for a wax figure, if it weren't for the stray locks lapping her face in the breeze, or her frightened eyes seeking comfort, or answers, in the dark recesses between the pines.

Later that night, Sanford returned from the hallway bathroom, moving jerkily, like a character in a flip book, in a white t-shirt and threadbare boxers that gapped in the fly. Manette read in bed, her pillow folded like a burrito beneath her neck. Sanford removed a dental instrument from his nightstand drawer. It was green plastic with a gum stimulator tip shaped like a rubber chocolate chip mounted to the handle. He sat on the bed, jiggling the instrument in his mouth.

"Can you do that somewhere else?" said Manette. "Whole bed is shaking."

Sanford rose, removed the instrument.

"What do you think of Jem Loud? For Laura?" Sanford said.

Fruit of the Vine

Manette clicked off her bedside lamp. The light from Sanford's lamp threw bruise-like shadows onto her face.

"Better than Bender," said Manette. "Jem's a good soul even if his parents are oafs. Were. Especially that mother who ran off. But you can't blame a kid for something he has no control over. Plus I can't help but feel a little responsible."

"For what?"

"For him. Always felt like I should take him under my wing. Teach him the lay of the land. He's got no one else to do it. That crab-apple dad of his isn't around anymore. And he wasn't exactly a stellar influence when he was alive." Manette shrugged. "We don't want another Joe happening again. Marrying the first fellow who asks. But Laura won't settle for Bender. She'll move on to the next guy before you know it."

Sanford's face paled. He blanketed his eyes with his palm. He still wasn't used to the idea of his daughters dating, though the eldest had been married for a few years already. The subject was something he preferred not to think about. Sanford was a young man himself once, knew what lewd thoughts crowded young men's minds. When Sandra was born, he vowed he'd raise a shotgun to any selfish, crotch-driven male who rang his bell. But the bravado was contained to thoughts, themselves short-lived. Sanford was doting. He couldn't bear to disappoint his daughters, and as they got older, he wouldn't embarrass them by screening and scrutinizing their dates. Sanford's personality tended toward laissez-faire. He armed himself with the knowledge that the girls possessed the good judgment to weed out the bad guys themselves. Yet, presented with Joe and Bender, it became clear that the girls' judgment was lacking.

"She doesn't need us to help her figure out her life. She'll do it on her own," said Manette. "I did."

Sanford gargled in the bathroom, wiped his face, walked back into the bedroom still holding the towel.

"You sure you want me to talk to Joe Silla?" said Sanford. Manette sighed.

She'd earned a horticultural degree, spent time in Italy among the sweeping cypress-edged Mediterranean landscapes pinstriped with grape plants. Had a small hand in developing stronger stock at the experiment station nearby. She met Sanford when shopping at the shoe store where he worked. He sold her a pair of boys' work boots.

The Hasslers weren't exactly whooping it up about Manette marrying a gentile, but they assimilated their culture right out of the next generation. The Hasslers had to accept that this union was the result. Protesting, if not hypocritical, would have been futile. Manette didn't care a whit what they thought of Sanford anyhow.

Back then, Hassler vineyard was a modestly steady grape-growing farm. That was until a huge California conglomerate bought out the largest winery in town, drying up the market for grapes like a raisin. The Hasslers almost quit the business altogether. Those were lean times, but they pulled through, thanks to Manette. Things improved when the folks ceded some control to her.

Manette told the Hasslers to include some of the newer European vinifera other local vineyards were growing—a supplement to the standard concords favored by the reluctant-to-change Hasslers.

"It's do this or watch the place die," said Manette to her parents. "Got to adapt to survive."

The year 1976 kick-started a new era. In the 70s, while New York's vineyards struggled, California's wine industry ballooned. In response, New York passed the Farm Winery Act, which allowed direct sale of wines by smaller, family-run farms. Manette and Sanford took some chances, took out loans, trussed up stout oak casks. The first crush yielded four and a half tons, from which they made Hassler's red and white dinner wines, and later dessert wines, sold them in the shop, hosted tastings, entered competitions, and even managed an honorable mention at one. But their success was marginal. They were a small outfit. Didn't have money for expansion. Direct-to-consumer sales could only take them so far. The state didn't allow wine in grocery stores. And selling to liquor stores was difficult. European wines were subsidized by their governments and therefore could be sold more cheaply. U.S. wineries were on their own. A farm subsidy might have helped, but the Hassler/Fillmore clan didn't qualify. By the standards of the state and the feds, they were doing just fine. It just didn't feel like it to them.

Sanford bunched the towel on the rack. "What we're looking to do is going to be a hell of a big deal," he said.

"A big deal is what we need," said Manette.

Cynthia Kolko

"Damn," Zack said from his perch at the Tavern. "Thick crowd. I ain't seen some of these people in years. Why they come out this Thanksgiving and none of the others?"

"Thanksgiving's always been a huge bar weekend," said Jem. "People come back to see their parents and all that shit. You don't remember because you get wasted and forget."

A lazy string of colored bulbs wearing last year's dust was draped high behind the bar, Bender's lone acknowledgement of the upcoming season.

"That Leslie?" asked Zack.

"Who?" said Jem.

"Leslie. Chick you fucked behind the church few years back," said Zack.

Jem's body hunched. He recalled how he practically threw Leslie onto the ground before climbing on top of her. Held both her hands over her head. Couldn't stop himself.

"Too fat. Leslie's skinny," he said.

"Times change, my brother. Asses get wide. Swear that's her."

The woman rotated her face toward the bar.

"Jesus," said Jem. "That is her. Holy shit. She ballooned. Like twice the size."

Russ emerged from the smoky near-distance. His loping gait was his signature. In the murky air, his slight stature made almost a feminine silhouette.

"Yo," said Russ. "Listen to what I saw earlier today on the road out near the dump. This dead woodchuck."

"You ain't never seen a dead woodchuck in the road?" said Zack.

Fruit of the Vine

"It had all four paws in the air. Its nose, too. Lying on its back, like it was doing some crazy stretching exercise. I ain't never seen road kill like that. Doing yoga. Like, slap a leotard on the bitch. Ha ha! That'd be something, huh? Roadkill yoga? Make a great kids' show. I'd watch that shit."

"You see over there? Remember Leslie DeGroat?" Zack pointed.

"Holy crap," said Russ. "Face is all bloated. She's been hitting the ho-hos."

"Aw, lay off her, would you?" said Jem. "Not like any of us is Fabio."

"You said yourself she swelled up to twice her normal size," said Zack.

"Hey! Come over to the Foxhole with me," said Russ. "You can pick up a chick there for pennies on the dollar. They're a little skanky, can't dance worth a shit, but what the hell. Between this place and there, you'll see practically the entire female student body of our class. And I mean bodies."

"I need to get up early. Going to Laura's in the morning. Working on a dresser for her," said Jem.

"Ought to work on an un-dresser for her," said Zack.

"You need to get way up for that," said Russ.

Zack and Russ exchanged high fives. Jem fished an ice cube from his drink, looked tired.

"What happened to that Meredith?" asked Zack.

"Nothing," said Jem. "She called the other day. Left a message."

"Just a shot in the dark here. You didn't return the call," said Zack.

Cynthia Kolko

"Not yet, I didn't," said Jem.

"Nancy," said Zack.

"The hell with the broads. Anyone got weed?" asked Russ.

Zack patted his front shirt pocket.

"So what we doing hanging around this piss can?" said Russ. "My place."

Jem peeled himself from the stool.

"You coming?" said Zack.

"Home. I told you. Laura."

nine

Meredith paced the hotel room. A gold-brushed chaise in a peachy medallion print sat in the corner, the bed crowded with pillows, a rectangular oriental rug over the gleaming wood floor. She took a drink of complimentary bottled water. Someone knocked. The peephole framed a rapidly-blinking Joe. Once in the room, he let loose.

"I got to hand it to you. You're really good at reeling in the rednecks. Like watching a maestro. Yelling at Jem like that up in the barn. Pissing vinegar all over the joint. No wonder he hasn't called you."

"What's the difference, Joe? It's just a lousy piece of land. Can't you let it go?"

Joe shook his head, chuckled to himself. He stood in front of Meredith, his voice low.

"You don't know the half of it," he said, nearly in a whisper, lips slack. "White deer, Meredith. Pure white deer."

Cynthia Kolko

Despite efforts to the contrary, Joe's face broke into a smile, relieved with the unburdening of this information he'd held solitary for too long.

"A mess of them," he said. "Maybe a dozen. You can't believe it. Moving and walking and chewing. Doing deer stuff. They're like anti-shadows."

"You sure they're real? Not an illusion? Why hasn't anyone else seen them?"

"There have been stories in this area for years about white deer sightings. But they've been one here, one there. Not a whole lot at once. Sightings are always near the Loud Farm. Always. Only a matter of time before someone else sees the herd. Knows where they hide. In those woods on the Loud property. Thank God hunting season's not too long."

A dreamy look frosted Joe's eyes. "They're so white. Not translucent, though. Opaque. Like ghosts."

Joe's expression heated back to its usual alert state, infused with urgency. "Don't you say anything! You hear? No one can know there are more deer on that land. It'll kill the plan! The hotel, the neighborhood, the open-air zoo. Pesky environmentalists, they'll turn the whole deal to shit."

The gravity of the thought pushed Joe into a chair. His stomach percolated. The rapid blinking resumed. He sprung up to standing.

"I have an idea," said Joe, his speech quick and forceful. "Jem's doing some work for my sister-in-law at her place. Refinishing an antique. Why don't you tell him you like antiques? Want to see what he's got in his dad's old shop? You

149

Fruit of the Vine

poke around for the contract. It has to be lying around in plain sight. Ed told me before he kicked that he had just signed it."

"With Jem there? He'll see me rifling through his papers."

"Give him something to drink that makes him sleepy."

"A roofie? Are you high?"

Joe sat back down. "Guess you're right. Jail would be a bitch, eh? So tell him you always wanted to sleep surrounded by old stuff. Bring some sleeping bags. How the hell is he going to resist you in the flesh? He'll remember your rendezvous, which I'm sure was unforgettable. Damn it, Meredith! Couldn't you have just cuddled?"

"What do you want from me? You're the one who's married. This whole thing is sounding ridiculous again."

"You have a better idea?"

"How about you get the contract yourself?"

"Listen." Joe put both hands on Meredith's shoulders, his words buttered with kindness. "All this, I'm doing for you. For us! We get that development built, you and I will be king and queen of this town."

"Whoopee. Two big fish in a puddle."

"Isn't that what you want? A puddle? To feel like a big fish somewhere you won't be swallowed up? Or would you rather always be Benson Payne's daughter? We'll be partners. Better! You'll be the big cheese. It'll be a woman-owned business. You get to call the shots. Big boss lady. Can win all sorts of business awards to hang in your office. Donate a little coin and they'll name a street after you. I'll just do the behind-the-scenes legwork. I'll fade into the wall."

150

Cynthia Kolko

Meredith scoffed, unconvinced that Joe would willingly fade anywhere. She put her hands on her hips.

"Show me the plans again."

Joe took a folded paper from a leather briefcase.

"There'd be a fence here, around the preserve," Joe said, using his finger to trace a freeform on the map. "Residents can see the deer for free. Same with hotel guests. Everyone else has to pay a fee. For preservation. Only most of it will go into our pockets." Joe patted his groin. "We can hire someone to give tours. Like Jem. He'd be great at that, seeing it was his family's land. Would lend an air of authenticity to the operation. We'll breed the deer into a massive herd. Eventually they'll need to be thinned. Managed. Day permits. Five hundred bucks a gun. Or a thousand to get the whole property to shoot up all by yourself. Work on that Jem kid, would you? Hook him in and find that piece of shit contract before the deer have a parade down Main Street."

Surrounded by the ivory-walled dressing room, Sandra tried on a short nightgown of sky-blue satin with black lace trim and tiny black buttons like squirrel eyes at the yoke. She draped her hair over the front of her shoulder, posed hip facing the mirror, and sucked in her stomach. She imagined dazzling the beholder, the garment being ripped right off her, buttons popping, rolling out of sight on the wood floor in the bedroom, disappearing under the bed or a velvet curtain, the blue satin puddling into a luxurious heap.

Fruit of the Vine

Sandra turned in the mirror, the scalloped lace grazing her kneecaps.

Too long, she thought, weighing whether or not to take it to be tailored or to forget about it altogether. Pink complemented her skin so much better than blue. Yes, she'd take the pink one with the diamond pattern.

Carrying the pink garment to the checkout desk, Sandra bit her teeth together in time to a song playing in her head, one in a litany of tunes that made up the soundtrack to her life.

Sometimes, Sandra imagined all she saw as through the lens of a movie camera. She would cast an actor or actress to play each part. At times, there was even narration, usually an omniscient buttery female voice, but occasionally a male voice, a half-whispered baritone with a fop-ish lilt.

As a child, Sandra had gazed upon her own red sneakers, kicking pebbles on the path from the camp bus stop to the first-grade shelter, and created a piece of a story about herself, the star. Those red tennis sneakers, the kind made of canvas, were the only style Sandra could wear, laced up tightly on her narrow foot so that the bow could be quadruple-knotted and still flop like bunny ears on top of Sandra's foot. Sandra had dreaded entering the shelter, rife with daddy longlegs spiders. She would shuffle her feet and center the sneakers in the frame, imagining this to be a supremely interesting snippet of a girl's life.

So when did it turn so uninteresting? Time was, she dreamed of a career in geology. It started with the gift of a geode from someone. Manette? Probably. One side of it was an ordinary rock. But rotate it, and a violet maw glittered a jagged, beautiful, grin.

Now, the geode resided in a box of similarly discarded childhood dreams in Manette and Sanford's attic. Replaced with newer dreams. Always something better to long for. Always another fantasy to become immersed in.

The shot rang through the air like a whip.

"Good one."

Laura relaxed the rifle. She pivoted to Bender and smiled. He returned the gesture with an expanse of teeth, moustache more straggly than usual.

Jem and Zack were at another shooting bay a few yards away.

"I still can't figure out what she's doing with that old hairy Bender," said Jem, sneaking a look at the couple.

"Shooting a whole lot better than you," said Zack.

Jem raised his rifle and shot the target three inches right of the bull's eye.

"Always right," said Zack. "That's because you're left-handed."

Jem gave the rifle to Zack, who fired a bull's eye.

"Suck on that," Zack said.

Jem found the soda machine. He smoothed a dollar and fed it into the slot, which regurgitated the bill.

"I got some quarters."

Jem turned to see Bender holding four coins in his gloved palm.

Fruit of the Vine

"Need to carry a roll to the shooting range. This machine don't like bills," said Bender.

Jem handed a dollar to Bender and took the quarters.

"You got two more? Zack ordered root beer. You can put it on my tab back at the tavern."

"Forget it."

Bender took half a roll of quarters from his jeans pocket and peeled two coins off like cards from a deck.

"Hear you're moving above the Hasslers' store," Bender said.

Jem nodded. "Manette wants a manager on site."

Bender folded his arms and gave an alpha stare that Jem recognized as a territorial mark. On Laura.

"I ever tell you my uncle dated her?" said Bender.

"Huh?"

"My Uncle Mike. Dated Manette. Way back in their early twenties. I remember," said Bender.

When Jem was a school kid in the early grades, Bender was cooler than cool. Bender smoked, put lit firecrackers in people's mailboxes, did handstands on his skateboard. He took girls behind the bleachers or into the woods around Franklin pond. How old was he now anyway? Had to be almost thirty-five. Or older. Ancient.

"Unc said she was frigid," said Bender.

Jem's face reddened.

"Right after they broke up, she married Sanford," said Bender. "Don't he just look like a devil? You look like that, what the hell you do for Halloween?"

The cola can clunked into the bottom of the machine like an anchor. Jem got it and pushed the half-lit root beer button. Bender slotted quarters into the snack machine, retrieved a bag of sourdough pretzels. Laura liked those.

"Don knows all about Manette. He used to kick around with her. Old friend of Sanford."

Bender pointed to one of the bays. Don fired a Civil War-era relic, a Springfield musket that shot mini balls. They looked like baby cannonballs. Sounded like a cannon too. Blew a heck of a lot of smoke with each shot. Don referred to the balls as grapeshot, but no one ever corrected him; grapeshot was artillery cannonballs. Jem didn't say hi. Didn't thank him for his work on the Loud homestead's collapsed porch. Don had his ear protectors on. He wouldn't have heard Jem anyway.

"You hear Joe Silla's cheating on his wife?" said Bender.

"Old news," said Jem. "Thought bartenders knew everything first."

"Just because I didn't tell you doesn't mean I didn't know," said Bender.

"Laura know?" said Jem.

"No," said Bender. "And don't you tell her neither. Wouldn't want her to tell Sandra. None of our business."

"I'm not saying anything," said Jem. "I don't spread rumors."

Bender folded the paper top of the remaining roll of quarters. He had a hard time cramming it back in his pocket, his jeans being so tight.

"Say hi to your great-grandma, all right?" Bender said.

"Yup," Jem said. "Thanks for the coin."

ten

Thanksgiving was finished, but Jem had a few more days off. He'd been packing, preparing to move to the vineyard. Jem surveyed the open boxes, the plugged-in stereo, the CDs in stacks on the floor. He'd thought it would take him half a day to get everything ready but he had more possessions than he'd realized. He couldn't understand how he had arrived at this point, owning all this stuff. It was like it had multiplied while he slept, or while he drank at the tavern. Bit by bit.

Jem stretched his arm to the furthest can in the kitchen cupboard and took it out. Baked beans. He noticed a piece of paper plastered to the inside back corner of the cupboard. Jem pulled the paper loose, leaving a scrap still stuck to a glob of old varnish.

Family Meeting
what happened in jail
medicine working? questions for doctor

Cynthia Kolko

JOB
saving money
ways to stay out of jail

Jem read it several times. Must've been a former tenant. He dug through an already-packed cardboard crate to find his cigar box of found objects. The arrowhead's point had scratched a groove into the box's edge. Jem nudged the arrowhead toward the center of the box and folded the note and laid it next to the arrowhead. Then he took the arrowhead out of the box and put it in his pocket. Someone rapped at the door.

"Hello?" Jem said.

Another knock. This time louder.

"It's open!"

Meredith's glossy hair rode high on her shoulders. A pristine white faux fur coat (or was it real?) grazed her knees.

Meredith perused the room of boxes. "You moving?"

"Hassler. They cleared out a place for me."

Jem unfurled himself from the floor.

"Sorry again I didn't call," he said. "Been so busy. Work. This move. All my dad's stuff to sort out. I'm not too good at this."

"Not good at all the work?"

"Not good at talking," Jem said.

"Ever take public speaking?" said Meredith.

Jem shook his head.

"So. Do you want go out again? Like, after everything's settled with your new place."

157

Fruit of the Vine

"Uh… yeah, okay. You want to call me? Except I don't know my new number."

"You still have mine?"

"Yeah. I mean, I don't know."

"You have a pen?"

"I got one here somewhere."

Jem fumbled at the counter by the phone. He knocked over a stack of old credit card and utility bills. Meredith scanned the pile for a green folder. None there.

Jem couldn't find a pen.

"You know where Hassler Vineyard is, right?" he said. "I'll be above the wine shop. Right side of the building. My door's the one with the sign that says 'private.'"

Meredith's face warmed and a sliver of bright white showed.

"Okay," she said.

"All right," said Jem.

"Know what I'd really like to see? The restorations shop."

"Huh?"

"It'd be interesting. All I ever see are antiques that are already pristine. Unless you count the ones that are left in a rustic state on purpose. I never see the in-between stages."

"Oh there's nothing in that place. It's a huge mess."

"I'm an antiques nut. Didn't you know that? I'd really, really love to have a behind-the-scenes tour."

"Well if you're that into it."

"We can spend the night in there. Wouldn't that be fun? Hope I'm not being too forward."

"Sleep in the shop? Place isn't exactly hospitable. Drafty

like you wouldn't believe. Gets awfully cold. Isn't a rug on the floor and the boards are all gappy. Walk barefoot, you'll get pinched. Might even be mice. You'll run out of there screaming."

"Don't you have a sleeping bag?"

"Sure, but—"

Meredith grabbed Jem's neck and drew him in for an open-mouthed kiss. It felt awkward to Jem, but Meredith seemed not to notice. She was an attractive girl, hard to refuse. Still, Jem had to force himself even to like her.

"Guess we could," said Jem.

"Tonight?"

"I got all this moving, unpacking—"

"Tomorrow."

"Yeah, okay. Be a good excuse to get in there and clear some stuff. Can't avoid it forever. For all I know there's a rat colony or a moldy pile of—"

"Well, I'll let you get back to your work," said Meredith.

Zack came up the stairs just as Meredith was leaving.

"He's in there?"

Meredith nodded.

Jem ran a length of packing tape over the top of a wine box filled with his toiletries: crusty toothpaste, shaving cream, linty towels, and an unopened bottle of Aqua Velva with the red Christmas ribbon still noosed around its neck. The only box left to seal was the one filled with cans of soup and mandarin oranges.

"Reheating the old hot plate?" said Zack.

"Tomorrow."

Fruit of the Vine

"Why you ain't jumped in head first with her, I'll never understand."

Zack picked up a box to hoist into his truck.

An hour later, the two men stood inside the new apartment, surrounded by boxes and tiny cold, dirty clumps from the treads of their work boots. Jem removed two beers from the fridge. A solid, silent minute hung over them as the beer was consumed. In unison, they smacked empty bottles onto the green Formica counter.

From the window, Zack saw Laura slide pie boxes into the back of her truck.

"Damn, you and Laura are really neighbors."

Jem almost tripped over a box to get to the window. He watched Laura as if he were gazing upon a wistful scene from a hilltop.

"She's cute," Zack said.

"No shit," said Jem. "But she's completely nuts."

"I'd wreck her anyway," Zack said.

"That so?" asked Jem. His face was hard.

Zack didn't answer.

In the morning when the sun had barely climbed above the horizon, Jem found himself at the window again. He could see Laura's porch: the turned fingers of the railing, the diamond lattice underneath.

Laura's door swung open, the wine bottle wind chimes tinkling away under a grape hook. The door remained agape for a full minute, blocking Jem's view of what was happening behind it. Finally, the door shut, revealing a dark-haired figure of medium height wearing a black jacket and jeans. Bender. He stepped off the porch and down the driveway, disappearing behind dense pines. Jem stood stalled at the window, digesting the situation. He backed up into the bed frame and sat down on the sheet-less mattress. In the time it takes a squirrel to dart up a tree, Jem's mood turned from surprise to chagrin. He flung a pillow against the window, hitting the top of the retracted blinds with a plastic-y clang. The pillow thudded to the floor like an overripe plum.

His radio alarm went off. A fuzzy "Dream On, Dream On, Dream On," screamed out. Jem ripped the cord from the socket to silence it.

Laura's wind chimes tinkled happily. The rattan swing rocked back and forth as if soothing an invisible infant to sleep.

Bender went home, thought Jem. Man about town. Back to his place to take a shower. Change clothes. Shave.

The sun slid up the sky. An icy stalactite dripped rhythmically from Laura's porch.

Hope he cuts his throat.

Monday evening, Jem rang Laura's doorbell, pressing the glowing circle bulls-eyed by embossed brass grapevines. He waited. One hand held his grandfather's scuffed black tool box while the other rubbed the scant stubble on his chin. He

Fruit of the Vine

occupied the same spot on Laura's stoop that Bender had. Jem hunched.

In the doorway, Laura's face was flushed by the overheated foyer. Cranking the thermostat was how she fought the old house's draftiness.

As Jem entered, his arm grazed Laura's. He felt fleeting but intense warmth, as if Laura were generating her own heat. A stubby, unadorned Christmas tree leaned against the front window. A box containing a haphazard collection of grape-themed ornaments sat underneath.

"I meant to stop up to your place this weekend," said Laura. She pointed a half-raised hand in the direction of Jem's apartment above the store, as if she weren't sure whether she wanted a taxi. "Didn't get around to it. You should have seen all the junk stored in there before you moved in. Should have used a dumpster for all of it. How do people accumulate so much stuff?"

"I was thinking the same thing when I cleaned out my apartment. Place was the size of a postage stamp. Don't know how it all fit in there. Or where it all came from."

Laura's ribbed crewneck clung to her chest under the unbuttoned corduroy shirt. Jem could just make out the "v" of her bra's front outline.

"You can stop by whenever you want," said Jem.

"Okay," said Laura. "Don't want you to think your neighbors are ignoring you."

The two stood there in the boxy foyer.

"Hey, remember when we talked about me doing some-

162

Cynthia Kolko

thing other than pies?" said Laura. "Been thinking about it. Sort of. Half-baked. Ha!"

Jem shifted his tool box to the other hand.

"I'd like to run this place someday," said Laura. "Think that's stupid?"

"You grew up here. Can do anything this place can dish out," said Jem.

"Be nice if Mom recognized that," said Laura.

"Why wait for her?" said Jem.

In Laura's back room, Jem sanded with the window ajar. A forceful wind rushed into the room, clouding it with sawdust. Jem closed the window and sucked up a good amount of the grit with the shop vac. He brushed stain onto the dresser. Laura came in.

"Need to let that dry," said Jem. "Soon you'll have a nice little dresser to hand down to your kids."

"Great, except I'm not having any," said Laura.

"What? Don't like kids?" asked Jem.

"I didn't like kids even when I was one," said Laura.

"Guess I always pictured myself with at least one," said Jem. "I got a few cousins who have kids. You ever notice when a little kid sits down next to you, they sit so close? They're practically in your lap. They're like dogs that way."

"I like dogs," said Laura. Her freckles weren't as pronounced as during the summer, as if the surrounding skin was assimilating them. Her lips were a salmon color.

"Going out tonight?" she asked.

"The usual gang."

Fruit of the Vine

"I don't understand how you can hang out with that Russ," said Laura with distaste. "I can't stand him. He spread a rumor about me. Said I was exposing myself in back of the ski club bus. I wasn't even in the ski club."

"He's not a bad guy," said Jem. "Got a chip on his shoulder is all. From when his sister got raped. Pissed they never found the perp. Couldn't get any justice. If it were up to him it'd be vigilante justice."

"Joe still talks about the way he punched that guy at Tap."

"Zack's mom thinks all Russ needs is to go to church."

"You go to church?"

"Only when I'm dragged there by Gram. You?"

"Remember, my mom's Jewish. Technically, that makes me Jewish too. And Dad. He's not into religion."

"I'm kind of that way myself," said Jem. "Though I think religion has a purpose. Think about history. People in medieval Europe, living in villages surrounded by woods, no roads. Most of them lived their whole lives never putting an arm outside those villages. Then someone comes rolling into Dodge wearing fancy robes and gleaming stuff. Stands in a huge church, most majestic building in town, tell the villagers how it is. They probably think they're listening to a messenger of God himself. Tells them about Heaven and Hell, gives them a bunch of rules to follow, what will happen if they follow them or if they don't. They'll get a reward or they'll get punished. Keeps everyone in line. Gives them the morals that they might not be able to come up with themselves. It's not a bad thing. It's a good idea, really. But that's what I mean about purpose. The purpose of God, at least how I see it, is

Cynthia Kolko

to try to get everyone to get along. Here on earth. In life. It's a theory of mine."

"Well, I disagree. I believe in God," said Laura. "Not any of this man-made purpose you're talking about. God is God."

"Just on blind faith like that?"

"That's what faith is, isn't it? I believe in ghosts, too."

"I do too. Well, not the floaty, two holes in a sheet kind. I believe there are spirits that wander the earth."

Laura liked that line. "Spirit" could be defined in so many ways, from an apparition to an indescribable force.

"You're deep," said Laura.

"Don't know about that," said Jem.

He'd never had such a conversation with a woman before. Or anyone, for that matter. He didn't want to leave, wanted to bask in Laura, kooky as she was, for as long as he could foresee.

"If you're Jewish, how come you weren't barely raised that way? Why didn't your mom insist or try, or..."

"Well, Mom occasionally pulls out lines like 'We are your vineyard, you are our keeper' and stuff. But it takes a lot for Mom to look to anyone, even God, for guidance. Mostly, though, I think she just thought it was easier. It's almost like all the hardship that came before her, like it was hardwired inside her. Passed down though the genes. She didn't want me to feel burdened. All that the Jews endured for all those generations, there's weight to it. She didn't want me to have to haul it around."

Laura shrugged. "You know, there are so many parts that make up who we are. Nature, nurture, and what we add.

Fruit of the Vine

What we do to affect the future. The fruits of all those vines, like Mom says. Yet she kind of let a lot die out. Let it rot on the vine. Not me. I never wanted that heritage to end with me. Mom has it wrong. It's not a burden. It's a blessing. And it makes you strong."

Jem thought of his own genetic baggage. The sorry history of the land that became the Loud Farm. His biological father's unknown identity. The pieces of the past that exist in him, but had yet to be revealed. How he could turn it into something positive. Something sweet and fine rather than bitter.

"I'm no philosopher," he said.

Back at home, Jem emptied his pockets onto the kitchen counter, examined the pile of coins, nails, purple-stained paper scraps. Took his fingers and spread the pile thin. He shook his pants upside down like denim carwash flaps, took a flashlight to his truck. He shuttled the seats forward and back, lifted the floor mats to unveil a heavy speckling of gravel and crumbs, as if he dislodged a rock from the dirt to find an infestation of bugs. Jem's arrowhead was gone.

Reports of an upcoming ice storm were usually met with skepticism by Sawhorn residents.

"I'm not worried," Jem said to Zack, eating lunch next to the space heater in the barn. "Besides, I could stay off the road if I have to. My apartment and my job are so close I could work from my bed."

Cynthia Kolko

But when day melted into evening, ice pellets pummeled the roof over Jem's apartment like giant handfuls of ball bearings. Jem turned up the TV to hear it over the clatter. The lights flickered, then went dark. The television silenced. Jem picked up the phone and heard a dial tone. He called Elba.

"I have power," she said. "If you want to sleep here I'll make up the cot, but it might be more prudent to stay put. Roads can't be safe."

Jem stayed home. By flashlight, he read a book of corny jokes—an odd and unexpected Christmas gift from Elba a few years back—before becoming bored. He brushed his teeth in the dim and climbed into bed. His lone blanket was an inadequate, flimsy sheath. Jem found his sleeping bag at the base of a closet. He tried to remember the last time he used it, thought briefly of Meredith and sleeping in Ed's shop, but his mind drifted to a scene in a book he had read. It was about Sherpas on Mount Everest, their backs toting supplies. Jem balanced the flashlight on the ground, bouncing light off the ceiling. He unrolled the sleeping bag onto his bed, revealing a furry mass inside a thatch of straw that voided forth a piercing stench. A mouse nest cradling three dead infant mice.

His skin crawling, Jem re-rolled the sleeping bag, wrenched open the window, the storm window and the screen, and hurled the mess of bag and critter corpses out onto the ground below. He fell asleep enrobed in his heavy winter parka.

In the wee hours, Jem woke shivering. He paced the apartment, trying to warm up. The kitchen sink's hot tap belched

Fruit of the Vine

frigid water. He jogged in place, knees high, the parka making a swish sound with every arm movement. He did jumping jacks. Jumped around like a wild clown. Felt like a fucking jackass.

He wrapped the flimsy blanket around his parka like an eggroll skin. He took in the scene out the window. The ice shower had stopped. It was peaceful and nearly dark, the moon glowing weakly, like it too might soon lose power. If he squinted, he could just discern smoke puffing out of Laura's chimney.

Laura had refashioned an old wagon wheel as a trellis and hung it next to her door. Artificial grapes were tethered to the circle with fence wire. Jem touched one of the rubbery orbs, which dropped to the ground on contact. He pushed Laura's doorbell. No sound. He knocked quietly, the sound muffled by his gloved hand. Jem waited. No answer. He tried again with bare knuckles and more force.

The door creaked open.

"My place is a meat locker," said Jem.

"You're making quite a habit of this," said Laura.

Laura was shrouded in an unplugged electric blanket. Her pillow and bed quilt lay heaped on the floor in front of the flaming hearth.

"You can go back to sleep," said Jem. "I'll just hang on the couch."

"Forget it. I'm awake now."

The two sat on the couch facing the fire. Warmth trickled through Jem's extremities. He closed his eyes, saw orange through his eyelids, opened them.

"How about a game?" said Laura. "My sister and I used to thumb wrestle. We'd even draw faces on our thumbs and cut scraps of fabric to tie around them like clothes."

"Great game," Jem said. What a nut.

"Look, you're the one rang my bell. Sorry I didn't have a ring toss and a band waiting. Why don't you go to Russ's place? He'll play beer pong and watch porn with you."

Jem couldn't disagree, as that was probably exactly what Russ would have on offer. Flames lapped the fireplace interior. Embers rose off the logs and wandered confused before finding passage up the chimney. Jem recognized an opportunity to make a move on Laura, but indecision glued him to the couch.

"I'm going to make pie dough for when the power kicks on. Almost time to get up anyway," said Laura.

"Yeah, I should get going," said Jem.

As soon as Laura left the room, Jem fisted the couch cushion.

❦

The phone rang at Tap. Joe answered.

"Jem stood me up," said Meredith.

"You need to be careful calling here. Roy could have answered, if he'd shown up, that is. With all that ice coating the roads, it's a ghost town. Not everyone's got the power of my SUV. Wait a minute, Roy can walk here. Lives down the street. Why isn't that damn fry cook in yet?"

"Who gives a shit?" said Meredith. "We were talking about

Fruit of the Vine

me. Maybe Jem got distracted. He's been spending time over at your sister-in-law's place."

"Got to nip that in the bud."

Joe fired up the SUV. From his driver's-side throne, he spied a compact car off the road, nose-first in a ditch with its back end skyward like a duck fishing in a pond.

"Suckers!" Joe shouted with glee as he passed the unfortunate vehicle. "Bet you wish you had this fine piece of machinery!" He patted the steering wheel like a dog's back. "Ha ha! You lame bastards!"

At Hassler, Joe pretended to need a lot of wine and made a big show of it, pointing to various bottles, saying he wanted a case of this, two cases of that. Commiserated with marvel about the storm. How so many Sawhorn households and businesses were without power, but how they must be pleased as punch that the grid that powered Hassler was back on. How it sure pays to live in the boonies sometimes, eh? How he owned a gas-powered generator he'd purchased from a catalog catering to the ski vacation home crowd, so it didn't matter to him. How he'd spent the night home watching TV with every light on while the neighbors, poor saps, shivered in front of their fireplaces, wondering why the pan of Jiffy Pop balanced on one of the logs wouldn't pop already.

Joe carried the crates to his car. It made him feel strong and young. It was as close to manual labor as he could fathom. Afterward, he hung around long enough to run into Laura outside the wine shop.

"Hear you've been spending time with that Jem kid," Joe said.

Cynthia Kolko

"He restored a dresser," said Laura.

"At Ed's shop?" Rapid blinking.

"In my house."

"You aren't interested in him, are you?" More blinking.

"No," said Laura. "Not that it's any of your concern."

A cold wind flailed. Laura pulled her grape hat down over her ears. Truth was, Laura liked Jem. A lot. Looked forward to his visits. Felt lonely when he left. She liked his face, the kiln-fired look of his cheeks, his thin lips, bony chin, kind eyes. She enjoyed talking to him. Was interested in what he thought. It felt comfortable. It was more than that.

"That's a relief," said Joe.

"What do you mean?" Laura asked.

Joe took off his mirrored shades, needless in the overcast light. He gave the glasses a quick chew before balancing them atop his head, chiding himself for nearly putting teeth marks into the fine frame.

"You deserve better than that farmhand. Hasn't made anything of himself."

"Jem's the vineyard manager. He works hard."

"So what? Everyone works hard," said Joe. "It's the American way, working hard. You need a guy who's got some gumption, who can earn a decent living, give you some security."

He plucked a stray pine needle off his pants.

"Things are changing, my girl. Old industries, farms. 'Unstable' is a kind word for it. You know what happened when the market for grapes collapsed a few years ago. I wasn't even living here, but I heard it a million times down at Tap.

Fruit of the Vine

Heard it up, down, and sideways. People out of work, no savings or investments. The unemployment steps crowded like they were giving away Stones tickets inside. Working hard isn't nearly enough. You've got to be able to reinvent. And you've got to have a nest-egg in case it all blows up in your face."

Laura's brow furrowed. "I haven't made much of myself either, if you look at it your way," she said.

"Different for a girl," said Joe. "Women, it's okay not to be achievement-oriented. But not real men. No way. Something wrong with a man who's not gunning to be all he can be, as the Army says. Jem, he's not much younger than I am. But look what I've accomplished only five years since graduating college."

It hadn't occurred to Laura that it had been only five years since Joe and Sandra graduated, spent three months planning W-day, Sandra blinded by her fresh glittery diamond and Joe driving an ego-sized stake in the ground. At least they were happy with each other, a rare condition even in marriages ordained under more enlightened circumstances. Sure, they were shallow. But if they were pleased with the arrangement, Laura supposed she should be too. She was trying to be.

"You going to your five-year reunion?" asked Laura.

"Hell, yeah," barked Joe, his fleshy upper lip curled into a snarl, over-bleached teeth gleaming robotically. "Taking the convertible. That piece of ass'll really impress those losers. Which reminds me. Since Thanksgiving, I changed my mind about Bender. He's a decent guy. Got potential. His success

Cynthia Kolko

is marginal, but at least he has two good legs to stand on. How's it going with him?"

"Drifting," said Laura. "Always seems like he's got something else on his mind."

"With you around? Impossible," said Joe. "You might just want to hold onto him. At least for a month or so more. Where's Jem now? Couldn't find him out in the fields or in the bottling room or by the casks."

"Lunch," said Laura.

She retreated to her house. In the kitchen, she traced a line with her pointer on the flour-coated counter.

What'll they say about me at my fifth reunion?

You're living with your parents?

No, in my own house.

On the farm?

Well, yeah, but it's my own house.

Lame.

I got my own business.

Really? What do you do?

Sell pies.

Lame.

Married?

No.

You're a spinster baking pies out of a house owned by your parents? What do you do for fun? Feed pigeons from a park bench? Square dance? Lame, lame, lame.

Fruit of the Vine

Jem had escaped to his apartment. He flipped through the yellow pages, found an unbolded listing sandwiched between neatly-bordered rectangular ads: "Al Vargas, Private Investigations." He called the number, made an appointment for later that afternoon, told Manette he had some issues of his dad's to clean up. She didn't mind, still felt sorry that Jem was essentially orphaned.

When the time came for the appointment, Jem's throat tightened. He hunched. On the way to his truck, he walked across the parking lot in a cloud of uncertainty so thick he didn't notice Joe Silla.

"Jem," said Joe. "How you doing? You must have a butt load of your dad's crap to deal with. That where you're headed now?"

"I got an appointment."

"Must be a heap of papers and legal affairs. You do that yet? The papers?"

"Some. Dying is a huge deal. Insurance. Bank stuff. All his bills. Like you said, a butt load."

Jem opened his truck's door. He wanted to cut this short and get to his appointment, not chit-chat. But Joe pressed on.

"You come across anything else?" asked Joe.

"Like what? A treasure map to the pirate's booty he buried?" said Jem.

"I mean, anything he might have done recently. Like deals or papers he wanted to send off but didn't get the chance."

"For the last time, no. All his papers are in the shop. I'm going to look at it all soon. See if there's anything he might have sold."

Cynthia Kolko

"Sold?"

"Yeah. Like a piece of furniture. Someone might be looking for delivery on something he fixed."

"What's this appointment for?"

Jem got in his truck and drove away.

❦

Roy's blue pickup drove past Ed Loud's shop with the weather-beaten door, past Sawhorn Meadows with Mrs. Carpin's army of figurines, past a shuttered farm stand in front of which a prankster re-lettered the sign from "closed" to "coed." It climbed past Chateau Cobblestone's "Tastings Daily" sign. At the private entrance fortress, Roy rang the intercom bell.

"Roy Archer for Meredith Payne."

"One moment please," said the intercom speaker.

Cold from the open window fanned through the truck. After a minute, Roy heard, "Go ahead Miss Payne." Then the speaker barked Meredith's voice.

"What do you want?"

"Want to talk."

"About what?"

"I think you know."

The speaker exhaled loudly.

"Stay left. My door is the last one."

The gates to the cloistered residence opened. At her door, Meredith relegated Roy to the stoop. He stood hatless, but not cold.

175

Fruit of the Vine

"You tell me what Joe is cooking up," said Roy. "Tell me or I blow you both in to Sandra. And to Jem too."

⚜

Al Vargas worked at home, an early-1900s house built for farmhands. Scratchy lettering on the back door said simply "Investigations." Ed would have liked that, Jem thought. How it cut to the chase without any spin, any gilding.

Inside, Jem sat on one of a crowd of mismatched chairs. A hand-tatted doily covered the worn seat. Jem felt ashamed resting his butt on someone's handiwork, but it was the only chair that looked hefty enough to hold him. Jem was as nervous now as when he visited Ed in the hospital. He wasn't sure anyone else was inside the office until he heard Vargas on the phone in an adjoining room.

"Wha? Get out of town. Didn't you get the pictures? How can you say that? You don't need any more. Show them to the cops. Clear what's going on, isn't it? Wha? If you insist, but it'll cost you more money and you won't accomplish anything more. I'm not going to gouge you just for... Wha? Take another couple of days. Wha? Okay. Whatever you want."

Vargas hung up.

"Lunatic," he said.

Jem coughed.

"Who's there?" Vargas called out into the waiting area.

"Me?"

"Yeah, you! Who's there?"

"Jem Loud."

176

Cynthia Kolko

"You're up."

The office was a jumble of papers, photo albums, piles of unfiled photos. A dozen coffee cups, filled to varying degrees with rancid liquid, decorated the surfaces.

"So, you're looking for your mother," said Vargas. "Have a seat."

He motioned to an old wooden school chair. Jem sat, teetered on it.

"You're Ed Loud's son?"

"Yes."

"Sorry to hear of his death."

"Did you know him?"

"No, but I read every obit. Keep a file of them. Sometimes I wish I did know all these people. Would make my job easier. I've only lived here four years. Wife and I split up. Couldn't live in the same town, but needed to be nearby, because of the kids. Cheap place to live, Sawhorn."

"Property taxes suck," said Jem.

"I rent," said Vargas. "Tell me what you know about your mom."

"Well, she was born in 1950, because she was nineteen when I was born. Least that's what people tell me."

"Born here in Sawhorn?"

"Yup."

"Name?"

"Mary Girard. Her parents are dead. They were part of that food poisoning thing."

"What's that?"

"You never heard of the big poisoning in Sawhorn? Some-

Fruit of the Vine

time in the early sixties the firehouse put on a pancake breakfast. Something was wrong with the batter. People just started
dropping off their chairs. Literally falling out of them. Crumpling on the floor next to the tables. Right in the firehouse
where it was held. Bunch of folks died. Lots."

"Interesting."

"Some of my Loud relatives died there. Both grandparents.
You want to know about them?"

"Let's concentrate on your mother."

"Right. My great-grandma says she's dead."

"Easy to find out if that's true. What else?"

"She read a lot."

"Tell me more."

"She was into current events. Subscribed to magazines
like Time and Newsweek. Not politics, but manhunts and hi-
jacking and that kind of story. Never missed the six o'clock
news. That's what my dad said about her, but I believe it."

"Hmm." Vargas scratched notes on a pad.

"She had a friend."

"Who?"

"Dodie McAllen. Don McAllen's wife. Was like a mom-fig-
ure to my mom, I think. My grandma was kind of a screw-
up. Wasn't around her kids much even before she died."

"Where's Dodie McAllen now?"

"Dead."

"The hell is wrong with this town? Everyone dies," said
Vargas.

The same fact had occurred to Jem. That death marked the
area with curious strokes. The usual terminal illnesses, such

Cynthia Kolko

as cancer, claimed about as many lives as would be expected, though an undercurrent of finger-pointing singled out pesticides as the cause. And car accidents were a frequent cause of early demise. The popular sport of drinking, combined with country speed zones on skinny, slick winter roads made for at least one disastrous crash each year. Testosterone-fueled tailgating was an epidemic, and the bravado of a subset of SUV drivers, thinking their vehicles impenetrable, accounted for a number of bad bang-ups as well.

But then there were many odd deaths, deaths that seemed both disproportionately odd and disproportionately numerous to those in the population at large. Accidents involving farm equipment were not rare. One winery lost a bottler when his shirt collar got caught in the works, his feet slipping in the scramble to free the garment, which effectively hanged him.

Macabre occurrences of outlandishly slim probability were hardly confined to farms. One fall, hurricane-like winds drove hundred-foot trees to the ground, one of which hatcheted a roof on its downward arc, smacking the residents' bed like a colossal angry educators' ruler on the desk, where they tried, in vain, to escape the plummeting cudgel.

"Think Dodie had cancer," said Jem. "Don's still around. He was my dad's friend too. And he's buddies with Sanford Fillmore."

Later that afternoon, Jem stopped by the restorations shop

Fruit of the Vine

to call numbers from Ed's book, clients who might be looking for their furniture, the ones who hadn't already left answering machine messages, some pleading, some threatening, some meek. Jem got hungry. He decided to pack it in for the day, pick a pair of hotdogs from the yellow-lighted rotisserie at the Quik Mart for an early dinner.

A warm spell had caused some snow to melt. Main Street was a fabric of tonal tan and gray stripes left by tire tracks in slush. The inevitable drop in temperature as the sun set caused the mushy snow to freeze into ice. Local roads became treacherous when this happened. It was a mess compounded by precipitation that was rain one minute, ice the next.

Laura emerged from the bowels of the Quik Mart holding a package of feminine products. As she'd waited to check out, a light-haired man cut the line in front of her and then chatted up the clerk for what seemed an eternity while Laura steamed behind him, her foot tapping.

When she finally got through the checkout and returned to her truck, Laura spotted the man in a van pulling out of his parking space along Main Street. Laura hit the gas hard, to catch him before he disappeared down the street. She turned her face out the window to shout at him.

"Hey! You cut in front of me in line, you rude son of a—"

Laura's truck slid over an icy scrap of road, and amid the percussive beats of antilock brakes, careened off Main Street into another truck stopped on the shoulder. As she hit the broad brown rear, the bunch of grapes painted on Laura's hood receded into accordion folds. An Adirondack chair catapulted off the brown truck's bed and smashed Laura's windshield. The sound of the impact sent the truck's driver running out of one of the old buildings.

"Dang it all!" he said.

He hoisted the splintered chair off Laura's truck, grimaced at it and then let it fall from his hands like trash.

"Know how long that took me to build?"

He scratched at his goatee, looked at Laura's crushed hood designs, his pain fading, replaced with a spark of humor.

"Looks like you got grape juice now," he said.

Laura snarled, calculating in her head the repair costs and the insurance deductible. Jem, driving by, pulled off the shoulder in front of the brown truck.

"Is it still running?" he asked Laura.

She opened the driver's door, legs hanging out, right hip a fulcrum for her teetering body. She turned the key. The engine roared in affirmation.

"Follow me to the garage," said Jem.

"I can't see!"

"Take my truck. I'll drive it."

Jem drove Laura's crumpled vehicle with his head out the window like a dog.

At Loud Motors, Laura watched through a coffee-spattered window as Russ tinkered with his favorite wrench, a hammer.

"Sure I'm not keeping you from something?" asked Laura.

"I needed a break from my dad's stuff," said Jem.

"Must be a huge pain. I can't imagine."

"There's more," Jem said. "I hired a detective. To find my ma."

"A detective? Couldn't you just find what you need to know around here? By yourself?"

Fruit of the Vine

"Some things are worth the money," said Jem.

"Just don't get your hopes up like some people do," said Laura. "They find their birth parents and it isn't what they expected. The parents don't want anything to do with them."

"I wasn't adopted."

"What are you going to do if…when the detective finds her? Are you going to show up at her door or something?"

"Just want to talk a little. I'm not interested in any kind of relationship."

"That's the story of my life," said Laura.

"Huh?" said Jem.

"Never mind."

He bent to the floor to retrieve an empty plastic creamer cup, tossed it into the unlined garbage can.

"Well," said Laura. "You can always talk to me. If things get rough."

"Thanks," said Jem.

Jem wished he had kept his search quiet, didn't talk about himself. He felt awkward, embarrassed. Like he was looking for sympathy. Or help. It was weak. Unmanly. He could run a few things by Zack, simple things, nothing deep. But opening himself up to Laura? Now he looked like a pussy. And worse, she had implied that he needed to talk. That she saw a frailty in him. That he was so pathetic, so broken, he needed the help of a woman. Jem's complexion reddened. He hunched in the wobbly plastic chair. He could hardly contain his shame.

Russ came into the waiting room through a greasy-knobbed door taped with a sign that read "Absolutely No

Customers Allowed through This Door." He left a trail of black prints from one of his heels.

"Might not want to waste your money on this one," said Russ.

"It's totaled?" said Laura.

"Unless you wanna spend a few grand in repairs. Truck's had it. Ain't worth it. What's your insurance policy like?"

Russ scraped dark gunk from under one thumbnail with the too-long pinky fingernail of the opposite hand.

"Cheapest policy I could find," said Laura.

"If I was you, I'd junk it," said Russ. "It'll never pass inspection. Could fix it enough for you to get around, but people ain't going to want to buy a pie from a girl driving a junky rickety truck. They'll think you bake in a mousetrap."

Laura threw up her hands, then let them fall to her sides as if she just couldn't hold them up anymore.

"If that isn't a reason to quit the pie business," she said. "God's sending me a sign."

Out the door, Jem said, "See? Told you Russ was a nice guy all-in-all. He could have taken you for thousands there, but he didn't. No one's completely bad or completely good. People you think are evil, they have it in them to do right. And even saints have something stinking up their closets if you dig deep enough."

◈

Joe bought black sneakers for the occasion. In his basement, he unearthed a dark ski mask from an unpacked box

Fruit of the Vine

marked "vacation stuff." He found a roll of electrical tape one of the handymen left in the garage, taped a black strip over the white logo on his jacket. Sandra was in Rochester with her girlfriends, drinking cocktails with umbrellas in them, and flirting with blue-collar men down on their luck. Dime a dozen, those guys.

On the bedspread—custom sewn from Tuscan yellow silk modeled after an antique Fortuny print—Joe fanned the black garments: pants, turtleneck, socks. He removed his shiny watch and put it in the nightstand drawer. Joe dressed in front of the mirrored reproduction armoire.

He drove to a secluded spot behind a defunct lawnmower resale shop hidden by overgrown shrubs. He sidestepped from shadow to shadow down one of the streets perpendicular to Main Street, sprinted, sidled into the alley between Ed's restorations shop and the building next to it. He took a crowbar to the shop's window, wedged it under the jamb, and pushed with all his strength. Joe wasn't as strong as he thought he was. The crowbar slipped, sending Joe down onto the cold pavement. The bar clonked him on the head.

"God damn mother fucking shit," he said aloud, then looked around to see if anyone heard.

The alley was empty except for icy ridges of snow girding the buildings. A plume of white blew down the street.

The crowbar had created a thin stripe of an opening. Joe slipped his fingers into it, opened the window. You'd think they'd keep this locked. All those antiques. Rednecks sure are trusting.

Inside the shop, Joe shined his flashlight over half-finished nightstands, legless tables, piles of hardware. Worn planks of wood, barn slats perhaps, were piled at the base of a wall. Split-top dressers. A black-painted bed frame that couldn't be called vintage but wasn't yet an antique.

No wonder they kept the window open. Be a blessing if anyone took this crap.

The shop reeked of linseed oil and mold. In the closet, Joe found a box of papers marked "current affairs." He flipped through stacks of files, rifled through a rusty cabinet, piles of loose documents. He looked under furniture. Joe lifted a tool box from a table, revealing a dust-free rectangle underneath. He replaced the tool box exactly on the rectangle. No green folder. Exhausted, Joe left through the window. Delirious with wanton anger, he flung the crowbar into the alley with the sound of a steel pipe being dropped off a flatbed. He retrieved the crowbar, slipped home in the shadows without being seen.

The next day at Tap, Joe looked spent. He entered through the establishment's back door unshaven, eyes like sinkholes.

"I know what you're doing, Joe."

The door slammed behind Joe like an exclamation mark.

"Trying to buy Ed's land," said Roy. "Jem's land. You sure you wanna build up there?"

Roy held a chopping knife. Bell pepper pellets littered the counter.

"My money's the same color as anyone's," said Joe.

"I'm not saying you can't buy it. But build on it? Such a nice old farm. And before that, it was a village. You know that, right? It's historic," said Roy.

Fruit of the Vine

"Shit, what isn't historic?" asked Joe, irritated with lack of sleep, voice growing edgier with each syllable. "Everything here was the site of a damn village," Joe said. "Indians lived all over the place. Something happened on every square inch of this town, right? I don't see anyone yapping about all the other new builds around here. Anyone raise a stink when they built Chateau Cobblestone? You think Indians didn't live on that land? Bet the French took potshots at the Loud Farm from up there too."

Roy sighed. "Even if you're not concerned about what it means to American Indian history—and it should matter to you, but even if it doesn't—the Loud Farm itself is documented historic. Battle's in the history books. Got one of those blue signs there and everything. The state will never let you."

Joe's blinking started. "State's a bunch of pansies," he said, using his hand to slap away the imaginary obstruction. "I already have them in my back pocket. Besides, there's a lot of land there and not all of it is, as you say, a historic site. I'll be sensitive to it. Some of the land will stay and people can look at it. Take pictures. Whatever the hell they do at an empty field. I'm sure there'll be droves of them, like now. Just the other day, I was remarking at the enormous crowd assembled in front of the Loud family shack. Couldn't tear them away from the weeds and snakes."

"Be weird to stop at the blue sign and see a housing development," said Roy. "Kills the effect, don't you think?"

"Had it with those rusty blue signs," said Joe. "Every chicken coop that some old soldier pissed in has got a goddamn blue sign in front of it. Hell, even Loud's Tavern, that

Cynthia Kolko

stinking dive, is on the national registry of historic places. Can you believe that? That rat hole dump? This whole block is supposed to be historic, for Christ's sake. It's in a book about the state. The realtor showed it to me when I bought this building. None of that stopped all those big mansions from being subdivided into apartments with two-burner stoves and bathroom sinks you wouldn't wash a dog in."

Joe shook his head, turned his eyes to the ceiling, studied the rosette pattern in the tin.

"Just because something is old doesn't mean it's worth preserving," said Joe. "There's an old pile of rocks out behind my house. Maybe we ought to preserve that. And the tract my house is on? I didn't hear any flap about all that building."

"There absolutely was a flap," said Roy. "Habitat for birds, interfering with the natural watershed. I'm not saying they were right. You can't stop development altogether. People have to pick their battles. They had a point, though. By the way, how's your basement?"

"A little moist," said Joe, crushing his eyebrows together until the number 11 appeared creased between them.

Roy pointed his chopping knife, using it as a teacher's baton as he spoke. "Joe, you build on Loud Farm, and you'll have more bad PR than you can cram into a dumpster. You'll have Indian groups, environmentalist groups, not to mention the esteemed residents of Sawhorn, the old 'I like it the way it is' crowd who don't want anything to change."

"If you don't stop pointing that thing at me, I'm going to have to take you down."

Roy laid the knife on the counter, checked his pocket for

Fruit of the Vine

his pack of smokes. About this time most days, he'd head out back, outside the kitchen door. He'd stand, smoke, think of nothing in particular. These days though, his thoughts were dominated by the Loud Farm. The white deer he'd seen there months prior, that he suspected Joe had seen too. Couldn't get it out of his mind.

"The white settlers raped the American Indians and they raped the land."

"I never raped anybody. And how the hell can you rape land? Man, I hate it when people use that expression. You can burn it, scorch it, play baseball on it. You can't rape it! Besides that, aren't you mostly white? You saying you raped yourself? I wasn't there, and neither were you."

"I'm telling you, people hear of a development on that land, they'll beat you to death with their frying pans."

Joe didn't want to be unpopular. But making money trumped popularity. And wasn't money the easiest way to gain popularity?

"My ma calls those big pans 'husband tamers,'" said Joe. He shook his head. "You can't complain about lack of jobs and oppose development. It doesn't work that way."

"You know what your problem is, Joe?" said Roy. "It's not that you think you're better than everyone else. It's that you think you're better than the land. Well, it isn't true, man. None of us is better than the land. We're not even equal to it."

"I just want to make some money."

"And the rest of us, we pay for it."

"That land needs me," said Joe. "Look what I did to this place here. This decrepit, burned out building. I saved it.

Cynthia Kolko

Made it better than it ever was. Brought it back to life. Why can't I do that to the Loud house? And the farm?"

"Why don't you just set fire to that house too? Then you can pick it up for nothing, just like you did with the Brasserie. Operation Burning Bra. Worked like a charm."

"You're the one who rigged the wiring. It's your prints all over the works."

Roy took off his vinyl gloves, wiped sweaty palms on his apron. He squinted at Joe.

"Why do you want that land, anyway?" he asked. "I mean, there's plenty of other land here. What is it about the Loud Farm you can't do without?"

"Figured it'd be a good spot to build on. Nice view. That's all."

"Plenty of other nice views to be had," said Roy. Meredith had told Roy about Joe's plan to purchase the farm, but she was mum about the details. Never spilled whether Joe had seen a white deer.

"When they see what I'm going to do to that property, they'll be coming by the busload to live there," said Joe. "They'll wear out Loud Road with all the traffic. Bring money into this town. Probably carve a statue of me to put on Main Street, replace that sad old Elias Sawhorn that no one cares about, all pitted and covered in bird shit." Joe nodded, grinned. "Yeah. It's going to be something. Make a real mark on this town with that property. That and another piece of land I'm making an offer on."

eleven

Roy sprinted across Main Street to Jem's old apartment, momentarily crouching behind a parked car, the bumper on it sporting the region's most prevalent version of the Jesus Fish plaque, an ichthys bearing the words "Gone Fishing." Roy followed a serpentine of footprints to the apartment house, saw "Loud" next to a black call button, pushed it and prepared to talk into the intercom, but a buzzer sounded before anyone spoke. He pushed the double doors, climbed the stairs. A bulky woman waited at the top.

"Jem moved. Lives at Hassler Vineyard now. Try him there."

Jem heard the footsteps first. A knock at the door sent him clambering to hide piles of laundry and dirty dishes. He was surprised and disappointed when he answered the door.

"Mind if we talk a minute?"

Jem let Roy inside.

"Joe Silla tell you anything about a deal?" asked Roy.

"Huh?" said Jem.

"Think he had something going on with your dad. Anyone say anything about it?"

"No. But Joe's sure been acting strange. Questions about my dad's affairs. He thinks I'm an idiot, obviously."

Roy thought back to the white deer, its angelic coat, the joy that filled Roy's soul with each step of the animal's hooves.

"Joe didn't say anything about buying Loud Farm?" said Roy.

"Buying Loud Farm?" said Jem. "Why didn't he just say something outright?"

"Because he was pulling the wool over your dad's eyes," said Roy. "Me and Joe, we're friends and all, but we're strange bedfellows too. Don't see eye-to-eye on a lot of stuff. I don't usually get up in his business. But this time, it's personal. It means something to me."

"The Loud Farm means something to you?" said Jem.

"Don't you know the history of it?"

"Yeah, I do," said Jem, wearily. "Believe me, I do."

Jem sat on the nearest piece of furniture, a creaky mission-style chair with worn cushions. He pushed his hand to his forehead. If there were another chair in the apartment, he would have offered it to Roy. But Jem figured he was the one with the weight on his shoulders. He deserved to be the one sitting in the chair.

"You know what I saw in those woods, Jem? I saw an American chestnut tree," Roy said. "Not a horse chestnut. An American chestnut. Big tree. Forty feet tall, I figure. You know how rare that is? A big one like that? Blight usually gets them before they're anywhere near that tall. Bet no one but

Fruit of the Vine

the two of us knows it's there. Joe wouldn't recognize it if it ran up to him and said 'howdy.'"

As Jem listened, he could feel the circles under his eyes darkening, denting his face like the impressions of table legs on a rug. The mental tasks of the past weeks exhausted him to a much greater degree than any physical labor. Mere weeks ago, aside from the responsibilities of personal health and hygiene, all Jem had to concern himself with was doing his job and keeping his truck running. Now, the bestowal of a piece of dual heritage hinged on his actions.

Jem already felt he had aged a decade since his father died. This was not a decision to honor the past, or even the people, from ancient Americans to Jem's own brood, who marched in history's army. The land—its life, its spirit—depended on his patrimony. He was as much the guardian of the land as he was of his great-grandmother, though the continuum of earth and creature would extend far beyond any of them.

"He wants to build on it," said Roy.

"What I figured."

"If I were you, I'd find out exactly what he's planning. Real quick. Putting a bunch of boxes up there on that land, that'd be a crime."

Roy felt in his pocket for his pack of smokes.

"You may not like to think of this," said Roy, "but soon enough, you'll be the last Loud standing. Your great-grandma may be in good shape today. But how old is she? Ninety?"

"Eighty-five."

"Eighty-five is old," Roy said brusquely.

Cynthia Kolko

"You're not God. You don't know anything," Jem said.

"What happens to that land will be your legacy," Roy said. "Good or bad. And if Joe gets it, it isn't going to be good. He might throw some bills at you, but believe me, you won't be happy with the result. Nourish that land. Do that and it'll nourish us all."

"Thanks for your concern, and for telling me about the chestnut, but I've got to work this out myself. If and when Joe comes to me with something. It's my land."

Roy was not ready to give up. "Jem, that land's full of treasure, and not the kind Joe's thinking of. Apply for a land trust. You've got to. It'll keep the land safe. Your dad never did it. Wanted to keep his options open, I guess."

A land trust would have been out of the question for Ed, but for a broader reason than a desire to make money off the land someday. Ed distrusted the government. He couldn't bear giving it any more of a foothold in his life than it already had. He hated taxes. For years, his truck's bumper held up a sticker: "If this is the Land of the Free, why does it cost so much?" It was all a symptom of what Ed called "Government Bigfoot," an autocratic bully who impinged on a litany of rights from employment practices to land use. And Bigfoot's main weapons, overtaxation and overregulation, were entirely to blame for the region's woes.

"Bigfoot's killing New York," Ed would say. "Without firing a shot. Scaring off business. Driving out the people."

Ed wanted to keep the imposing creature from Albany from tromping all over his land, directing what he could and couldn't do with it, wrestling from him a proud badge of freedom, sliding its sticky fingers over one of the last things Ed thought he controlled.

"New York's just one move away from being a commie state," Ed said. "I'm telling you, if that Bigfoot comes here from Albany, comes onto my land, I'm going to shoot him square between the eyes, least while I still got the right to own a gun."

Jem thought that if someone were fortunate enough to have something to sell, you could hardly blame him for doing it in these times. What would be so wrong with letting a few acres go to the folks looking for a piece of what they imagined was the charmed, healthy life they'd glimpsed from the car or seen on TV? If someone offered you some nice dough for a fraction of land, money that would allow you to keep the rest, pay down debt, or even get rid of it all and move the heck out of town, well, who's to say that'd be selling out? Who among those who called Sawhorn home weren't descendents of someone who took a chance, ventured far from home to start something new amid uncertainty, not to mention bodily danger? Was Joe so wrong?

Roy spoke. "With a land trust, you could get a big tax break. Might not cost you barely anything."

"The hell it won't. It'll cost me the money I won't be making from the sale," said Jem. "Assuming that's what I'd want to do; and we're not making any assumptions here."

"What are you talking about? You get a land trust, you can still sell the land. Course you won't get as much money for it if no one can develop it. And, there's eminent domain, where the government can take any property it wants. That might not be a bad thing here, Jem. If the land's historic enough for a trust, maybe the government can do something good there."

Jem thought he heard Ed kicking in his grave.

❦

"Awesome," said Laura, opening and closing the top drawer of the dresser. "Just great."

Jem was proud of the work he'd done on the piece. He'd taken something old, and by adding some new parts and a little effort, extended its life, ensured its continued utility. Honored its history. Became part of its future.

"Sure I can't pay you something?" asked Laura.

"Forget it," said Jem. He scrubbed away a drop of stain that had spattered on Laura's floor.

"Can I at least give you a pie?"

"Now there. That's something I will take," said Jem.

In the kitchen, Laura removed a pie from the freezer.

"Directions are on the label," she said.

Jem nodded, noticed skis propped in the corner of the kitchen near the back door.

"Hitting the slopes this weekend?" he said.

"Yeah. Should be great snow. Want to come?"

"Wish I could."

"You should take a break sometime."

"That's what this dresser project was," said Jem.

"Why don't you come here some night and we'll get a video?"

Fruit of the Vine

Jem pictured the two of them sitting on the purple couch, lights off, the television flickering on Laura's face like candlelight.

"Yeah, okay," said Jem.

Laura held Jem's gaze. Her eyes seemed to brighten with each blink as if her eyelids were polishing them.

"You want to do it Saturday night? If you've got something already, we can plan for another night. I don't want to cut into your weekend."

"You're not cutting in," said Jem.

Take that, Bender. Chew on that. Get it all over your moustache.

✿

Joe's thick black tires spewed tiny, snowy pebbles which pelted the car's underside. The convertible top was up, still too cold even with the heater on, but the snow had been cleared on most of the roads, making garaging the SUV for the day plausible, if not desirable. Sandra had her arm hooked through an Italian leather purse, its color billed in the fashion magazines as "British Highlands Green." She gazed out the passenger window into the side mirror at the tall grass above the snow recoiling in the wake of the passing car. Their car. Shiny yellow so it couldn't be missed. A blue spruce swayed in the harsh northerly wind.

Sanford waited in the kitchen, looked out the window, drank black coffee from a Syracuse Orangemen mug with a lip-shaped tan stain at the rim.

Cynthia Kolko

"Howdy," Sanford said, as Joe and Sandra walked in.

"Where's Mom?" Sandra asked.

"Still asleep. Laura's up, I bet."

Sandra left, walked across the driveway, purse slapping her thigh, hair flowing out behind her like a yellow towel on a clothesline. Daylight had broken an hour ago, but Laura's porch light was still on. The timer hadn't shut it off yet.

Joe kept his hands in the pockets of his suede jacket, quilted inside for extra warmth.

"Coffee?" asked Sanford.

"No, thanks," said Joe. "Already had some."

"Into the study then."

The two men walked through French doors stained a honey oak. Shelves flanked every wall, even the spaces over doors and windows, crammed with books. Manette consumed books like glasses of water, chiseling out the time in the scant minutes before bed. Sanford closed the study doors and sat at a desk that was neat but cluttered with short stacks of paper and several photos in small pewter frames.

"Where's Manette?" asked Joe.

"She wants us to work out more of the details before she says yea or nay. She'll have lots of questions. Though, I don't have to tell you."

"We need to talk price at some point."

Sanford cocked his head, made his mouth a wide line and raised his eyebrows in a gesture Joe recognized as a concessionary "yes."

"Does anyone else know you're thinking of doing this?" asked Joe.

Fruit of the Vine

"No. You and Sandra are the only ones who know we're looking to get out of this business. I don't want to tell Laura yet. Not until we get a firmer idea what would happen to her. Her place and all."

"Laura's house is pretty much shot," said Joe. "Practically a lean-to. Even if we did keep it, we'd have to fix it up like a son of a bitch. Major overhaul. Too expensive to do that. Cost prohibitive. Have to work that into the deal."

Sanford pushed his lips together. The beard pointed forward.

"We'd keep the big barn like you wanted, and this house would become a B&B," said Joe. "We can build a nice ranch house for you and Manette. Sandra's talking about having some horses when we build our own place on the property. Sure you'd like to gaze out onto some of those. Nothing wrong with a view of some of nature's finest. The horses, I mean."

Sanford remembered the two girls in childhood, dressed in shorts and t-shirts, blowing bubbles in the barn, pretending they were dancing on the Lawrence Welk show. Sanford's face drooped.

"You okay, Sanford?"

"Guess so," he said.

"I know this is a change. But you have to keep moving forward."

"It'll be different," said Sanford.

"Different doesn't mean bad," said Joe.

Sanford recalled how Manette had uttered those very words to the elder Hasslers all those years ago. He splayed his palms on the desk and used his arms to boost himself from the chair. When he stood, he was still slightly crunched, knees flexed, like he might sit back down.

"Not a word to Laura about any of this," he said.

"Now, Sanford. What kind of loudmouth do you think I am?"

Joe rang Laura's bell. Sandra flung open the door a second after the single chime. She bolted outside, as if someone lit a fire in the foyer.

"It's getting bad out again," said Sandra.

Joe petted his hair. "Looks like it was bad in there. Where's Laura?"

"In the kitchen. She's peeved. Got mad at me. I told her not to get too involved with that Jem."

"That's what I've been telling her. What did you say?"

"Tell you in the car."

Joe opened the car door for Sandra and then slammed it with a slight flourish.

"What I told Laura," said Sandra, "I told her to get out once in a while. Looking for a guy here in Sawhorn is like shopping in your own closet."

"True, true," said Joe. "But what about Bender? He's not all bad, besides the fact that he's a two-bit barkeep. And he sure isn't good-looking. Not even if you dressed him in an expensive tux. Not even close."

"Ecchh. Terrible." Sandra stuck out her tongue but retracted it quickly, not wanting to contort her face into an unattractive expression.

Fruit of the Vine

Joe's mind bubbled. Maybe it wasn't so bad, Jem and Laura hooking up. When Joe bought Loud Farm, Laura would learn from Jem about how good life can be when you make a bunch of money. That might make the sale of Hassler Vineyards easier.

"She needs to dress better if she's going to hold a guy's interest," said Joe. "Let him see what's under there. You ought to help her. Tell her what to buy."

"I'd take her shopping, but the stores she goes to," said Sandra. "I can't stand the smell of cheap material."

She checked herself in the sun visor's vanity mirror.

"What did Mom say?" she asked.

"She wasn't there," said Joe.

"Oh no," said Sandra.

"I know," said Joe. "Talking to your dad, no offense, but it's like I'm talking to Manette's stoolie. She's the one who owns Hassler. It's her decision. All hers. Damn it."

In the big house, Manette padded down the floral stair runner in a zip-up bathrobe that looked as if it were constructed from old towels. She took an English muffin from the shiny aluminum bread box and creaked the toaster oven dial to dark. She removed a squat yellow teacup from the cupboard. It had a gold rim faded and etched by years of dishwasher assault. No saucer. The toaster dinged. She spread strawberry jam onto the muffin's singed bumps, filled the stainless steel kettle with tap water. The stream sounded to

Cynthia Kolko

Sanford like pissing in a can. He leaned against the obtrusive monstrosity of an old cast iron stove. Manette and Sanford kept it partly for nostalgia, but also because it was too damn heavy to move. Neither had any memory of it working. The kettle emitted a shrill whistle, first as bursts, then a steady protest. Manette filled her teacup with the steamy water.

"Joe Silla have a price?" said Manette, dropping a bag of black tea into the cup.

"Not yet."

"What about Laura?"

"Still working it out."

Manette flattened the teabag against the side of the cup with a spoon. A cloud of muddy tea seeped into the liquid, dyeing it brown.

❦

Jem had barely slept the past few nights. The weekend was a few days away. He pushed Laura's doorbell.

"You got a minute?" he said when she opened the door. "Want to run something by you."

He sat on the couch. Kept his cap on.

"Your brother-in-law. He wants to buy Loud Farm," said Jem.

"That's a terrible location for a bar."

"Guess he wants to develop it. Hasn't approached me yet. My dad and him had a sweetheart deal I gather. But he's just going to have to deal with me directly. Seems like he's in a hurry. I figure he'll come to me any day now."

"Houses? Well, that makes some sense. I always thought

Fruit of the Vine

he'd try to go into his father's line of work. But why there? That's a nice property and all, but it's desolate up there. And it isn't like there's no other land to build on. And there's that big battle, the old village."

"He might offer a bunch of money."

"Money? Can't you sell your Dad's house and his shop and everything and make money that way? And live on the farm yourself?"

"Couldn't make enough that way. Property taxes on the farm will eat it up. I may not have a choice."

Laura understood. Upstate New York had the highest property taxes in the nation. Even more than downstate. It never seemed to get any better. Each legislative term, promises of tax relief went unfulfilled, while more and more people and businesses fled the region for friendlier climes. It was the sort of subject you could bring up to just about anyone, in line at the Quik Mart, at the shooting range, out in the fields, and face the universal eye roll in return.

"There's got to be a way," said Laura. She examined her fingernails, starting biting one of them. "How come no one ever moved back to that farm? You'd think one of your family would have kept living there like they did for so long."

"My dad. His generation. Not the farming type," said Jem.

Ed's brother, Jem's uncle, died in Vietnam. Ed returned, his personality altered, strapped with palpable self-woe. There was a cousin, Louise "Loony Lou" Loud, who'd spent a short adolescence in the old farmhouse experimenting with mind-altering drugs and favoring twangy sitar music before mov-

Cynthia Kolko

ing to California to chase down the like-minded free spirit who'd knocked her up.

No one could argue that farming wasn't a tough way to earn a buck. Rising fuel prices, a tangle of state regulations and a sour economy killed profits. Some farmers tried to fill the gap with agro-tourism. A tractor ride out to the pick-your-own apple fields, a petting zoo of goats, chickens dyed green and purple, mazes of corn stalks. Larger-than-life scarecrows. Pumpkin catapults. Anything to reel in money. Vineyards didn't need gimmicks. Tourists in limos from all corners of the globe roller-coasted from vineyard to vineyard, the well-known ones mostly, but occasionally smaller outfits like Hassler. Some folks were fresh from city living, savoring the scenery and even each shanty barn and wasp-infested cobblestone schoolhouse on the way, gawking at the wildflowers, tasting, sampling, toasting each other for another successful year, a new baby, or an enduring friendship. They bought cases upon cases of wine. Great wine. And came back for more.

For some farms, agro-tourism worked well. One mother–daughter pair, saddled with three hundred acres of sagging fruit trees and another hundred of soggy hayfields and purple loosestrife, put out a catalog peppered with Shakespearean verse, offering lavender wreath-making classes on the farm. They were pictured in long skirts under barn beams heavy with hanging yarrow and hydrangea clusters, hawking promises of sun-spattered afternoons of jams and farm-fresh quiche with chutney. Ladies came from far and

203

Fruit of the Vine

wide to wear straw hats and sip tea in a barn, listen to a harpist imbue the musty air with serenity and beauty.

"You ever think of putting out some picnic tables?" said Jem.

"What?"

"Under some grape arbors. Make Hassler a little more like that ladies' apple farm. More genteel."

"Is this a joke?" said Laura.

"Forget it," said Jem. On second thought, Manette wasn't one to greet guests with poetry about clouds and the seasons.

Laura pushed at her cuticles, picked at a hangnail. She had never had a manicure. Wouldn't know where to go and wouldn't ask Sandra.

"How's it going with the search for your mom?" asked Laura.

"Not much has happened yet," said Jem.

"I can kind of understand that, with your dad gone, you want a connection to a blood relative. He was really the only one you had besides your great-grandma, right?"

The silence hung between Jem and Laura like a fog. Jem opened his mouth as if he were going to say something, but closed it. Laura noticed.

"What," she said.

"Nothing," said Jem.

"It's not nothing. I can tell," she said.

Jem considered making up a story. Tell Laura he was going to ask what new truck she was considering. Make believe he was concerned about Manette's health. Contribute another idea on how Hassler could make itself competitive with the thriving wine operations in the area. He tried to conjure up something, anything else but the subject he truly needed to share. It was a futile effort.

"Ed's not my father."

Jem was relieved not to feel as embarrassed as he'd anticipated. It sounded offhand to Laura for Jem to mention it like this. But it wasn't for Jem. The subject had hovered at the forefront of his thoughts for weeks.

"I found out back when he was in the hospital," said Jem.

"Oh man. Oh man," said Laura.

She wanted to take Jem's hand, but did not.

"Do you know who your real father is? Real's not the right word. Not what I mean."

"Biological," Jem said. "I've got no idea. That's mainly why I'm looking for my mom."

Jem didn't mention that he wanted to find his mother not only as a means to find his biological father, but for scientific purposes, that it was a quest for DNA on both sides. He was interested in what she was like and what her interests were and so forth, but only as it related to him. He was curious what parts of his personality he might have inherited from her, seeing as she wasn't around long enough to impart much of anything on him environmentally. Except perhaps through happenstance.

Laura was suddenly thankful for her own situation. Thankful she had two parents who had stayed together, who worked together and had a strong relationship. She was even thankful for her sister, who lived her life on her own volition, who got married when she wanted to, and to whom she chose.

Fruit of the Vine

And now, she felt the luxury of family could not go to waste. It was a gift bestowed on her, and it was her duty to do something other than merely consume it, to be child-like in her dependence. She needed to use the life she'd been handed as a foundation on which to build something more, and to build herself in the process.

"I've got something to announce too," said Laura. "I'm going to take Jewish classes."

"Jewish classes?"

"I want to learn about it. From someone other than Mom."

"That's nice. That's a good idea."

Jem ran his hand under his square-ish chin, lightly washed with stubble. Out of his green eyes gazed his ancestors, whoever they were, settling the land, building lives with pluck and a pickaxe, creating their own destinies—good and bad—by their own accord. Ain't going to end with me.

Jem's phone rang. It was Joe.

"Got something I want to see you about. When you can come to my office? We'll sit down, have a cigar. I got some bourbon that you'll seriously think is the nectar of the gods."

"I'm not interested," said Jem.

"Not interested in bourbon? That's okay. Perfectly fine. I have a full cabinet of top-shelf booze."

"I'm not selling Loud Farm."

"Hold on, now. Who said anything about Loud Farm?"

"I know what it is you want, Joe. And I'm not going for it."

Cynthia Kolko

"Now, listen. This might not be what you're imagining. No sir. We can hammer this out together. We can negotiate. Make whatever deal you want. I'll make you a rich man, Jem Loud. Back up the Brinks truck. Beep, beep, beep."

"I'm not negotiating," said Jem. "Land's too important. I want to see it and more stuff like it preserved."

"I'm not dropping a bomb on it, Jem. I'm making it better. And your life will improve like nuts. I assure you."

"Making it better means growing on it, letting nature take its course on it. Animals. Our history's more than just stuff we used or wanted, what we did to get it, the furniture we built, the houses we lived in. We have a natural history too. And I want to make that property part of the future. The least I can do after all it's done for us."

As Roy cooked in Tap's kitchen, Joe paced behind the bar, forehead corrugated. The more Joe thought, the angrier he got. The blinking became furious. He pushed open the door to the kitchen, his steps thundering and deliberate.

"You talked to Jem, didn't you," said Joe.

"What makes you say that?" Roy looked up from a half-mixed bowl of house dressing.

"I can tell. I called him to talk about the land. Gave me a load of crap about it. History. Responsibility. All that shit. Like he was channeling you."

Roy stifled a smile.

"You watch yourself, Roy. I know too much about you."

Fruit of the Vine

"That a threat? Because I know a lot about you too."

"I'm clean, buddy. I'm the good Samaritan who saved this building. Brought another business into this town. There's nothing to tie me to that fire."

"Nothing except motive," said Roy. "You got to buy it for practically nothing. And there's your crooked insurance agent friend, the one who tipped you off about the building owner letting the insurance lapse."

Roy stirred the contents of the bowl.

"You're one to talk," said Joe. "You practically jumped for joy when you saw that stack of hundreds I gave you. Didn't exactly say 'no' to doing it."

"When times are tough, people do what they need to. No one got hurt."

"That's right," said Joe. "No one got hurt. Same with this Loud land deal. Won't hurt anybody. Isn't that right?"

Roy dropped his whisk, his face less-than-conciliatory.

"You need me, buddy. I know too much," said Joe.

The phone rang in Jem's apartment. Jem expected Joe's voice spewing some sales tactic or other. A last-ditch effort.

"Jem? Al Vargas. You got cable?"

"Yeah."

"Turn it to CNN."

It was a story was about American soldiers in the Middle East. On screen, a rumbling military truck fanned dust. A motley wave of civilians, soldiers, children, and a dog ran after it.

"There! There!" said Al.

The picture had cut to a studio newswoman, a freshman to the network. Light brown hair formed ruffles around her ears and hung suspended over her shoulders. Her face was perhaps too thin, like she was undernourished. A name popped at the bottom of the screen: Mary Sawhorn, correspondent.

"That woman," said Al, his voice low and solemn, having regained its composure, "that's your mother."

twelve

Jem kept it quiet for some time. He didn't tell Zack, didn't tell Laura. He tried not to think about it. Sporadically, the coiffed, serious image on the screen would emerge as a character in his dreams. Sometimes her role was central: Mary Sawhorn working at the Hassler wine shop, chatting with Jem, offering him free Coke. More often she had a bit part: Mary Sawhorn, the angry driver of a car whizzing by him on Franklin Road, flipping him the bird as she passed.

Jem's days became heavy. He felt little enjoyment. His eyes glazed over with a murky glass through which everything appeared duller. He began avoiding the television altogether. Not just CNN, but the whole contraption. Even at the tavern, where the sets were tuned to a sporting event or turned off, he sat with his back to the screen.

Jem took his gun to the woods behind Hassler Vineyard. He didn't call Zack or Russ, just loaded several empty beer cans into a knapsack and took off. He set the cans on a downed tree trunk, blew away can after can, then set them back up. He repeated the exercise until each can was a sorry, shredded mess which had long surrendered. Jem ate an apple, hurled the core into the woods, exulted as it hit a tree and split in two. He went after the pieces and stomped each one until the pulp flattened onto the cold soil. Then he stomped some more.

Jem was seething at himself. For searching out his mother. For hiring Al. For not knowing instinctively what to do now that he'd found her. Jem was angry at the injustice that Mary had found such success after the dastardly deed of abandoning him. She'd dared to move on, dared to have experienced any happiness after casting Jem aside like a piece of spent fruit. He shot into a few amoebas of smashed apple.

Alone in his apartment, Jem removed from his pocket a worn piece of paper he had folded and unfolded several times since getting an eyeful of his mother's visage. Al had presented Jem with a manila envelope containing both the bill for his services and this paper, both of which incited foul language from Jem. The paper had Mary's phone number on it.

Jem hoped, as he heard the electronic rings, that it would be a wrong number. That Mary wouldn't answer.

"Hello," said the female voice.

"Is this Mary Sawhorn?" said Jem.

The voice answered more robustly than at first, "No solicitations at this number."

"I'm not selling anything. This is your son, Jem Loud."

The seconds of silence mounted like a child's wooden blocks, one on top of the other, until they fell under their own awkward weight.

Fruit of the Vine

"Jem?"

The voice sounded fragile.

"Yeah."

"Well, this is like being hit with a two-by-four."

The words Jem had rehearsed in his mind vanished, erased by anxiety. He'd probably have trouble tying his shoes at that moment, he was so thrown off course.

"Your husband. Ex-husband. He's dead. Ed. My dad. He died. Was about a month ago."

"I heard."

"What?"

"I have sources. Up there in hell. Is that why you called? To tell me about Ed?"

"Man, this is weird."

"You're telling me."

"Well, I wanted to ask you some stuff."

"Okay."

"Find out about my history. My genetics."

"Genetics?"

"Thought it would be good to get some medical history, in case I need to get checked for diseases. Or if I get sick."

"No genetic diseases in my family. No cancer. No diabetes. My people live to ripe old ages. Unless they eat bad pancake batter."

"What about my father? Anything you could tell me about him?"

"Didn't he talk to you about anything himself?"

"Uh..."

"I don't have much to tell you, Jem. You were a good-looking boy. Premature, but still well over six pounds. You skinnied out, but you were always strong. Ate like a lumberjack. What do you do for a living?"

"I'm a lumberjack," Jem said.

"You serious?"

"I'm the vineyard manager at Hassler," Jem said, the pride in his voice knifing through the angst the conversation provoked.

"You work for Manette? Oh, that just takes the cake."

"Huh?"

"That foul-mouthed shrew. She drove me out of town. And I was so young and spineless. Back before you were born, when Ed was in Vietnam, Sanford and I had a thing going. Nothing serious. When Ed came back it was over. A few years later, Sanford, whipped as he is, comes clean with Manette. It was dead on the vine, but he confessed the whole thing. Well, didn't she just go ballistic. She comes over one day when you were napping and Ed was working. She points a shotgun at me. Tells me if she sees my face again, she'll blow it off. And let me tell you, I believed her. You should have seen her. Eyes all bugged, teeth clenched. Holding that rifle with both hands. She looked like a freak. Insane. Kind of person who needs a straitjacket and a padded cell."

"Later that night, I went out. Told Ed I needed to clear my head. Not easy being home all day, I said. Driving Loud Road, I saw the ghost of a deer. Never told anyone about that until now. I stopped the truck. It stood there like it was made of marble. Spoke to me. Told me to get the hell out. It told me, Jem."

Jem was about to interject, tell Mary that there have been

Fruit of the Vine

rumors of white deer swirling for years, but another thought crowded the story out.

"I left that night, while you and Ed were sleeping. I walked to Route Twenty and hitched a ride to the train station. Took the train to Florida, then Georgia. Changed my name."

Jem hardly heard. His mind was busy calculating. If he were as big as a full-term baby and Mary had been having an affair with Sanford...

Mary spoke again. "Nice talking to you, Jem. Take it easy, now. I wish you good luck. But I have a nice life here. Do me a favor. Don't talk to me about Sanford. Okay?"

"Do you a favor?" Jem asked, but the resounding click told him that Mary Sawhorn had had enough.

She didn't answer the phone after that, not once in the dozen or so times Jem tried.

The bloated sun eased itself below the horizon, leaving watercolor waves of pink, peach, and indigo. Jem stood in his window. A smoky stream of flotsam from Laura's chimney puffed through the scene. If Sanford was his father, that made Laura his half-sister. Jem enumerated the problem in his mind again and again, hoping for a different outcome each time. The conclusion remained constant, yet somehow it kept getting worse.

In the big house, Joe handed a stack of papers to Sanford. Manette scowled, whipped the papers from Sanford's hands. "How much?" asked Manette, flipping the pages.

214

"Now, why don't you just read the proposal first? Then we'll talk numbers," said Joe.

Manette stopped flipping, glared at Joe.

"How about you tell us a number first so I'll know if reading this thing's a waste of time?"

"Wasn't expecting such a direct shot. Guess I should have. Been part of this family long enough to know the players. Heh heh! Yeah, I can do that. I was thinking something like eight hundred."

"What?" said Manette.

"Joe, with all due respect, that's peanuts for a property like this," said Sanford. "It's less than peanuts. It's peanut crumbs."

"That's what I'm offering," said Joe, thrusting his chest forward even more than usual, like armor against the Fillmores.

"Less than two thousand an acre? This isn't exactly a swamp," said Manette.

"Recall the laws of supply and demand," said Joe, finger raised. "There's a hell of a lot of land around here and nobody's buying it."

"This farm's like part of my family," said Manette. "My parents escaped the pogroms, just ahead of the Holocaust, with little more than their lives. Settled here. Where we're standing. Toiled, endured, died. Now I'm supposed to let it go just like that for a handful of bills?" Manette snapped her fingers.

"We're talking current market value. Numbers don't get nostalgic," said Joe.

"Well, I do," said Manette, pushing the swinging door into the kitchen and folding herself inside.

Fruit of the Vine

"I knew this was a bad idea," said Sanford.

"She going to be okay?" said Joe.

"Yeah."

"She'll change her mind?"

"Doubt it," said Sanford.

"Give it time," said Joe. "It's a win-win for everyone. Read the proposal. Talk to her some. Doesn't have to be next week."

When Joe left, Manette reappeared, thick wrinkles etched around her mouth.

"He thinks we're stupid, doesn't he?" she said.

"Not stupid. Desperate," said Sanford.

"How insulting. Thinks he can blow in here, take advantage, and we'd just go along with it since we're toothless hicks. Doesn't he understand what it takes to run this business? All the know-how, the talent, you need to turn a profit this way?"

"Apparently not," said Sanford.

"You're not going to believe this," said Jem, scanning the tavern for eavesdroppers.

Zack stood, beer in hand, eyes like oversized laundry tokens.

"Sanford might be my father."

"Holy shit!" Zack blurted. He took a sip of beer, swallowed and then repeated in a whisper, "Holy shit."

Cynthia Kolko

"She said I was over a month premature, but I was too honking huge to be a preemie. Way I see it, I was conceived earlier than we thought, before Dad came home from Nam."

"Your mom was taking it from Sanford?" asked Zack.

Jem gave Zack a weary look. "Seems that way."

Zack was as close to a brother as Jem ever knew. Still, the conversation was hard for Jem. There was the lurking possibility that Jem might reveal vulnerability, express too much of his feelings. Something girls did.

Zack fit his bottle into the shin pocket on his painter's pants, sawed his sleeve over his brow. He rested his hands on Jem's shoulders, shook his head gently, stared at Jem with empathy.

"Holy shit," Zack said. "This mean you're Jewish?"

"Huh?"

"Ain't Sanford Jewish?"

"No. That's Manette."

"What? I always thought he was the one. That's why he got that beard."

"You don't have to have a beard if you're Jewish. That's just for the really religious ones, I think. With the black hats. No, Sanford has the beard because he's weird. It's a weird beard."

Zack laughed at the bad joke. "Good thing you ain't Jewish."

"Why do you say that?"

"Christmas."

"Tell you the truth, I wouldn't mind giving it up. I only do Christmas for Gram's sake. She likes it so much, what with the music, the decorations and all."

Fruit of the Vine

All December, Gram's house basked in the ancillary glow from Mrs. Carpin's circus of lights that adorned every tree in her front yard and framed the garage.

"You'd have to wear a skull cap."

"That's like saying you have to wear a crucifix. You don't have to do anything. Man, you're ignorant. You've got to get out more. Meet people who are a little different from you. Explore. Find out what they believe. What makes them happy. Find out they're just like you."

"Speak for yourself, Magellan."

Jem floated about the farm in a daze. He pruned vines, removing unneeded straggly shoots until a queue of clean umbrella skeletons remained. Each minute of the morning plodded toward lunchtime. When a distant firehouse wail indicated noon, Jem entered the wine shop looking for Sanford. A customer pointed out a display of figural bottle openers to his young boy. Some were shaped like people, others like animals. A woman, presumably the mother, added a bottle of wine to a small assembly of others on the counter. The man grabbed the boy's hips and swung him upright side to side like a bandleader's baton. The mother looked as if she were watching the kid dive from a cliff.

"Whee! Whee! Whee!" said the father.

The boy emitted a gleeful sound, "Scraw!"

Jem remembered his dream from the previous night. Laura had his baby. He'd dreamed of the kid sitting in a stroller with a lap blanket, his feet poking out from under it, each one with twelve webbed toes.

When the family left, Sanford and Jem were alone.

"Mind if I ask you something?" said Jem.

"Yeah. I mean, no I don't."

"I talked to my mom yesterday."

"Oh," he said. "That's quite something." He glanced toward the door to Manette's office, though he knew she was out in the field.

"She said you had an affair," said Jem.

"What? Absolutely not," said Sanford.

Sanford's face withered like a balloon with a slow leak. It seemed to lose elasticity with every passing second. Jowls became pronounced, the lines between the nostrils and outer corners of the lips deepened. Sanford seemed to have aged five years in a second.

"I'm not here to blame you for anything," said Jem.

"Nothing to blame me for. She's full of it," said Sanford.

"I'm not out to get anyone," said Jem. "I just want to know if you might be my father."

A sunburned hue crossed Sanford's face. He shook his head furiously, the skin beneath his chin waddling almost imperceptibly behind the beard.

"No, no, no. Impossible. I'm an honorable man. Always was. I knew your mother, but we never, you know. When were you born?"

"Sixty-nine. July fourth."

"Fourth of July, eh? It's a blur that far back. Laura was born that fall. Didn't Ed come back from the war not long before?

Fruit of the Vine

Maybe a year earlier. Round Thanksgiving time? Is he listed on your birth certificate? Guess that doesn't mean anything. Why do you think it isn't Ed?"

"Something at the hospital. It ain't him."

"I see," Sanford said.

"They have tests for these things," Jem said.

Sanford shrugged. "Waste of time. Waste of money, too. But if it makes you feel better, I'll take the stupid test. Can't be easy, not knowing who your dad is. Lord knows you've had quite a pile of dung tossed on you already. Do what I can to help. But I'm telling you, Jem. She made the whole thing up. All wrong."

Sanford came out from behind the counter and put a hand on Jem's shoulder.

"You know me, know I wouldn't yank your chain. I'm going to tell you something, and I mean it with all the respect I can say it. Your mother. She was a certifiable loon."

Jem's heart felt like it was beating in his Adam's apple.

"And there's no way I'm your father."

Jem felt an intense heat in his throat and fell into a coughing fit. Hacking, unable to speak, Jem pointed his finger in the air to signal "wait a minute" but feeling woozy, he loped away toward the bathroom sink in the barn.

Jem scooped water with his hands, drank it like a dog lapping from a bowl. His head pounded in time to a low beat deep in his ears, ungh ungh ungh. He folded to the floor in front of the sink. The pounding faded and was replaced by a cloudier pain that diffused into every cell like a noxious gas.

It was still merely a theory, no matter how plausible. But

hearing the words out loud, seeing them spelled out before him, "I'm your father"—even though they were preceded by the negative, "No way"—seemed to make it closer to a solid, jarring fact. A strong possibility.

"Jem."

Sanford's voice roused Jem as if from sleep.

"We're keeping this test thing between us. Okay, Jem? You and me. No good can come of telling anyone else. No good at all. Don't tell Manette. Don't tell Laura. Jem? You hear me? Don't talk about it to Laura."

Jem stood, tugged his belt, scratched a hand through the fine buzz of his hair. He took a deep breath and exhaled like a truck releasing its air brakes. "I never was a big talker."

"That's what I like about you, Jem."

thirteen

Christmas passed. The pewter winter cast a melancholy pall over Sawhorn. Faces fell. The drugstore filled more prescriptions of antidepressants between December and February than all the other months combined. Like a mass seasonal-affective disorder.

It was ten degrees outside, just cold enough for the late season grapes, the ones used for ice wine, to be harvested by hand. Pickers' hands swirled like windmills over the cold vines, picking off several bunches at a time, tossing them into picking boxes. These workers were paid by the box, so the faster they picked and the more boxes they filled in a short time, the more they earned per hour. Jem found them a convivial group. Picking was as rote as breathing, leaving their minds and voices open to engage in whatever struck them. Laughter and lively talk were usually heard over salsa music playing from a weathered boom box atop the dashboard of the pickup truck, parked nearby between two rows of icy vines. Jem didn't understand Spanish. For all he knew,

Cynthia Kolko

they were dissing him, ridiculing him, declaring him a pansy. Planning to stuff him in a barrel and roll him into town. Family men, most of these guys, plus a small percentage of women. Jem couldn't imagine the industry surviving without them. It'd be like losing a limb. Like the old Loud homestead porch, rotting and falling off.

The harvesting effort ran into the night. A gibbous moon shone its lopsided countenance unobstructed in the cloudless night sky. Like a gang of cold-weather Zorros, five pickers, headlamps strapped atop their ski hats, wielded shears with the precision and speed of a ten-armed machine, dropping frozen grapes like marbles into boxes waiting to be loaded onto the narrow vineyard trailers to carry them back to the winery to be pressed.

Jem stood pouring the already-picked grapes into the press outside the barn. Orbs rolled noisily like jawbreakers into the metal funnel-like opening. He watched the press extract each precious drop of juice from the barely-yielding grapes.

"Jem!" Laura called. "You were going to come over. See a video. Talk some more about the land."

"Sorry," Jem said, his manner curt. "Be here all night. Grapes need to be pressed right away. Temperature's supposed to rise tomorrow. Manette doesn't want this harvest to be late. Got her eye on a gold medal."

"So how about tomorrow?"

Jem didn't answer.

"I said, how about tomorrow?"

"I'm busy."

Fruit of the Vine

"Didn't seem to bother you before."

Laura hung by the presser for a minute. Annoyed and be-fuddled, she slipped back to her house.

"Next time, we're going back to the tavern," said Jem. "I've had it with this joint. With Joe Silla. The whole scene. Not my fault you got too big a tab with Bender."

"It ain't the tab. I told you, better class of ladies in here," said Zack.

"Don't you have anything better to do than chase skirts?"

Zack put his bottle down, faced Jem squarely.

"Now why you ask me that? You know I ain't got nothing better to do than chase skirts."

"Dude, I didn't mean anything by it," said Jem.

"Maybe I like to come in here and forget that my life sucks. You got to remind me how bad it is?"

"Calm down. You're life doesn't suck and you know it."

"Yeah? That's something coming from you, with your good job. Your chicks. Probably end up marrying Laura. Got some money coming to you from that land. Me? I got nothing. Job's hanging on a thread. Stuck in this town 'cause there's nothing I can do anywhere else. My landlord wants to turn my apartment into a seasonal rental. What's up with that shit? I've lived there four years and now the rent in the sum-mer's going to quadruple. So don't tell me my life don't suck. All's I got is alcohol and drunk girls. And the older I get, the less girls I'm going to have. Then what? What's going to happen to me when all the farms go bankrupt in this crappy economy? Or get sold to developers? And I'm too old a dog to learn a new trick?"

"A, I'm not marrying my half-sister," said Jem. "And B, the wine business here is on the verge of booming. It already is. Wine's got to be one of the only industries upstate that isn't shrinking. It's getting huge. Everywhere. Not just here."

Zack flipped his bottle to his lips but nothing came out.

Jem continued, "You know what your problem is, man? You always believe the worst of what you hear. Even if you want to be like that, all doom and gloom, like the whole region's going to hell in a baggie, it still doesn't mean your life's over. Know what happens when an industry dries up? When a town dries up? You find a new industry or find a new town. And you. You can work at the laundromat."

"Yeah, great. A laundromat in a town where no one gives a fuck what their clothes smell like. Working with all them chemicals would cut a decade off my life anyhow."

"You're twenty-two. Your life's hardly over. And who's stuck here? You got legs."

Zack looked unconvinced, as if he were a teacher listening to a student explain that the dog ate his homework.

"You want to know whose life is in the shithole?" said Jem. "Just look right here at me. Dad's dead. I don't have any ma, least not one who wants me. And Sanford might be my dad. My ma was a two-bit slut screwing that pointy-bearded Sanford. Worse, she did it for free."

Zack nodded. "That is pretty bad shit."

"What the hell happened to my life?" said Jem, on a roll.

Fruit of the Vine

"I used to be a regular guy. That's all I ever wanted to be. Now I don't know who the fuck I am. Got no real family. Everyone's looking to me as some sort of guardian of the town's history. Like it all depends on what I do or don't do. I never bothered anybody. Never asked for anything. All I want is to go to work and go home. Never asked for all this shit. And now that I got it, hell if I know what to do with it."

"No one's life turns out the way you figure it will," said Zack.

"Mine did," said Joe.

How long he had been standing there behind the bar, neither Jem nor Zack knew.

"I'm the happiest man on earth," said Joe.

Joe walked away, passed Sandra leaning over the bar and grabbed her behind, causing her to yelp.

"Least someone's got it made," said Zack, defeated.

"Here's a question," said Jem. "How come you never tried to make more of yourself, huh? What's keeping you from learning something new, getting a better job? What's really keeping you stuck?" said Jem.

Zack held up his hand like a traffic cop signaling stop.

"Forget it," he said. "You wouldn't understand."

"I wouldn't understand 'cause there's nothing to understand," said Jem. "Can't change where you came from, but you can change where you're going."

"You know what?" said Zack. "Go fuck yourself, okay? Walking around like some kinda sad clown with all the answers for everyone else. I don't see you raising yourself up to any high level. Not without help."

Cynthia Kolko

"I ain't getting help," said Jem.

"You kidding? Anything you got, and anything you're going to get, is what's been dropped in your lap. Someone asking questions about why I don't get educated or leave town, you sure ain't doing a lot of running around yourself. Only reason you're where you're at is 'cause someone else put you there," said Zack.

When the door to Tap opened, no one expected Laura to come through it. There were two reasons she received so many stares. One, the pure novelty of seeing her in Tap. Two, the careless outfit she wore—shirttail dangling out from under the jacket, sweatpants—more suited to walking a dog than bar-hopping.

"Well, what do you know? There's your lady friend," said Zack.

But Laura didn't stop to talk to Zack and Jem. She wasn't looking for them. In the dim light, she couldn't distinguish their faces from those of a dozen other patrons. She strode to where Sandra and Joe seemed to be arguing.

"Do you know about this land deal with Mom and Dad?" she asked Sandra.

"Laura, not now," said Sandra.

"We were going to tell you when we thought the time was right," said Joe. "Now isn't the time."

"Yes it is. Because I know. I saw the papers at their place. How could you not tell me? Do you think I'm a little kid? Like, I shouldn't have any say? My opinion doesn't count?"

"It isn't like that, Laura. We didn't want to worry you, get you all worked up," said Sandra.

227

Fruit of the Vine

"I'm worked up now!"

A handful of patrons near the bar turned to look at the small young woman with the booming voice. One well-dressed lady scurried off, drink in hand.

Laura said in a half-cry, "You two. Why do you have to throw a monkey wrench into everything? This town, our family. My life! Can't you just leave well enough alone?"

Sandra tried to calm Laura. "It isn't like it's a done deal. Mom and Dad rejected it. They might never go for it. You're making a big stink over nothing."

"It's the principle," said Laura.

She nearly sprinted out the door.

Jem dug a bill out of his pocket, gave it to Zack, and ran after Laura. He caught up with her outside the bar.

"What's the matter?"

Laura sobbed. "They want to buy the vineyard."

"What?" said Jem. Plumes of his breath hung in the cold air. Laura's eyes were rimmed in red. "Let me take you home. Doesn't look like you're in the best condition to drive," he said.

"Forget it," said Laura. "I'm fine."

She moved fast, like a speed walker, down the street toward the tavern.

Almost at daybreak, Laura was inside her parents' front hall. Who cared if they weren't up yet? She'd been awake all night, restless, thinking about Joe and Sandra owning the

228

farm, building on it, making it a miniature city of McMansions.

"Were you going to let me in on your little secret?" she yelled up the stairs.

"Laura?" Sanford called.

"Or were you just going to tell me after the papers had been signed? Throw me a bone? Stick me in a doghouse out back?"

"What are you talking about?" said Manette. "Are you okay?"

"No, I'm not okay!" Laura's knees seemed to give out. She sat on the floor, leaned her arms and face on the steps, and collapsed into sobs.

"Wait. I'm coming down," said Manette.

She arrived in the towel bathrobe. Her white lips were almost indistinguishable from her skin.

"Who told you? Sandra?"

"It doesn't matter!" Laura blurted.

"Laura, your dad and I, we're getting old. And we need money to retire on."

Sanford trudged down the steps.

"What about what I want? Did you ever think maybe I'd want to run this place?" said Laura.

Sanford and Manette looked at each other.

"Doesn't matter who's running the place. We can't afford it," said Sanford. "Least this way, we get what we need from it."

"Can't you sell off part of it?"

"Wouldn't make enough," said Manette.

"Then sell it to someone other than Joe."

Fruit of the Vine

"Someone else won't take care of you like he will," said Sanford.

"Take care of me?" said Laura, screaming in disbelief. "I'm a grown woman! I don't want anyone to take care of me! Least of all Joe!"

fourteen

Jem hadn't been inside the hospital since Ed's death. When he entered, the weight of a thousand could-haves and should-haves fell over him. A middle-aged woman with a head of loose curls—which Jem thought looked rather unkempt for a clinical setting—gave Jem a swab and told him to work it into one of his cheeks for a count of ten, then took it and sealed it.

"Redundant to do this. The police already got my DNA when I was in the jail."

"Yep. It's a waste," said the technician, "but there's government for you. S'what they do best. Waste money."

Jem didn't want to get into an argument, but it was his money that'd been wasted. He was the one paying for the test.

"A few days is all it'll take. You'll get the results certified mail," she told Jem. "Go get a drink, honey. Looks like you need one."

On the way home, Jem retraced the route he took the day Ed died. He almost passed right by the octagon house, stand-

Fruit of the Vine

ing unremarkable and messy behind wearied trees that looked like they might succumb to death right where they stood. But after a short stop that sent a near-empty snack bag sprinkling salt and pretzel shards onto the passenger foot well, he pulled into the driveway, its gravel stirred with snow.

The main entrance had two doorbells. Jem rang the bottom one. A young woman holding an infant opened the door without asking who was there. Jem thought this oddly trusting, wanton even. In a flicker of fantasy, he wished he were without a conscience. He would direct the woman to put the baby in a crib or pen or whatever. Then he'd screw the hell out of the woman. He'd leave, telling himself she'd asked for it, opening the door to a stranger like that.

"I'm Jem Loud. This might sound strange, but I wondered if I could take a look inside this house."

"You buying it?" the woman said. "Guy who owns it is evicting me. Says he wants to sell the place. I think it's 'cause he hates kids. Ain't like he's a real prince to live under. All them cigars he smokes stink up this shack something fierce." She waved her hand in front of her nose, wafting away the memory of the stench.

The woman let Jem inside. She kicked aside a dropped pacifier, which crashed into a stuffed ape splayed against the wall as if it had been shot. The house smelled of diapers and mildew. Jem scrutinized the structure. Everything, the floors, window casings, moldings, seemed to be original, aside from the wall that was erected around the staircase to separate this apartment from the one above. That wall bowed when Jem pushed against it. He figured he could knock it down in minutes, even without a sledge hammer. The front parlor was decorated with what appeared to be the original wallpaper. It was faded, stripped in spots and stained some, but in remarkable shape considering its age.

"Think the owner would let me see the upstairs?"

"Go ahead and try," the woman said. "Old bastard never goes nowheres."

Jem tried the upper bell. A scowling, grizzly man answered.

"The hell you want?" he asked.

"Just seeing if I could take a look upstairs. I know it's an unusual request, but this house, it's—"

"It's in the shape of an octagon," the man answered, suddenly cheery, his sour expression wiped away by Jem's half-declaration. "My kin built it in the late 1800s," said the man. "A doctor and his wife. They believed it was good for your health. Well, I'm living proof. Ninety-eight years young."

The man straightened his back, protruded atrophied pecs. Took a deep breath and exhaled. Rapped his chest with a fist.

"Come on in, I'll show you the rest. You are in for a treat, m'boy. By the way, I'm Benson Frechette. You are..."

"Jem Loud."

"Loud! Henry's grandson?"

"Great-grandson," said Jem.

"Who-ee. I'll be dipped. That name goes way back. Knew him from the Rod & Gun Club. Damn. Isn't that something. Elba still alive, is she?"

"Yep."

"Course she is. Built out of steel, that one."

Fruit of the Vine

As Benson spoke, Jem surveyed the place. It was shabby, but well-preserved. Something about the shape, the design, struck Jem as magnificent. He'd take a house like this over that Chateau Cobblestone fool's castle any day.

"This house, it's one-of-a-kind," said Benson. "It's an architectural gem. Not only the shape. The philosophy behind it. The manner in which it was built. The methods they used were unprecedented in those times. You'd be hard-pressed to find a house with a foundation like this one or walls this thick anywhere in the region, let alone in those cheapie new houses they got springing up like clover. And guess what? This house is cool in the summer and warm in the winter. That's without any fancy air system. It's because of the octagon shape. The circulation. All you need is one fireplace going or one window open, and you're all set. Comfortable as a bird in a nest. Course, the air would circulate better if we didn't have the stairwell cordoned off, but you get the picture, right m'boy?"

Benson led Jem up shallow, steep steps to the cupola.

"Now, this room gets hot," said Benson. "You've got to open all the windows up here. But look how far you can see. On a clear day, I bet you can even see the Loud Road pinnacle, where your family's house sets."

Jem couldn't see much but snow, but he understood the potential.

"Great place to smoke a cigar. You want one?" said Benson.

Jem declined, thanked Benson for his hospitality, and left with Benson's phone number on a folded paper much like the one with Mary's number, the one he'd thrown away with little ceremony beyond a walk to the dumpster outside

Cynthia Kolko

Manette's office, hurling the garbage bag containing the phone number with more zeal than usual and a barely-noticeable cross between a grin and a snarl.

※

Sandra often found the task of shopping between seasons odious. Depressingly horrid merchandise, Christmas leftovers, droopy dolman-sleeved sweaters (all sized extra-large) hung forlorn on rack after rack, wasting floor space, the time to hang them, and even the resources it took to craft them in the first place. It brought on a lonely despair that would have completely repelled Sandra from shops, if not for the thrill of finding something fabulous tucked between rags, or even the more mundane quest for any new material object that was worth more to Sandra than the money it cost, or the time it took to seek it. But things were looking up. Any day now, the first spring catalogs would arrive in the mail, proffering strappy tops and strappier shoes. Sandra reminded herself to schedule a pedicure and leg wax.

And Sandra had been thinking, after watching some television advertisements, how fabulous it would be to have her own summer car like Joe had. Why should he have all the fun? Joe didn't let Sandra drive his yellow convertible. He barely let her lean against it. Yes, she needed her own convertible. Something in a dark color to contrast with her light hair. She'd wear a red headscarf and oversized sunglasses. But maybe a white car would be more striking? Yes, a white con-

Fruit of the Vine

vertible. She'd wear a white headscarf. She'd look like a goddess driving that car.

The snow wasn't as high as it had been a few weeks ago, didn't extend as far up the trunks of the trees in the backyard. What time of year was best to build a pool? She scrutinized a clearing that would make the perfect spot for it. Something organically shaped. A clover, perhaps. With a flagstone surround and iron lounge chairs. And a fountain like the ones flanking Meredith's entry.

Poop. Why weren't the spring lines out already? It was almost April. Sandra needed a new bikini or two. A triangle top? A balconet? Both.

fifteen

Early spring burst open like a pinata. One day it was
frigid, the next it was so warm that people were out
walking, saying "Hello! Beautiful day isn't it?" and
pumping air into bicycle tires. Crocuses smiled from lawns.
Noisy clouds of blackbirds swept through, landing on roofs
and yards, pecking at the ground and moving on like spills
of floating, cawing ink.

Jem draped his elbow over the lip of his truck's open window. On Franklin Road, the snow had almost completely receded. Winter was evident only in the serrated edges of co-
conut fluff on the road's shoulder, where, poised to cross the
road, stood a rabid raccoon.

Jem thought back to a weekend afternoon sitting at the
kitchen table with Ed and a cousin who'd long since skipped
town, learning the craft of creating a coonskin hat from
hides Ed had hung from fraying twine knotted to a nail in the
garage in wait for a purpose such as this. Ed cut two patterns
from a brown paper grocery bag, fashioned them into a

Fruit of the Vine

temporary fez on each boy's head. He helped the boys extract pins from a plump cloth tomato that looked like a voodoo doll for hexing produce. They skewered pattern and hide together, the occasional pin pinging to the floor. Jem sliced slowly around his pinned pattern with the hunting knife Ed had bestowed on him for his ninth birthday, rust corroding the green handle.

Getting the hang of it, Jem took swifter swipes at the hide. Then the boys crowded the cab of Ed's pickup, Jem gripping a towel to the bloody fissure left on his index finger by his errant hunting knife, and Ed drove to the hospital, sputtering about safety and the necessity of patient, careful work. A freckly doctor sutured Jem's finger with thread that to Jem resembled the fishing line Ed had just used to demonstrate a blanket stitch on a raccoon tail.

Jem rotated his hand, regarded the white scar. He flicked a grasshopper off the side mirror, sending it careening airborne.

Cleaning Ed's shop was a dirty job. That damned bean-counting lawyer wanted Jem to sift through Ed's financial and property files for statements and deeds. Lucky for Jem, Ed wasn't much of a bookkeeper, stowing important papers in one plastic file box that he'd stashed safely atop a high shelf in the shop's lone closet. Jem kicked aside the stepladder and pulled the file box down. A mist of sawdust breathed into his eyes. Jem blinked away the irritating grit.

Jem found bank statements from the previous quarter. He found another copy of Ed's will, and in a folder marked "disputes," a half-dozen parking tickets. He almost didn't find the green folder. It had become moist, causing a white sheet of paper to stick to its cover. Inside was the agreement with Joe for Loud Farm. Here it is, thought Jem. Joe's golden ticket. He read the numbers, almost couldn't contain his laughter. Clearly, Jem was not Ed's son. Jem would never go for this joke of an agreement. The sale amount was ridiculous.

The folder also held a map, marked with a few words labeling the property: hotel, preserve. Jem couldn't imagine why Joe thought this plan, the collection of buildings outlined on the map, the nature preserve, would make a viable investment. He also had a hard time believing that Joe was in any way concerned with preserving nature. In fact, Jem found the whole phrase "build a nature preserve" oxymoronic.

Another folder had the word "photos" crossed out, with the word "personal" replacing it in thick black permanent ink. Jem rifled through a handful of photos before sitting down with the file, examining each picture before adding it like a card to the growing fan on the table. A few subjects he didn't recognize, old people in old-fashioned clothes. One young man's photo looked like Ed, but Jem realized from the ancient vehicle grille nosing into the frame that it must be his grandfather Isaiah. Was that the blue shirt Gram talked about? Couldn't tell in black and white.

There was a dog-eared picture of the octagon house, unmistakably Benson Frechette's, the same house Jem toured. The cupola peered out over the roof like the handle of a pot lid. Jem couldn't understand why the picture was there. He turned it over, read the writing on the back. Girard Homestead.

Fruit of the Vine

Jem found other items in the folder. A dollar bill old enough to bear the marks of a silver certificate. The first dollar Ed had earned? Jem would never know. He opened a letter. The groovy flowers decorating its border seemed withered on the paper's stale edges. The penmanship was loopy and adolescent.

> Dear Ed,
> You know this is a long time coming. I can't stay here which should be no surprise to you. Treat Jem like he is your own son. You will do a better job than me. Don't try to find me. I can't come back and it's better that way. I'm going south. The snow here kills me.
> Mary

Ed knew. Aware that he wasn't Jem's father, Ed still raised Jem and did the best he could. Did what he thought was right. Just plodded on. Responsible, hardworking, upstanding Ed. So what if he had craggy teeth and never got over the war? Who was Jem to judge, or anyone who hadn't, as Elba said, ever truly been scared to death? He was a Loud, for sure. He did what he could with the life given to him. Took the raw materials given at birth, the circumstances of upbringing, and created something fresh from it all. Didn't have to be earth-shattering. Just had to be his.

sixteen

The weather had broken in earnest. Robins had been spotted. Winter coats were hung on hooks, not packed away just yet, but already looking like the wrong season's garments, too heavy, too dull-hued. Cherry trees budded.

Laura confronted Jem walking to his truck outside the wine shop. Her cheeks blazed, eyes quizzical but angry.

"What's with you, Jem? Do I disgust you or something? Is it the land? You don't want to talk about it with me? Don't you like me anymore?"

"It's complicated," said Jem.

"Sure, if you make it that way," said Laura. She stormed off with a gait remarkably like Manette's.

A man's hand on Jem's shoulder made him jump. It was Don, holding a bag. Inside, two wine bottles clinked together like glass castanets.

"Heard you talked to your mom."

"Who told you that?"

Fruit of the Vine

"Let's just say I know. It isn't important how. I wanted to tell you, if you need something, I'm here. It's what your dad would have wanted."

"Thanks."

Jem spent the weekend sorting Ed's stuff, staying up too late, falling asleep in his clothes, then wearing them again the next day. Monday, he felt like a zombie. He worked with barely a thought, his actions automatic, as if he were directed by remote-control. After work, an invisible tow line dragged him up the stairs to his apartment. He took a beer from the refrigerator, dialed Meredith's number.

The gates to Chateau Cobblestone were agape, just like Meredith said. Jem entered between them, ascending the long, steep driveway to the residence. Before he had a chance to ring Meredith's bell, she opened the door, let him in. Easy as anything had been lately.

"Saw your friend Zack Saturday night," said Meredith from the bed.

In the adjoining bathroom, Jem swished mouthwash, spat into the scalloped sink and turned off the faucet. He wiped his face on a flowery towel.

"Where was that?" he called out the open door, hanging the towel onto the chrome ring.

Cynthia Kolko

"In town. Getting into his car. He was with that girl from Hassler. Joe Silla's sister-in-law. What's her name? Laura?"

Jem stopped cold in the doorway separating the bathroom from the bedroom, feet nailed to the floor.

"Laura? You sure?"

"Yeah, I'm sure. Are they dating? They looked kind of close. That's new, isn't it?"

"Definitely new," said Jem.

"Good for him. All that prowling around. About time he found a nice girl. The kind he can settle down with."

Jem's face blazed. His throat itched. He thought he might vomit.

"You okay? You're all flushed," Meredith said.

"Never been better," Jem said.

"Aren't you going to kiss me goodbye?" Meredith called to the closing door.

At Hassler, the early morning light glinted off the dew like fireflies in the grass. Jem walked up the cobblestone path next to the main barn, saw Zack in the field. Jem stopped, stared like a bull. Zack stared back and then sauntered in the opposite direction, looking pleased with himself.

An hour or so passed. Jem handed out the work schedule, inspected the barrels, stopped into the bottling room, and repaired a trellis wire.

Right before lunch, Zack's shadow appeared against the light square of the barn doorway. He shuffled his hands to-

Fruit of the Vine

gether to loosen the caked dirt. Jem was in the barn, absorbed in something on a clipboard. He scribbled with a pencil, threaded it through the clip, and hung the board on a nail. He heard Zack, turned to see who it was and immediately re-aimed his gaze to the clipboard. Zack swaggered over to Jem, cleared his throat. Waited. Tapped Jem on the arm.

"What?" Jem said, face forward.

"You going to avoid me all day?" said Zack.

"Matter of fact, I am."

Jem took a deliberate step toward the barn door, cuffing Zack's shoulder with his own. Zack extended his arm like a crossing gate to block Jem's passage, but Jem flung it out of the way and kept walking, his face serious.

"C'mon man," said Zack. "You can't go out with your half-sister. What if you shot one past the gate? Your kids'd come out all cracked."

"Ain't the point," said Jem.

"It was Laura's idea. I swear. She came on to me. I just went along with it is all."

"That don't make it right," Jem said.

Just walk away, he told himself, feeling the adrenaline rising. Plenty of better things to accomplish than this.

He turned to exit through the gaping barn doors, the sun shining through them like a spotlight over the scene.

Zack called to Jem's back. "What's the difference, man? You were never going to get Laura anyway."

Jem wheeled around as if standing on a lazy Susan, took two giant steps and drove his fist into Zack's face, knocking him to the ground. Jem leapt atop Zack, throwing three or four wild

Cynthia Kolko

punches before Zack grabbed one of Jem's arms and tossed him aside. He rolled over to pummel Jem, but Jem's foot jerked up into Zack's crotch. Zack curled inward and Jem delivered an upper cut that sent Zack flying into the barn wall. The clipboard fell down onto Zack's head. Zack took the clipboard and smacked Jem's face with it, drawing blood from Jem's nose.

"Spick," said Jem.

"White trash," Zack punched.

"Son of a bitch," Zack punched again.

"Son of a whore," Zack hit Jem's jaw.

Jem fell back. Zack jumped onto Jem, but was wrenched onto his feet from behind.

"Hold it right there!" said Sanford, arms clamping Zack's shoulders.

Blood covered Jem's upper lip. A lone drop traced a red track across his cheek.

"Just what the Sam Hell is going on here?" yelled Sanford.

It was the first time either Jem or Zack had heard him raise his voice, and they froze momentarily, shocked at the outburst. Jem scrambled to his feet. He breathed labored gusts.

"I know what this is about," said Sanford. "Know more than you think I do. I'll tell you this: you two keep it out of here. Out of my barn, out of my farm. I don't want to see any of it, or you'll both be looking for jobs faster than a dropped fork finds the floor."

Zack and Jem exchanged hard, hateful stares. Sanford released his grip on Zack.

"I got too much to do to play daddy to grown men," said Sanford.

Fruit of the Vine

The remark hung in the air like a twisting inchworm on a thread. Sanford glared admonishingly at both of them.

"When you come here, you leave your personal business back on the road. You pass that Hassler Vineyard sign, you work for me and Manette. You act like a man. No fighting like tomcats."

Jem wiped his bloody nose with his shirtsleeve. Zack looked down to the dirt floor and saw a pair of dime-sized blood drops on the toe of one of his boots.

"Got it?" Sanford raised his voice again, though not as loud as before.

"Yeah," said Zack.

Jem nodded.

"Now get the hell back to work before I kick you off my land. Jem, clean yourself up. And clean up this barn."

Sanford noticed the cut on Zack's chin.

"You. Go into the washroom out back."

Laura rolled pie dough, draped it over a tin, and dropped violet filling into the center by tablespoons. She listened to the radio, a talk program about African music interspersed with snippets of singing. She found the harmonies beautiful and comforting, though not enough to cut through the indecision, the angst, that hung over her like a cloud. Couldn't she run this farm? If only she could find a partner, a peer, someone to help share the burden. If only Sandra wasn't such a ninny, the sisters could have taken over the vineyard together. But Laura didn't want to blame anyone else for her misfortunes. Not Sandra, not Joe. Not Sanford and Manette. One had to earn the right to be treated as an adult, as a citizen. As someone capable of making her own contribution to the community, to the machine that is the American system.

Her house—this house—was cute but silly, filled with the trappings of someone caught in a purgatory between adolescence and womanhood. Her kitchen cabinets were stocked with purple mugs, dishes wreathed with grapes. A purple sweater hung on a hook. Even her gun sleeve was purple, although it was not leaning against the corner of the coat closet as usual. There was a rubber-banded American flag in there, but the rifle was gone.

Zack spotted Jem's cap bobbing above a loose crowd of tourists milling outside the wine shop. Zack skirted the mob and caught up with Jem on the driveway.

"Heading to your dad's shop?"

"Yeah," Jem answered cautiously. "Lots of projects still to clear out. Be a miracle if I finish by fall."

"You going to move out of the apartment here? Live in your dad's house after you shovel it out?"

"Walking in there makes me puke," said Jem. "I'd be happy if it burned to the ground. I'm going to sell it, but I won't get nothing for it. Place ain't much more than a souped-up trailer."

Fruit of the Vine

"You got all that land, though, right? Up on the hill. That shit's gotta be worth a mint."

"S'only worth what someone's willing to pay for it. I might make a few cents off it eventually, after I pay off taxes. And lawyers, damn bloodsuckers."

"And your dad's debt."

"Dad didn't have any debt. Always believed that what he couldn't pay for, he couldn't have. He didn't like to owe nobody."

"No debt! Man. That's the American dream right there."

They were both quiet, Zack watching Jem's face, Jem looking off toward Laura's front door. Zack broke the silence.

"Shit, man. I gotta tell you—and I'm sorry that this is the way it is—but holy crap, you sure can profit from someone's death."

"Watch it. That's my dad you're talking about."

"You got a short memory or what? Ed's wasn't your dad."

Jem snatched Zack's coat in both hands and pushed him backward all the way to the store, smacking him against the siding. The crowd of tourists murmured and floated in the other direction en masse.

"Daddy!" a girl's voice broke above the buzz.

Jem's expression darkened. His lowered voice was studded with anger.

"Ed was my dad. Not my biological dad. But my dad."

Zack, aware of the spectators, played the pacifist. He lifted both hands as if being arrested.

"Whatever, man. You're scaring the tourists."

The wine shop's door jingled and opened, revealing Laura,

248

Cynthia Kolko

who pivoted to see what the devil the tourists were so engrossed in. Jem held Zack fixed to the barn wall. She frowned like a disapproving schoolmarm, impatient with the boyish horseplay of her charges. Jem released Zack, who smoothed his shirt.

"Ain't worth it," said Zack.

He stepped away, around the shop to the field.

"If you're going to work together, you have to stop beating each other up," said Laura.

"Sorry," said Jem. He couldn't look Laura in the face.

He adjusted his cap and walked on to his truck, leaving the crowd to comment to each other on the skirmish they'd witnessed. One guy, eager to document every aspect of his trip, snapped a picture of the truck's hindquarters as it departed and blew exhaust over the scene.

seventeen

Joe stowed the rifle inside his overcoat. He quietly turned the unlocked knob of Zack's apartment door. No one was home. Joe perused Zack's Spartan digs. He was surprised at how spare the apartment was, and how clean. Zack was a neatnik, perhaps to an obsessive degree. Not many people knew that about him. He scrubbed the kitchenette daily, even if he hadn't been cooking. He tucked his sheets and blankets into his bed, which consisted of a mattress and box spring on the bedroom floor under a sparkling set of bay windows.

Joe opened the refrigerator. The shelves gleamed under neatly-rowed beers, ordered by brand. He perused Zack's collection of heavy-metal and 80s glam-rock, a genre Zack called "grilled cheese," alphabetically displayed on the apartment's lone bookshelf. This from a guy who in recent years had had a two-by-four for a front bumper, though even with the sandbags in back, Zack's truck tended to be spotless.

There was no artwork in the apartment. No photos. Not

Cynthia Kolko

one poster or even a refrigerator magnet. Aside from the beer, there was nothing to show what Zack's interests were. Joe took in the scene, disappointed at—aside from the cleanliness—how unremarkable it was. How uninteresting. As a bachelor pad, it plain stank.

Sandra would never go for this. She's all about ambiance.

Joe parked a few houses down from his own and tucked the rifle back into his coat. At his house, he tried the back door handle, found it open.

How many times do I tell you, bitch? Always keep the doors locked!

Joe sidled inside, heard creaking upstairs. He climbed slowly, one foot at a time, on the soft floral stair runner. I knew that extra carpet padding was worth the money.

A woman laughed, followed by a few words spoken in a male pitch.

I should have brought a camera instead of a gun. Hell no. This'll scare the shit out of that wetback.

Joe stood silently at the threshold of his bedroom, drew the rifle, and kicked the door open.

"Surprise, you fucker!" Joe yelled, an angry eye squinting through the gun's sight. "How'd you like a load of buckshot?"

Sandra screamed, "Put that down!"

Her companion froze, his mouth hinged ajar under his handlebar moustache.

"Bender!" shouted Joe. "Fucking Bender?"

"Oh my God!" Sandra shrieked.

She leapt naked over the pink diamond-pattern nightie

251

crumpled on the floor, and into the bathroom. The lock sounded with a flimsy click.

"Earl, run!" she whined meekly from behind the door.

Bender slid off the bed. One hand held a sheet to his waist, the other was extended. He approached Joe. His voice was measured.

"Joe? Come on Joe. You don't want to shoot that thing. Give me that."

Joe changed his grip, held the gun like a battering ram. He lunged it into Bender's crotch. Bender wailed, dropped to the floor as if his legs gave out.

"What's happening?" Sandra called from behind the bathroom door.

"I'm hurt," Bender groaned. One of his testicles was swelling rapidly. It was already the size of an orange.

"Get out of there!" Sandra yelled, her voice echoing off the bathroom tile.

"I can't, you stupid bitch! I need an ambulance! Call an ambulance!"

"Hey, now, you don't talk like that to my wife," Joe said.

"There's no phone in here," said Sandra.

Bender groaned at Joe, "You call."

"I'm not calling an ambulance for you! And you don't need an ambulance, Nancy. Like you never been hit in the balls before!" said Joe.

"That's how I know I need an ambulance," said Bender.

Bender unfurled himself and stumbled toward the phone on the nightstand. Joe watched Bender push the numbered buttons.

Cynthia Kolko

Joe left the house, head clouded with scenarios that floated like fragments of surreal dreams: jail, a prison jumpsuit, a cellblock riot, escape, living on the lam. Joe got to his car as an ambulance wailed by. One of two patrol cars slowed and turned.

eighteen

Joe sat in the town holding cell. White paint coating the cinder block walls couldn't expand the tight quarters. Joe wondered who else had relieved himself in the cell's toilet, a steel lidless bowl tinting the water gray as weathered pavement. If he weren't bailed out soon by Sandra, or someone else, he'd be transferred to county facilities where he'd share a cell with Lord knew what variety of hoods.

The lawyer said Joe might serve time for assault. He recommended a psychiatric evaluation, noting that poor old cuckolded Joe only meant to frighten adulterous Sandra and her bedfellow. The crotch pounding was an accident, a matter of temporary insanity, brought on by the grievous notion of losing his one and only love to another man. It may have been the truth.

Footsteps approached. Joe checked the white-faced clock on the wall outside his cell. Too early for lunch. Was it Sandra?

"Visitor, Mr. Silla."

The cell bars cut Roy Archer's weathered visage into strips.

Cynthia Kolko

"Old buddy. Thanks for coming," said Joe.

"You don't look so bad. Sandra said you looked like death."

"How would she know? She hasn't shown up. Supposed to come by this morning and bail me out."

"Said she heard it from Alvin Southcomb. He's the policeman who booked you last night. Old townie. Played football at Sawhorn Regional. Anyhow, besides seeing how you were, I was wondering what you wanted to do with the bar. Sandra's not in the best shape. Keeps crying every time I try to talk to her. Ask her what to do, she just rocks back and forth, says 'I don't know, I don't know' and then there's more crying. I've never seen her without all that black makeup around her eyes. She keeps crying it off. So Tap's been closed."

Joe had been thinking of Tap only sporadically this morning. His mind was far more concerned with what would happen to him if he were sent to jail. He could get four years. More, even. What would happen to Sandra if he did? Would she arrive for conjugal visits? Would she dump him? Get remarried? Would he rot in there and look twenty years older when he got out? Would surgical procedures have advanced enough to erase the outward signs of the stress? What if it didn't? Who would he get then? He thought about a career change. Politics, maybe. Life sure can go down the shitter fast.

"Open Tap or keep it closed for the time being, your choice," said Roy. "The tavern's going to be open all weekend."

"Keep it closed tonight," said Joe. "Let that shitcan tavern take care of the ambulance chasers and rubberneckers. We'll open tomorrow. Saturday's a better money night than Friday anyhow."

Fruit of the Vine

"Reporters will bring extra bodies into the joint," said Roy. "This is their only news story, after who won the needlepoint show at First Baptist."

"Reporters?" said Joe. "Then we're definitely opening tomorrow. Hell if I want anyone to think I'm beaten down. See if you can scrape up a few people to help out at the bar for the night shift. Could get crowded, what with the publicity of the situation."

"I'll get in there tonight to do pre-prep. Make it less of a headache tomorrow. We need all the head start we can, with you here in the brick house."

"It's 'big house.' Brick house is a—"

"I know."

Some of Bender's buddies volunteered to run the tavern on Friday. Bender was still in the hospital, watching network television from bed. He shared a room with a fellow recuperating from a complicated knee operation. The thin curtain between them wasn't enough to buffer Bender from the guy's phone conversations with his wife, drawn-out strings of defenses against one complaint after another. The television wasn't enough of a diversion, either. Bender had a cassette player, a book about Yellowstone National Park, and a few motorcycle magazines. Visitors trickled in to see him, mostly guys in canvas overalls and work boots. They tried to keep the subject off Bender's throbbing balls. Laura didn't show up. Neither did Sandra.

Cynthia Kolko

Bender had had surgery to drain the water balloon that was his testicle. Although he was still in pain, he couldn't wait to get out of the hospital. He put on a good show for the staff that came to check on him. He mustered all the strength he had when the physical therapist arrived to watch him amble around the room seemingly effortlessly, but with his teeth gritted behind his closed mouth, caging the pain from on-lookers. When the therapist had left, Bender collapsed with exhaustion. He was still recovering from the anesthesia, which made him feel anemic, tired him so easily. Coupled with the boredom of being largely bed-bound, he slept like a cat until receiving the okay that he could go home. The nurse gave Bender a sheet of instructions and several ice packs, though she recommended frozen vegetables. Peas to be exact.

That night, the tavern was teeming. A few reporters, hungry for the slightest drop of juicy news, came by earlier in the evening, but left after a few good sound bites, video pans of the sticky bar's interior, and photo stills of the worn clapboard exterior. Regulars came in partially as a show of solidarity with Bender, but also to partake in the camaraderie. They knew droves of their fellow townspeople would be there.

With Tap shuttered for the night, some of that establishment's patrons, motivated by curiosity or just a cold beverage, came to Loud's Tavern too, sitting in groups and muttering over the drink list, or standing in clumps when all the tables filled, the ladies' high-heeled boots making their calves ache. They talked about Sandra, poor lost soul. And Joe, over-stressed and jealous. A tragedy. By midnight all but the most

Fruit of the Vine

adventuresome Tap patrons had gone home. But the tavern was still rife with locals, mostly men, most drunk, others well on their way.

"I ain't never seen the place like this," said Russ.

"Sure you have," said Jem "Day after Thanksgiving, remember?"

"Oh yeah. That's a good bar night," said Russ.

"See you later, buddy," said Russ when Zack entered. He met Zack just inside the door, slapping his palm. Neither Zack nor Jem approached one another.

Talk of Joe and Bender dominated the tavern, and as a result, there were more guys shifting uncomfortably on their stools, more hands protectively moving to crotches. Amid the drunkenness, there seemed to be a proliferation of minor accidents, more so than usual: little slip-ups like bottles dropping to the floor, people losing their steps in the slick puddles, and tripping into each other. The background noise inside the tavern gained volume and crept to the foreground. Jem could barely discern any single voice above the rumble of voices, the bang of a bottle on the bar, the slap of a chair that had tipped to the floor. But sporadic shouts could be heard cutting through the din like headlights through a fog, gaining momentum until a battle cry seemed to be taking shape.

"Poor old hairy son of a bitch Bender...He's our boy, Bender."

"Can't do this to one of us—"

"Maiming Bender...Didn't he say he wanted a bunch of kids?"

"How's he going to do that now? Took his manhood. It's an assault on us all."

Cynthia Kolko

"The brotherhood of Sawhorn."

"Damn transplants...Ruining our town. Whacking us in the balls."

"Can't let it go unanswered. For Bender! Gotta do something for Bender. Ol' black-n-blue balls Bender!"

"Let's go! Let's fucking do it!"

It was hard to imagine a circumstance that could empty the tavern before closing time, yet a shouting, tripping whirlwind of parkas, caps, beard stubble, and BO trampled out, leaving Jem, a handful of other guys, and the few women present rattling around in the tavern like holdouts in a theater after the last curtain.

The crowd prowled the street like a rock concert audience on parade, brandishing lighters that flickered, went out in the wind, and were re-lit. The men assembled outside Tap like a raucous bubbling stew. A dark, thin, sunken-eyed man in a Skidoo hat jiggled the knob on Tap's locked door.

A shout from the crowd—"Fuck the knob!"—and two or three men simultaneously kicked in the door, the gang flooding in like water through a broken dam.

What happened next was shattering, splintering mayhem. Bottles were stuffed into pockets, smashed onto the floor. Men stomped the glass-topped bar like a line of clumsy barmaid dancers, kicking through it with an explosion of glass, shards etching blood from their own feet and legs.

Declarations were made, followed by the exclamation points of rash actions, and approving howls.

"This is for Bender!"

A stool windmilled into the coat racks.

Fruit of the Vine

"For all the working stiffs in this town!"

A bottle of gin christened the bar.

"For anyone who's ever fucked a whore!"

A roundhouse-kicking work boot split the ladies' room door. Whistles and roars.

Display taps were snatched. Someone dribbled triple sec in crude cursive on the counter behind the bar and lit it with a lighter. "Brotherhood" spelled out in flames ignited a mass howl from the motley mob, and others followed suit with their own bon mots: "RIP TAP," "U Suck Joe," and the incomprehensible "YANKEE GO HOME."

The bar itself became a pyre. A few men tried to douse it with draft beer or a wimpy hand water shower from the steel bar sink. By the time someone found a fire extinguisher, the flames had already leeched to stools, tables, the walls. The hapless fellow operating the extinguisher only weakly sprayed white gunk in the wrong direction. Half the men had already fled the smoldering joint.

"Fucking get the hell out of here before it blows!"

Outside, grammar deteriorated into an unruly string of cusses as the lumbering mass fled on foot, shedding stolen bottles and food, and drove away in pickups and rusty sedans, or the occasional tricked-out sports car. Miraculously, no accidents were caused by all the drunken driving, except for a dented "raise plow" traffic sign knocked off the threshold of a bridge into the murky creek below.

Firefighters killed the fire. The sanity of the dawn crept into the cloudy minds of those responsible for the evening's destruction, and a stunned but somehow unsurprised town learned the news by telephone, television, and police warrant.

In a way, the Tap fire was good for Sawhorn's economy. A sizable chunk of the town's working population was in the pokey for arson, assault, and inciting a riot, thanks to security cameras hidden inside the bar's recessed lights, which were themselves shielded from the heat by the metal cans that surrounded and held them in the ceiling. The heretofore unemployed and underemployed residents of Sawhorn could now find scores of jobs in the want ads. Lift operator. Construction crew. Part-time bottler.

There were, however, no cameras in Tap's kitchen. So aside from the hapless doofus who served top grade filet mignon at a barbeque the following weekend, many thieves of food, booze, and flatware remained at large. And when, on the night of the inferno, firefighters found Roy Archer's body in Tap's freezer, a crude attempt at a scalping apparently aborted in favor of a throat slitting, that perpetrator too remained elusive.

nineteen

Jem watched Laura wander up and down the grape rows, as if her mind were somewhere else, or as if she wished she were somewhere else.

"Just wanted to say sorry," said Jem. "About Bender and your sister and the whole mess."

"What's the difference?" said Laura, kicking a clod of dirt. "Bender and I were on the way out anyhow. He wasn't into it. I was just something to do. Should have known."

"You couldn't have been into it either. What did you ever see in…" Jem stopped himself.

Laura looked annoyed. "Why does everyone ask me that? Like it's so unbelievable that he was nice. Or that I liked the way he talked. The way he listened, joked."

Good reasons as any, Jem thought, still having a hard time believing that Bender was merely the passive recipient of Laura's pursuit. He guessed Bender wasn't so much interested in Laura as he just wasn't uninterested. Like being tossed a pretzel. Chances are, you'd eat it. Laura was Bender's answer to the question, "Why not?"

"I got a knack for pushing people away," said Laura.

"No, you don't."

"I pushed you away, didn't I? There must have been a reason. Tell me the truth. Don't worry about hurting my feelings. I can take it."

"You don't wanna know," said Jem, aware that he had just revealed too much.

"Aha!" said Laura, pointing her finger at Jem. "There is a reason! Now you have to tell me. Spill it. Give it up."

"You really want to know," Jem said, as a statement of fact.

"Yeah."

"Well you asked for it." Jem broke a sucker off a grape vine, ran his finger over a bud that perished before having a chance to bloom, then flung the branch into the bleak distance. Laura stared.

"Shit, I can't," said Jem.

Laura hid her face in her hands. "You're killing me," she wailed between her fingers.

Jem steeled himself to deliver the conjecture he believed as fact. He couldn't meet Laura's eyes, so he looked beyond her to the blood-red barn. His voice became a murmur.

"I think we're related," he said.

"Related?" asked Laura, her voice frantic. "How? Cousins?"

"Shh!" said Jem, checking around for eavesdroppers, as if they could be lurking behind the vines or under a hill of dirt. "Closer than that," he said. "I mean, uh, your dad and my mom."

Fruit of the Vine

"My dad and your mom what?"

"Um. Laura? You might wanna sit down."

"Here on the ground?" she said, face incredulous, impatience winning out. "Just tell me already."

"I think you're my sister. Half-sister."

"Is this a joke?"

"Like I said, your dad and my mom. Seems they had an affair. You see, Ed's not my real, not my biological father. I think it might be Sanford."

Laura took a few backward steps, tripped over a rock and fell into a sitting position on the ground, all the while not taking her eyes from Jem's face. He extended a hand to help her up.

"Not true. I don't believe it," she said. "That's not him. Never. Ridiculous! Besides, we don't look alike, and you don't look like my dad."

"Genetics work in odd ways. You never can predict what drops of the gene pool you're going to end up with. You and Sandra ain't exactly twins."

"That's only 'cause she went under the knife a million times. Dolls herself up. You should see our baby pictures. Can't tell one from the other."

"Now you're just in denial. Shit. What kind of idiot am I? I knew I shouldn't have told you. I was going to keep quiet, but you made me say it."

"I made you?"

"Yeah. 'Spill it' and all that."

"Aren't there tests for these things?"

"Already took it. Should get the results back in a week."

"My dad took the test?"

Cynthia Kolko

"Yup."

Laura sat back on the dirty ground as if someone had shoved her. "I'm going to be sick." She inserted her nose between her knees, rested her cheeks there, and closed her eyes.

Jem was about to ask Laura if she wanted some help walking back to her house, if she needed water, but she lifted her face to speak, her skin washed with a green cast.

"Does Mom know?" Laura's voice was thin.

Jem squatted down, didn't like his towering position over weakened Laura.

"I didn't tell her anything, but she probably knows. Can't imagine there's something she couldn't figure out."

"Oh God," Laura groaned. Then, conjuring up a flash of strength, "It isn't true!"

"This isn't what you want to hear, but chances are, it is true. I mean, how many affairs could my ma have had all at once? Plus, she didn't mention any other ones."

"Well of course not. Hasn't talked to you for how many years? And she's going to just run down a list of her floozy escapades? She didn't want you to think she's a tramp. Did you ask about any others?"

"Uh, no, I didn't."

Laura pointed at Jem, but didn't say 'aha' this time.

"Well, this might get awkward when we start working together," she said.

"Huh?"

"Didn't Mom tell you? She and Dad decided not to sell to Joe. You know, with jail and Bender's crotch and all. I'm going to be shadowing her. Helping her run the place. I told

Fruit of the Vine

them I was full of ideas and really wanted to learn all I could to really make a contribution here. Take it to the next level. Continue the family tradition, but modernize the place the way we want to do it."

"You'll be my boss?" said Jem.

"No, no," said Laura. "Your co-worker. Mom's the boss. Next year, I'm going to Italy. Study there like she did. Learn about vinifera."

"Italy?"

What about me?

But Laura kept talking.

"It'll be part of my enology degree. I'm going back to school. Spend a year or so in Italy and another few years back upstate. There's so much to learn. This isn't a simple business."

A year or so in Italy? His throat got hot. He pictured an Italian man, handsome, suave, with one of those accents chicks dig. The man would sit with Laura in a café, swirling a glass of wine, teaching her an idiom in la bella lingua, one that meant "love," or "devotion," or some such crap. And Laura would fall for it like a sack of potatoes over the porch railing.

"Sounds great," said Jem.

"It's a lot all at once, but sometimes change happens fast. Especially when you're the one doing the changing," she said. "If something doesn't screw it all up." The few rays of sun in her expression were snuffed out by dark.

"I thought you wanted to learn about being Jewish," said Jem.

"You can learn a few things at once, you know. And it's all intertwined to me. All about figuring it all out."

Cynthia Kolko

That night, Jem sat on his bed holding the green folder in his hand. Laura had taken control of her life like taking a bull by the horns. Sure, she had help. Lots of it. She had her parents right there across the driveway, owed them volumes for being in a position to be able to choose the path she did. But isn't that what life is? Taking the raw materials, the situations one has been presented or saddled with, and forming them into a new pursuit? Creating something oneself from all the challenges and opportunities?

Jem had been lazy, he thought. He had let his own opportunities pass him by while he dawdled. Procrastinated like a champ. Everyone—Ed's clients, the lawyers, Joe, Roy—had implored something of him. He chose the easiest path. The one most comfortable, the one that would challenge him the least. Zack was right. If something weren't dropped in his lap, he didn't do anything. And Laura was right. Change either happened to you or you made it happen yourself.

The door down the long hallway closed with a thundering echo. Joe Silla was the only soul held in the facility. The fellows rounded up after the Tap inferno and Roy's murder had either been released or moved to a more secure, larger facility in Geneva.

High heels clicked down the hall and stood by Joe's cell bars. They were boots, patent-leather, immaculate.

Fruit of the Vine

"You've got balls coming here," said Joe.

"I do whatever I want," said Meredith.

"Sandra finds out, I'm in the shitter."

"You're already here, aren't you?"

"She isn't a smart girl, but she'll put two and two together."

"This place bugged?" Meredith circled left and right, face to the ceiling, her silky hair sweeping like the streamers of a maypole.

"What is this, Sing Sing?" said Joe.

Meredith smiled. Her pretty face seemed to shine warm light into Joe's cell. He basked in it, then became serious.

"Sandra's pregnant," he said.

Meredith's light clicked off. "Oh God," she said.

"You're sure it's yours," she said, a question in the form of a statement, her arms tightly folded.

"Sandra's not, but I am. She's getting an amnio. Find out definitively."

Meredith scrutinized the ceiling, the fire detector, the sprinklers. No cameras that she could discern.

"We need to talk," said Joe.

"Now what?" Meredith pursed her lips.

"Think we ought to cool it," said Joe.

"You're dumping me?" said Meredith, voice laced with poison. "After all I've done for you?"

"It's Sandra, okay? Sandra! You might find this difficult to believe, but I love that broad. I'm a damn fool without her. Don't know what I'd do. Wasting away here in jail, you do a lot of thinking. Take stock of your life. The choices you've made. What you've done with what you've been given. I'm a changed man. Sitting right here, this is not the same Joe Silla you knew yesterday. Same clothes, different Joe."

"What a load of crap."

"I'm serious. I'm starting a new phase of life. Going to be a better husband, a better person. Going to stop all this sneaky stuff. I don't want to be like my dad. Philandering. Involved in all kinds of shaky shit. I've got to be higher brow that. More of a pillar of the community. Someone who gets buildings named after them."

"Go to hell," said Meredith. "I can't be dating a jailbird, anyway."

Down the hall, she saw Jem's tall figure approach, holding a green folder. Jem's face blazed as he got closer to her standing outside Joe's cell.

"Well look who's here," said Meredith. "Mr. Wham-Bam, Thank You—"

"Stop. Please," said Jem.

He slipped his eyes at Joe, who looked pathetic. Joe's sad visage instilled sympathy in Jem rather than the derision he had been feeling since he'd read the land agreement which Ed had, no doubt, been duped into thinking was a good deal.

"Oh, Joe! Your patsy is here!" Meredith called.

Joe kept his eyes to the floor. "Stop making a scene."

A cop came to the cell. "Didn't think we'd need complex security procedures here, but I guess there's a first time for everything," he said. "Let's go, Miss Payne. Your time's up."

"What a two-bit jail," she said. "No real visiting room. I've never seen anything like it."

The cop took her arm, but she wrenched it away.

Fruit of the Vine

"Don't worry, I'm leaving," she said. "And believe me, I don't plan to come back here."

Jem's gaze alternated between Joe, who still had neither acknowledged his presence nor looked at him, and the steel toilet in the corner of the cell. Why Jem hadn't gone to the bathroom before coming here, he did not know.

"These the papers you been asking about?" said Jem.

He held up the green folder, opened it, flapped the contents, slid them across the cell bars as if he were playing a gliss on tubular bells. Sitting on the cell's bench, Joe looked broken. His posture was sickle-shaped.

He spoke without raising his eyes to meet Jem's. "I'll give you same deal. Plus ten percent."

"Make it twenty-five and I'll do it."

"That isn't the only piece of land in this region. Not by a long shot. Dime a dozen, old farms like yours."

"Yeah, but you want this one, ain't that right? This one's special. You don't want some other farm. Just Loud Farm."

"Have you been talking to Roy again? From beyond?"

"I've been talking to my own sense of reason."

Joe smirked.

"Well. Jem Loud. Look at you now. Calling the shots. Rising from obscurity. Maybe I underestimated you, Jem. Underestimated all you townie bastards. Twenty-five percent it is."

Jem held the folder under his armpit. Something in him told him not to shake Joe's hand.

Cynthia Kolko

Jem's phone rang late, ten-thirty or so.

"Mind if I screw your girlfriend?"

"What?"

"Meredith," said Russ. "Can I fuck her?"

"She ain't my girlfriend."

"So it's okay, then?"

It wasn't okay. Not that Jem was truly interested in Meredith. But somehow, he wasn't not interested, either. Even if Meredith had essentially given Jem his walking papers back at the jail, he didn't want anyone else to have her. Especially one of his friends. Besides, wasn't passing her around skanky? But then, this was a small town. There weren't enough girls to not have shared one or two. Jem thought of Laura and Bender, then just Laura.

"Whatever," Jem said.

⚜

Jem knew the instant he saw the blue uniforms. They'd been dropping by the farm every few days, throwing questions at anyone who might know a morsel of information about the fire, and especially about Roy's murder. Even before the two officers stood at the edge of the field, following Sanford's pointed finger to Jem, who stood solitary like a log post at the end of a tangled row, Jem knew it was his turn to be questioned. He had run his story in his head numerous times, rehearsed just the words he would say, and although he had nothing to do with the sordid events of that night, he had watched enough cop movies to concoct the fear that some-

Fruit of the Vine

times the truth didn't come out the way it should. Sometimes the truth did hurt, put innocent souls in jail, or worse.

One officer was older than the other by a good twenty-five years, maybe more. The younger one looked like a kid, his freckled face and red hair reminding Jem of Opie from the Andy Griffith show. The kid cop was vaguely familiar to Jem. Maybe he was one of the kids around town, the ones who skateboarded in the parking lot of the firehouse, the ones who bought lemonheads at the Quik Mart, or loitered behind it hacking on the smoke of their first cigarettes. Maybe Jem had seen this kid a hundred times but had never locked him into memory, so the kid faded into the landscape of the streets like the façades of a dozen buildings Jem passed every day but couldn't describe if called upon to do so. And now Opie was all grown up and a cop. Coming to question Jem about one of Sawhorn's sorriest nights, a fresh stain on a spattered history.

"Jemison Loud," the elder cop said. Opie was silent. "We'd like to question you about the night of February 23rd. At the station."

"The station?" Jem asked. The cops questioned all the other guys in Manette's office, releasing them like netted butterflies fifteen or twenty minutes later. Less, even.

"How long this going to take?" Jem asked.

"Hard to say," the elder cop said. "But if you come willingly, we won't need to cuff you."

Jem's oaky complexion, already faded by winter, blanched further. He hunched.

In the squad car, caged like a dog behind the steel fencing

that separated the front seat from the back, Jem saw Laura standing just outside the wine shop's front door. Her face was inquisitive. He imagined she was thinking much the same thing he was: Why is Jem being taken to the station instead of the office?

At the station, Opie led Jem to a room. "This whole case. Everything. It's just 'cause someone's marriage went sour," Opie said. He turned to Jem, spoke low as if he were telling him a secret. "Stuff sure goes to hell when a woman craves the strange," Opie said and opened the door, his face sly. Suddenly, Opie didn't look so young and innocent.

The room was like a white cube, devoid of personality, windowless except for the large two-way mirror where the session could be observed without the identity of the observers revealed. It was a lot like TV, Jem thought, only dirtier, the legs of mismatched chairs ringed at the floor with dust, having not been placed on the table for floor cleaning. A drip-spotted coffee machine teetered on a plastic stand.

"Someone will be with you soon," said Opie.

Jem sat at a conference table. It was the second time in two days he ended up there. He dropped a heel to the floor, was startled by the resulting boom reverberating off the unadorned walls. The elder cop came into the room without Opie, but with another man, thin, middle-aged, comfortable in a suit jacket and tie. He reminded Jem of Joe, somewhat. It was the way the man stood like a soldier at attention, the self-assured expression that told Jem he was not one to back down. Jem guessed this man's confident presence was more than Joe's macho grandstanding. This guy looked like he'd earned it.

"I'm detective Iaculli," the tie man said. "Tell me where you were the night of February 23rd."

"The tavern," said Jem.

"Loud's Tavern?" said Iaculli.

"Yup."

"Met your buddies there?"

"Yup."

"And who might they be?"

"Zack Santiago and Russ, I mean Emmett, Roulette."

"Hear anyone say anything about Joe Silla or Tap or Roy Archer?"

"Yeah. A bunch of stuff. I mean, people were saying stuff like "poor Bender" and shit. No one said they wanted to kill anyone or torch the place, if that's what you mean."

"No one talked about getting revenge?"

"I don't know. Don't think so."

"And where did you go after the tavern?"

"Home."

"What time?"

"'Bout twelve."

"Your friends Zachary Santiago and Emmett Roulette? Where did they go?"

"Don't know."

Jem thought he was about finished when Mr. Iaculli strutted to the coffee machine and poured a cup. He didn't offer one to Jem. Opie rolled in a television and VCR. Mr. Iaculli turned the set on. A security video played inside the television's dusty box.

"Recognize this man?"

The video showed a lone man karate-chopping a gash in Tap's kitchen door. The perp had the poor judgment to look directly at the camera. The Norman Rockwell face was unmistakable. It was Russ.

"Mind telling me how you got that cut on your hand, Mr. Loud?" said Iaculli.

Jem examined the gash in the shape of a smile under his thumb.

"Opening boxes," said Jem.

"I understand there was a land deal about to go down. Joe Silla offered you a lot of money. Is that right, Mr. Loud?"

"Yes."

"And Mr. Archer. He was going to throw a monkey wrench into the whole deal, right Mr. Loud? You'd lose a bundle."

"Hardly. Not after taxes and shit. Archer didn't have anything to do with it, except try to convince me not to sell. Ain't no monkey wrench to speak your mind."

"Mr. Loud, we found blood on Mr. Archer we thought might not be his. Put it through the database. Now, the system is a new technology, and it's pretty good. Guess what came up?"

"What?" said Jem.

Iaculli leaned forward, eye-to-eye with Jem.

"Archer," Iaculli said.

"Okay," said Jem. A bead of sweat dripped down his back.

Fruit of the Vine

"That's not all," said Iaculli. He seemed not to blink, as if his eyes were glass. "Any guess what else came up?"

"Russ?" Jem said. He wiped his upper lip, but it still felt clammy.

"You," Iaculli said. "You came up, Mr. Loud."

The room pulsed. The paused security video shook. The ceiling tiles started to swirl, as if the whole place, Jem's life included, were going down the drain. Jem felt his throat get hot. He gripped the armrests of his chair, afraid to let go or he'd fall to the floor.

"I wasn't in there. Swear it."

Mr. Iaculli leaned back in his chair, folded his arms behind his head, revealed wet semicircles hanging under his pits.

"I believe you, Mr. Loud. We got witnesses who place you at Loud's Tavern. People who say you didn't set foot in Tap that night. People who saw your truck parked outside your apartment at Hassler Vineyard."

The swirling subsided.

"Can I go?" asked Jem, rising from his chair.

Iaculli put his hand out like a traffic cop. "Mr. Loud, do you know who your biological parents are?"

"One of them."

Iaculli took an 8x10 photograph out of a manila folder and pushed it across the table at Jem. It was a school picture perhaps, or an old police ID. The man in the photograph was a less-wrinkly, but no more smiley Roy Archer.

"That's your father, Mr. Loud."

twenty

Almost as soon as Jem returned to his apartment, there was a knock at his door.

"Police."

Opie handed Jem a manila envelope.

"Forgot to give this to you. Roy Archer's will. You're the next of kin, so you get a copy."

"Am I in it?"

"Easy, Bronco. It's over and done with. He left everything to the Seneca Nation. Almost a million dollars cold cash. 'For the preservation of a rich heritage' or some hot pile like that. Guy never spent much. Just saved."

That night, Jem rattled around his apartment not doing much of anything. He didn't turn on the TV. He picked up the phone to call Sanford, decided against it, and tried Zack instead. But there was no answer at Zack's place.

Jem went outside. Light illuminated the windows of the big house, delineating the right-angled shapes against the darkness like a student's rendition of a Mondrian painting. Laura

Fruit of the Vine

had changed the bulb on her front porch. The glow beckoned more brightly than ever.

Jem rang Laura's bell. She answered, hair loose, an unusual style for her. Jem liked it.

"We're not related," said Jem.

"You got the test back?"

"Got some information at the station. My biological father."

"He's the cop?"

"No. He's Roy Archer. Roy Archer is, was, my father."

Laura emitted a sound halfway between a sigh and a cry of anguish.

"Well, I've got to tell you, as much as I like you, I'm glad you're not my brother."

"Same here."

"Archer, huh?"

"Yeah. And now that I know it, I should have seen it all along. He was tall. I can't grow facial hair so well and neither could he. Probably other stuff we got in common that I don't know about yet. Maybe never will."

"Amazing."

"I feel pretty good about it," said Jem. "It's a relief."

"Did you tell Zack about it down at the station?"

"No. He was there?"

"Yeah. Some other cops came by here after you were picked up. Zack was yelling and cussing. Something about the cops being racist and that he knew he'd get blamed. Never seen him so mad. All red. But he didn't get charged with anything. He gets a bad rap, that Zack. Underneath it all, he's a good guy. Even if he did dump me."

Cynthia Kolko

"Huh?"

"Said he couldn't do that to you," said Laura. "What did he mean? 'Do that to you'?"

Jem noticed that Laura's toenails were painted lavender. She took the hair elastic from her wrist and bound her hair with it, leaving two or three strands unintentionally loose. Jem remembered his pact with himself to stop being passive, to not wait until opportunities dropped in his lap, but to create them.

"Want to watch a video?" asked Jem.

Laura clicked on the remote, turned it to a movie channel. They spent ten minutes watching an action flick about a lady spy who falls in love with the kingpin of a drug cartel. Jem felt something stab his backside and moved enough to see a pigeon gray point sticking up between two purple couch cushions. He picked the stone out. His arrowhead. He swore he saw it shine.

"So, Italy?" said Jem.

"Yeah," said Laura. "But don't worry."

Laura clicked off the remote, turned to Jem.

"I'll wait for you," she said.

twenty-one

The supermarket was well worth the forty minute drive from Sawhorn for those in search of a wider selection of wares than those offered on the Quik Mart's meager shelves. Things like ready-to-grill burgers. Bagels that weren't frozen. Fresh pineapple. Unsalted cashews.

Laura wheeled her shopping cart back to her truck, opened the passenger door, and crowded bag after bag into the foot well. It was a snug enough fit to avoid the clanking of bottles and jars. She hadn't noticed a woman sitting in the driver's seat of the adjacent car.

"I don't believe this. I can't get out," the woman said from her barely-opened car door, blocked by Laura's passenger door.

Laura loaded her last bag.

"I can't get out!" the woman said, her voice edged with anger.

"Tough shit," said Laura, slamming her passenger door and wheeling the cart around the back of her truck to the driver's side. "Couldn't wait a second? Couldn't just get out the other side?" Laura asked under her breath.

"Dumbass!" the woman directed at Laura as she locked her car and headed for the supermarket.

Laura sat in her truck, rifled through her bags, and found what she wanted. She got out and sprawled the word "BITCH" on the woman's windshield with the jumbo squeeze-bottle ketchup.

Half behind a van, holding a paper bag and a case of beer, Jem saw the whole thing.

"You boys, you get together, you're like a pack of hound dogs," said Mrs. Carpin, sitting in Elba's green velvet easy chair. Can't blame you for misbehaving. It's like a gang mentality. No one's fault. It's the gang's fault."

"But each person is responsible for his own behavior," said Elba, index finger raised for emphasis.

"Bah!" said Mrs. Carpin, with a disgusted look. "Boys get crazy in groups."

"Jem, how is it going with that girl? Laura is it?" Elba asked.

"The Fillmore girl? Oh, she's attractive," said Mrs. Carpin. Jem's face reddened.

"Well, would you look at that face?" said Mrs. Carpin. She chided, "Oh Elba, he doesn't want to talk about girls with his great-grandma."

"Well, why not?" said Gram. "Are you dating?"

Fruit of the Vine

Jem shrugged. Thought of Laura's bad temper.

"You're finding out she's a real person, aren't you? Boy, the reality can never live up to a fantasy."

"That's the truth," said Mrs. Carpin.

The two ladies nodded, cackled. Jem's face flushed a deeper red. He hunched.

"Did you see they pulled a fossil off one of the hills around here?" said Mrs. Carpin. "A three-foot long millipede. Could you imagine? A bug big enough to ride a bike. If there were creatures like that still roaming this town, things would be a whole lot different."

"Jem, I was going to ask you if you were planning to keep up the flags?" Elba said.

"The flags?"

"Like your dad did," said Elba. "Replace the veterans' flags at the Loud family plot. He kept them nice. Meant a lot to him. You can get cutie little ones at the VA. They're free."

Sandra waited on a cold molded plastic chair in a bleak room. The guard led Joe to the seat facing her. There was no screen between them like on the cop shows. Just two chairs squared off, as if they were about to play a game of Password.

"Fifteen minutes," the guard said before leaving Sandra and Joe.

"What a mess," said Joe.

"No kidding," said Sandra.

"I get the paper in here. And the guards, they tell me stuff.

Cynthia Kolko

Nice guys. I'd have a drink with them if it weren't for the circumstances."

"They made a few more arrests," said Sandra. "Destruction of property, looting, bunch of other stuff."

"That Zack kid part of it? Always knew he was no good. I'm a great judge of character."

"He's clean," said Sandra.

Joe looked annoyed. "Any for Archer?"

"Picked up Russ Roulette. Think he acted alone. Something about revenge for his sister. Some weird thing he'd been stewing about and he just blew. Not sure how he's going to plead."

"I believe it. He always looked like one of those nice kids who underneath it all could spit fire. But damn. I loved that old fucking Indian. Like a cousin."

Joe's mind saw Roy, the newspaper photos of his decimated bar. He pictured the state of the kitchen when Roy's body was discovered, Roy's corpse, the autopsy. Scenes he'd never beheld. Didn't need to. The ones his imagination created were chilling enough.

"Saw the doctor. She says I'm healthy. Baby too," said Sandra.

She waited for an embrace, but Joe remained still, aside from his eyes, which drifted down Sandra's body.

"When do your boobs start to grow?" he asked.

"Is that all you care about?" said Sandra.

Joe folded his arms. "You better start taking care of yourself. No drinking! Play classical music, get the kid smart. Might be good for you too, seeing as you're not exactly a brain trust. Pray the baby gets my genes. I mean, damn. If I were any smarter, it would be freakish. But what does it matter? Kid'll be good looking."

※

The next morning, Joe's cell door opened with a loud clang.

"You're a free man, Mr. Silla."

"Hot damn! I knew someone would come through. I got connections. Know the right people. Who do I need to thank?"

"Earl Bender. Told the DA he won't testify that it was attempted murder. So you've just got the assault charge now and Bender paid your bail on that. Said something about kids needing dads, and why make a whole bunch of people miserable. Hell of a guy, I'd say. Don't know that I'd do the same in his situation."

Sandra waited in the station's lobby, a cold-tiled space of mismatched folding chairs huddled around a squat coffee table spread with issues of Consumer Reports. She gave Joe the car keys. The parking lot was barely bigger than a welcome mat and empty, save for a trio of turkey vultures picking at a deceased squirrel.

"What, no reporters?" said Joe.

※

Roy Archer's funeral was a low-key affair. His wishes were to have his ashes spread over the Loud property. There were perhaps ten people assembled on the field. The evergreens had shed some of their snowy cloaks, and the ground swelled with the moisture of the falloff. Joe and Sandra stood slightly apart from the rest.

A Seneca elder presided over the ceremony. He passed out cigarettes to everyone present, telling the group it was permissible to light up if they wished, that Roy had requested it. Jem declined, but Joe took a cigarette, looked like Andy Capp dangling it from the side of his mouth. The Seneca man read some words thanking the earth for its gifts. He said that Roy was going on to another life, gave some history of the property, read some words about the divinity of creation.

The Seneca man took Roy's ashes and sprinkled them over the wet, weedy ground. Jem caught a flash that cut through Joe's solemn expression, something devious. Joe's eyes met Jem's. Joe winked and then showed Jem a thumbs-up. The Seneca man spoke more about the correlation between nature and happiness. Jem, a gloveless hand fingering the arrowhead in his jacket pocket, felt as if he might vomit.

twenty-two

Jem's muffler bellowed as he pulled into Benson
Frechette's driveway. Benson puffed a cigar on the porch,
which had been cleared of debris. Someone had been by
to fix up the yard as well. Trees were trimmed and the grass
was coiffed. The fresh landscape smelled like a rapidly-ap-
proaching spring. It was a hopeful, cheerful scent.

"That old truck sounds like hell," Benson said. "You'll
scare all the little children, driving around like that. I heard
you coming down the road and thought it was a tank. Had
flashbacks to the war."

"Haven't had a chance to get it fixed," said Jem. "Not with
the deal on the Loud farm going through."

"How'd it go with your dad's house? Get it sold?"

"It just closed. Didn't get what I wanted for it, but let me
tell you, I'm glad to be rid of the joint. The shop was a rental.
Landlord doesn't even live in state, let alone in Sawhorn. I
managed to get it all settled and the stuff carted away. Anything that customers didn't claim was sold to a lady from

Cynthia Kolko

Rochester. She's one of those people buys a whole estate's worth of stuff. I thought she was going to sweep up the sawdust on the floor and put it into a box, she took so much. Maybe there was a piece or two there that made it worth it to her, but again, I'm just glad to be finished with it."

"Any idea what's going into that space? Don't tell me it's another goddamn lawyer's office."

"A gym," said Jem. "Some kind of high-end workout place. Landlord didn't tell me who was behind it, but he did say he sold the whole building to whoever is putting it in. Said it was part of the gentrification of the neighborhood that started with Tap. I ain't never heard that word, gentrification, but I figured out what it meant."

"It means all kinds of overpriced shops selling gizmos for people who like to spend money," said Benson. "Makes a division between hoity types and regular folks. Between new and old. Course, who's to say it can't all exist together? One big happy family, right? Beats an empty storefront. That just looks bad. Hell, of a lot of them in the state these days. Empty warehouses, factories like ghost towns. Anytime I hear of a new business going in anywhere around here, I'm surprised. Who can afford to do business in this state anymore?"

Suddenly, Jem missed Ed. Jem imagined that had he lived to be Benson's age, Ed might resemble him quite closely. Benson was an opinionated man. He mistrusted the government. Hated anyone who disagreed with him. Had a wife once, but never remarried. Just wanted to be left alone.

"What exactly is a high-end gym anyhow?" asked Benson. "The YMCA stocked with golden medicine balls?"

Fruit of the Vine

Jem laughed. "Stuff like wooden lockers, sauna," he said. "Make it look like hot springs are sprouting out of the walls. Get people to teach whatever the latest fitness fad is. This is just a guess on my part. I play basketball in the middle school gym and lift a few weights."

"I got the number," said Benson. "The men will wear them nutters in there. The shorts they wear to ride a bike. I don't mind the women in them, but the men? No thanks."

Benson stood. "Well son," he said. "I'm pleased as punch you're buying this here house. Can't think of anyone I'd rather sell it to than someone who's descended from the people who built it. Dr. Girard and his wife. You'll take good care of it. It sure took good care of me. Maybe I'm a crazy old coot, but I truly think this house had an effect on my health. I'm raring to go somewheres else now. Got a nice little home in Sawhorn Meadows. Great deal, too! It's subsidized by the government. Have to ring your great-grandma's bell. She's got all kinds of time to spare. Needs a little spice in her life. That would have been a good nickname for me. Spicy!"

Benson snuffed out his cigar in the crimped ashtray resting on the arm of his Adirondack chair.

"Too bad you don't smoke," he said. "I'd a thrown a box of Cubans into the sale."

"Thanks, Benson. But I have to get the inspection done, so if you don't mind, I'm just going to let myself in and start."

The house had already been through a professional inspection, but Jem wanted to go over the house himself as well. He didn't trust that the inspector was on the up-and-up,

288

that his work wasn't shoddy, or that he wasn't on the take. It was something Ed would have done.

"Jem!" Benson called up the stairs.

"Yeah?" Jem yelled.

"Forgot to congratulate you on the land deal! Think it's great you did it. And you didn't seal the deal with that squirrelly Joe. Doing the right thing. Your dad would've been proud."

Which one?

The house movers inched toward their destination. For a good hour or so, it looked sketchy. Power lines had to be lifted, the truck had to detour across one section of field to bypass a too-narrow thoroughfare between two homes, and this was one of the steepest climbs in the county. Each member of the crew feared the truck slipping backward, spilling its historic freight. Eventually Franklin Road flattened out. From the sky it might have looked like a thread pulling across a field of amber fabric dotted with grape plants. Almost home.

All the while, the restoration crew, including Jem, worked on the Loud farmhouse. Sections of missing molding were replaced, walls patched, painted, de-bugged. Overhead, kettles of hawks migrated en route to their gathering spot along the shores of Lake Ontario. The teeming birds were wired to not cross the large body of water, but to go around it.

Fruit of the Vine

The once beaten and bereft portion of the Loud property that was reserved for the octagon house seemed complete when the house was lowered into place. Jem had sold the land to the Seneca tribe, which purchased it by way of Roy Archer's largesse. The state declared the property a living museum of viticulture and area lore. Future plans included a park, hiking trails, and a longhouse replica. The aim was to draw tourism, lift the area up like the rising tide and the boats. A new blue historical marker went up not thirty yards from the existing one highlighting the Loud property.

AMERICAN INDIAN VILLAGE
Site of a Seneca village and
meeting place for five Iroquois Nations
from antiquity until 1650.

A small number of Sawhorn residents gathered as spectators to the house-moving. Most were too knee-deep in spring chores to spare the time. Elba Loud stood at the road's edge, remarked that the house didn't look so grand all trussed up on the flatbed of the colossal truck that toted it, but that she had faith in Jem to see it preserved. She couldn't have realized that one of her own comments reverberated in Jem's mind when the idea for this venture came to him.

The fantasy never lives up to reality, Elba had told Jem.

But what good is reality without a little fantasy in it, thought Jem. My reality could use some fantasy.

Laura walked to the property with her new dog, a male sheltie named Carruthers, purple bandana around the pup's

Cynthia Kolko

neck, paws muddy with spring's draff, happy to have so much to see and sniff.

Jem exited the Loud farmhouse, its siding stripped, to murmurs ranging from disbelief and disdain to admiration. Laura cheered, waving her arms like flailing tree branches. Jem, sweaty and reeking, hair seething with sawdust, recognized Laura's silhouette against the road.

He approached, asked "Whaddya think?"

"Cool," she said, unable to steal her gaze from Jem's dirty face.

Sandra carried two takeout containers and put them on the kitchen table. Joe poured a glass of wine.

"I'd pour you some too darling, but we don't want a screwed-up baby."

He sat at the kitchen table.

"I thought of some names today," said Sandra. "Brooke if it's a girl."

"Brooke. Sounds classy. A little sexy. I like it."

"And how about this for a boy? Bogart."

"Huh. Got an old Hollywood flair to it. A screen star."

"Exactly."

"Don't know if it goes with the last name Silla though. What do you think of the name Jordan?"

"Jordan?"

"Yeah. Like Michael Jordan. Athlete. Ladies' man."

"Maybe we should get a baby book. A naming book."

291

Fruit of the Vine

"Yeah. See what's under the heading of 'classy' or 'cool,'" said Joe. "Or 'successful.'"

Sandra let ice from the automatic dispenser plop into her glass. She pushed another button, filled the glass with water.

"When's the last time you've gone over to see the space for the gym?" asked Joe.

"It was locked up tight the other day," said Sandra.

"Aw, that's not right. I'll get a key made for you. I want you to put the finishing touches on the design. Especially the women's retreat area. Make it feminine. Smell nice. Like sandalwood. Or vanilla. What's the hot scent these days?"

"Eucalyptus," said Sandra. "You know, Joe. I was thinking, now that I'm so far along, that maybe I ought to go stay at my parents' house. You know, until the baby is born. Until we know for sure who is the father."

"That's my kid," said Joe. "And that's what we'll say at the reunion."

"You still want to go to our reunion?"

"Hell, yeah! Show everyone I knocked up this hot number."

Sandra sat down at the table, her legs together, crossed at the ankles.

"You really do need to say something to Earl," she said.

Joe put his glass down, gave Sandra an incredulous expression, shook his head.

"What are you, high? I'm not talking to that scumbag. That low-rent Tom Selleck."

"He was so nice to say what he did to the DA, pay your bail. Did it for us. Our family."

Sandra put a palm on her abdomen.

Cynthia Kolko

"Nice? You are one dumb broad, Sandra. He didn't do it for you or me or the kid. He did it for himself. Feels guilty for screwing another guy's wife. He's a selfish, no-good dick. You think most people are good for good's sake, or because they think being that way is going to get them into heaven? That they do nice things because they're going to get a return for it?"

Sandra's voice was small. "I think most people are good."

Joe shouted, "No, they're not! That's why man, all those philosophers in their old-time suits, why they invented heaven. As a reward to get people to do the right thing. Because if you left it up to them, they wouldn't."

"That's what non-believers say," said Sandra. "I'm a believer. I think people are good and heaven was created by God. God guides people to do the right thing. But it is their choice to listen or not."

Joe drank the last of his wine, took his takeout box into the family room, clicked on the TV.

"Dumb broad," he said.

A clap of thunder shook the house. Sandra took it as an admonishment.

※

On Hassler Vineyard, crooked talons of lightning traced across the sky. The tangled locks of grapevines flanked by proud fence posts quivered with each thunder clap. Drops like Mardi Gras beads pinged Laura's grape-painted window box and streamed under the window she left open in order to glean the scent of basil if she happened to pause there.

Fruit of the Vine

The rain covered the sill with a wet sheen and soaked the tired bottle-bordered throw rug below.

Laura was not home. She watched through Jem's metal blinds at the rain that dripped off the crooked roof overhang like water from a faucet. Told Jem she liked rain. Made for sweeter grapes.

Jem was the Quick Mart's first customer in the morning. He took his coffee, drove Main Street on autopilot.

Jem got out of his truck on Loud Road. He carried a flag next to his hip like a golf club. In the small Loud family cemetery, Ed's headstone was so polished it reflected Jem's torso, like a neck-down cutout for tourists to pose behind for a photograph. Edward Isaiah Loud, 1946–1992. Jem crouched, rammed the flag into the ground at the base of Ed's stone.

The wind pried Jem's cap off in a scampish playground joke, sending it skittering like a tumbleweed toward the woods and Franklin pond. Jem darted after it. He grappled at the air, grabbing handfuls at each spot the cap inhabited, a mere second after it flew onward out of Jem's reach. Finally, the air stilled and Jem lurched to step on the briefly-resting cap. Yes! He folded the cap into his pocket.

A collection of thin white tree trunks under the splayed tent of a green pine caught Jem's eye. The trunks walked, revealing the body of a white deer, which opened its mouth to pull a leafy limb from a nearby tree, let go to chew, sent the limb springing back into place. The deer resembled a paper

294

Cynthia Kolko

cutout against the deep browns and greens of the forest, a study in negative space, white as a doily. The deer turned to Jem, and their two faces, man and deer, froze in regard, the animal's chomping jaw the only movement.

The deer ran, vaulting over downed trunks, its flapping tail waving goodbye. Jem watched the woods, felt a calm contentment in his chest, the warmth of a fire in the hearth. Then the woods themselves seemed alive. A symphony of rustling chimed into the air. Boughs parted like the arms of an usher and deer after snowy deer, intermixed with a peppering of brown ones, strode from the forest, bucks wearing crowns of antlers, smooth-headed does, a herd of sugar and cinnamon, bounding away like wind to where that first deer led, woods swallowing them one by one until Jem remained, abandoned like a lonely scarecrow.

He couldn't wait to tell Laura.

About the Author

Cynthia Kolko graduated from Hamilton College with a bachelor's degree in English. She has worked as a corporate, advertising, and editorial writer as well as a graphic designer and photographer. Her writing has appeared in such varied periodicals as P.R. Journal, How, Interactivity, Progressive Railroading, Rochester Business Journal, and the Democrat and Chronicle. She brings her keen ear for dialogue, dark sense of humor, and penchant for eccentricity to her first novel, Fruit of the Vine. Mrs. Kolko lives in western New York State with her husband and two children. She enjoys gardening, birds, history, and winter, and is currently busy crafting her next novel.

CPSIA information can be obtained at www.ICGtesting.com
260260BV00001B/31/P